Booper and Harry
Book 1

Be Careful What You Wish For

Booper and Harry Book 1

Be Careful What You Wish For

Robert L. Perry

A Pleasant Oliver Media Adventure

Published in the United States by Pleasant Oliver Media LLC , Reston, VA
For information on special discounts for educational or bulk purchases, email: booperandharry@gmail.com.

The author is eager to speak with young adult audiences. For more information or to book the author, email booperandharry@gmail.com or use the contact form on the website: www.booperandharry.com

Cover design assisted by Susie Hancock, https://www.susiehancock.com

First U.S. edition

Library of Congress Control Number: 2019902978
ISBN-13: 978-1-950518-00-5, ISBN-10: 1-950518-00-0
Robert L. Perry
Be Careful What You Wish For
1. Young Adult Fiction, Social Issues. 2. Young Adult Fiction, Adventure, 3. Young Adult Fiction, Soccer
Pleasant Oliver Media LLC, Reston, VA

Dedication

To All the Courageous "Harrys" of the World
Who Care So Much for What Is Right and Good

Gratitudes

Booper and Harry and their thrilling and profound adventures would never have come to life without the steadfast support of Lynne Tarakan, Kirk Treakle (Head Librarian at Rachel Carson Middle School, Herndon, VA), Michael P. Wall, Julia Wall, Jerrold Zimmerman, John Houghton, Meg Dombro, and all of my loving and courageous friends in Northern Virginia and Annapolis, MD. You know who you are! You are truly my brothers and sisters, and I am deeply grateful to each of you for your unfailing belief in me and your constant love. You triumph over tragedy one day at a time with more love in your hearts and more dedication to your fellows than can be expressed with mere words. You are angels who walk the earth!

To the many members of the support teams at Draft2Digital, Amazon Kindle Direct Publishing, Word Press Live, and Bluehost, every one of you has made a significant contribution to giving Booper and Harry the kind, considerate and professional attention they deserve.

To all, thank you and bless you!

Chapter 1
How I Got My Name, But Not My Dog

I've wanted a dog more than anything I ever wanted. Again, Mom had said no. We had just finished dinner one fall evening. She seemed to be in a fairly good mood, so I thought I would go for it. It wasn't working.

I pleaded with her, "Mom, why can't I have a dog? I'm 12 now and in the 7th grade. I know how to take care of it."

She said, like always, "No, the answer is still no. Who's going to walk the dog twice a day in the rain and snow? Who's going to take it to the vet and take care of it when it's sick? Who's going to pay the outrageous vet bills? Did you know it costs more to take a dog to the vet than for me to take you to the doctor? Who's going to pay for its food? Me, that's who. We're already on a real tight budget and we can't afford to pay for dog food and vet bills!"

As always, I promised, "I'll get a part-time job. I can deliver newspapers, or cut grass for the neighbors, or bag groceries at the grocery store, something to pay for the food and vet bills."

Then I made a big mistake. "Maybe we could ask Daddy."

"Don't start that again. You know I won't ask your father for any more money than the child support check. I have a hard enough time getting that out of him much less more for a dog."

My mom is tall and thin with curly reddish-brown hair that always looks like she just slept on it. She always looks tired and unhappy. She has circles under her eyes that never seem to go away. She doesn't sleep much and often works overtime and weekends at the factory to make more money.

That evening, she wore a loose cotton dress that was wrinkled and frayed at the edges. I should have known I was pushing her too hard. I should have just stopped. I don't know why I didn't.

I made it worse. "But, Mom, didn't Daddy tell us that he would help us if we really needed it?"

She snapped at me, "We don't really need a dog, so I'm not going to ask."

"But I can ask him to do it for me." That was it.

"Henrietta," Mom said sharply. "Enough! I said 'No' and that's final! Now, go do your homework before I get really cross."

"Oh, all right. I'm sorry I even brought it up."

I knew I had pushed her too far. She never called me 'Henrietta' unless she was really getting mad.

I got up from the small, wobbly kitchen table and shuffled down the narrow hall from the kitchen to my bedroom. I opened the door and slammed it a little too hard, just to make a point. I could get mad too. I threw myself down on my twin bed and the rusty springs creaked and screeched.

I rolled over and sank into the deep hole in the middle of the old mattress. "Mom can be such a witch! I know I would do great with a dog. I'd brush him every day and walk him twice a day and take care of him when he was sick. I just know it would be the best!" I grumbled.

I didn't know then I was going to find out the very hard way that getting a dog was going to be far more difficult and more dangerous than I could have imagined. I know now. You know what? I would still have done everything, endured everything I did for the dog I love.

By that night when I had irritated Mom—again—I had wanted a dog for more than three years. Mom and Daddy separated and divorced three years ago. I remember that when I was about three, one of my first memories was they had a screaming fight. I don't remember how I felt, but I must have been terrified. Their fights kept on and on.

I always knew something terrible was wrong, but I didn't understand until I was 8; my father was a drunk, a really bad one.

Mom and Dad had tried to hide the truth from me since I was born. They usually sent me to my room. It was upstairs in our large house in the St. Brendan neighborhood, one of the best in our town. I couldn't make out what they were yelling in the kitchen; it was on the far side of the house from my bedroom.

One late night, I was already asleep when my father came home hours and hours after he should have been home. My mother, of course, waited up for him so she could yell at him.

This time they were so loud they woke me up. Startled, I thought, fearfully, "Not again! I'm sick and tired of this; they're driving me crazy!" I decided to march downstairs and tell them exactly what I thought about their fighting all the time.

I left my room, marched down the long hallway in a rotten mood, and started to go down the stairs. Just then, Daddy lurched out of the kitchen and collapsed on the floor. I stopped and just stared down at my father like I was peering through the longest, most horrifying tunnel in the world. I plopped down onto the second step and curled up in the corner, hoping Daddy and Mommy didn't see me.

My Mom walked around the corner and stood over my father.

She growled, literally growled, "You blasted drunk! Every freaking night! I am so sick and tired of your stupidity. You are the world's biggest fool, and I am done, done! I've done everything I can do to help you! I've done everything I can do to protect Henrietta from this craziness. I dropped out of college for you. I married you because I loved you madly.

"We had a deal, and you've broken your promise thousands of times. The only bigger fool than you is me. I knew you drank too much in college. My friends told me you were an alcoholic and to stay away from you. I'm more stupid than you for believing every stinking, maudlin sob story, every promise you made when I threatened to leave you. I believed every lie you told me. You are exactly what you say you are, a rotten bum, a worthless father! I'm done, I'm leaving."

I let out a small sob, and Mom jerked her head up and saw me curled on the top step.

"Oh baby, I'm so sorry," she said as she ran up the stairs. "Your Daddy isn't feeling well. He has a bad stomach ache. He's going to sleep downstairs tonight so he can be near the bathroom. Honey, it's alright, so let's go back to bed. I'll tuck you in and read you your favorite story."

She took my head, and we stepped up onto the hallway. I turned around and looked back down the stairs, as Daddy groaned and flopped over on his other side.

He wailed, "I'm gonna die. Get me a drink!"

"Is Daddy really a drunk? I thought only bums and the homeless were drunks?" I pleaded with my Mom.

"No, no! Daddy isn't a drunk. He just drinks a little too much sometimes. He's going to be fine, sweetheart," Mom said.

"But you just called him a drunk and said nasty things about him!" I protested as Mom gently led me into my room and shut the door.

"I just felt a little upset with him for coming home late. That's all. I don't hate your Daddy. I love your Daddy and I especially love you, my wonderful Henrietta," she cooed at me as she lifted me up onto the bed and pulled the covers back over me.

She turned on the Little Pony light next to my bed and started reading my favorite story about the adventures of Ramona Quimby. I loved her at that age because she had a funny name like mine and she wasn't very good at following the rules like me either.

I shut my eyes and pretended to fall asleep, breathing softly. Mom read a few more pages, put the book down, kissed me on my forehead, and whispered, "I love you Henrietta more than my own life. I'm always going to take care of you…"

After she left and shut the door, I lurched straight up, shocked by what I had seen and heard. My father WAS a drunk—he came home like he did tonight almost every night. They had been fighting about it for years, probably since before I was born. Worst of all, my Mom lied to me! How could she do that? Maybe she wanted to protect me, but she always insisted I tell her the truth! Doesn't she owe me the truth, too, now that I'm old enough to know the difference!

I felt betrayed! I was scared because I had only one other person in the world I could trust, Grandpa. But he lived on a farm more than 50 miles west of town and he wasn't feeling as well as he used to.

I felt enraged at my Dad for being a drunk! How could he do such a thing? Didn't he care at all about me and Mom! I was afraid the answer was a big, fat NO! I had heard some other kids at St. Brendan's whispering about their dads drinking too much and how their Moms had divorced their dads and forced them to give them more money than I could imagine!

My mom—of course, liar that she was—didn't leave my Dad then. She kept giving him "one more chance" for another year. Once I knew the awful truth, I started listening to their fights every time they got started—which was almost every day. It was always about the same thing—his drinking and coming home late. Usually he was broke so we never had enough money.

That didn't make any sense because he had a great job as the general manager of the largest department store in town. We lived in a large house in what I was told was the part of town where all the lawyers, doctors, and bankers lived. I had a huge bedroom and my own bathroom.

We had a large backyard with a 150-year-old oak tree. Dad built me a tree house where the enormous trunk split into five branches. I practically lived in that treehouse when the weather was warm. It was my private palace where I ruled a peaceful world of green fields and birds singing me to sleep every night.

I attended the elite Catholic elementary school, St. Brendan's. Our nickname was the Navigators or 'Gators' to make us sound tougher than we were.

The real name honored an Irish monk who supposedly discovered America about 500 years before the Vikings showed up in what is now Canada and a thousand years before Columbus tripped over the islands in the Caribbean. The dummy–Columbus, that is—thought he had reached India. That's why those islands south of Florida are called the "West Indies." The ancient written records strongly favor St. Brendan and his hardy band of monks who sailed in a tiny boat, so good for them!

We weren't Catholics—we weren't much of any kind of religion—but my parents didn't want me to go to public school because they thought the public schools had bad reputations for not teaching very well. Actually, I think my parents didn't like poor people; they seemed kind of conceited that way. St. B's, as we called it, wasn't as expensive as the super prep school, Briarhurst Academy, but it had a solid academic reputation.

We had so many wonderful things, but I learned that nothing could stop my Dad from drinking. I listened when he was too drunk to get into the house by himself. Lots of times, he banged on the door for Mom to let him in because he couldn't find the key.

A few times, he fell down and passed out in the front yard. Or his so-called friends dumped him in the front yard because he was too drunk to drive and they could not get out of the car without falling over. It's a miracle they never crashed and killed themselves or somebody else.

Mom had to go out to the yard and drag him inside before he embarrassed us before the neighbors. But they all knew anyway— by the time I was 9, the kids at my school, even the ones whose dads were drunks themselves, used to torment me.

The time my Dad was passed out in the yard, and the sprinkler system turned on and soaked him became unbearable for me. He screamed and cussed so loud that he woke some of the neighbors. They stared at him from their front yards like he was a crazy man, which is exactly what he was at the time. And I heard about my Dad "going for a swim in your front yard" at St. B's for weeks!

I also learned then that for a couple of years, he had been taking afternoons off from work to drink. He started missing more and more days of work. His bosses in another city often couldn't reach him when there was a problem at the store.

Finally, the headquarters sent someone to check up on him. They found out about his heavy drinking and how much time he spent drinking at his favorite bars instead of managing the store. Mom told me later that his bosses warned him time after time, but he never listened and kept getting drunk. When I was eight, it all hit the fan; his company got tired of his behavior and fired him.

That was the last straw for Mom. A few days later, while Daddy was out drinking with his buddies, she packed up our clothes and we left in the middle of the night. We went to stay with Grandpa at his small farm, the place I loved more than anywhere in the world!

That was more than four years ago. It seems like forever. I had hoped Mom would begin to get over their bitter divorce. But whenever I talked about asking Daddy for anything, Mom got very upset.

At least, I got to see my dad on Wednesday night, two weekends a month, and a month in the summer. He never drank in front of me when I stayed at his house. I sneaked around looking for his hiding places, but I never found any booze. I was happy he had quit drinking, but for a long time, I had no idea how that had happened.

Mom apparently knew he had stopped drinking, but that didn't help her feel any better. Once I heard her tell her sister on the phone, "I couldn't help him. I was such a failure as a wife. I'm so afraid I can't take care of Henrietta and lose her, too. Oh, Sis…." She cried softly into the phone.

Maybe she felt so bad because Daddy had been doing so much better for more than two years, she was working in a factory, and we lived in a small house in what we used to think was a "bad neighborhood."

Mostly, I think she was upset because Dad was about to marry Kim. Kim is nice to me, but it will be weird for her to be my stepmother. Kim is really young, maybe young enough to be my older sister. But she is pretty—long brunette hair, blue eyes, slim figure, fair skin. She looks really fit, like she works out at the gym all the time.

After Mom found out about Kim, Mom and Daddy got into a huge fight about Kim so she and I hadn't gotten to know each other very well. The fight was about me visiting Dad when Kim was there at the same time. He had started going out with her about a year after they separated, while Mom and he were still fighting about the divorce.

When Mom found out that Kim was staying over when I was there, she hit the roof. She stopped letting me go to Daddy's for the weekend. To retaliate, Dad refused to pay child support for months. Mom refused to let him near our house. They sued each other in court. Without Daddy's support checks, we had so little money we even had to get food stamps one month.

Finally, some guy they called a mediator got them together. Mom said he convinced them how expensive and painful it would be if they kept fighting with each other. Neither one of them could afford to spend thousands of dollars on lawyers to fight over me.

Mom said if Kim would not stay overnight, I could go back to visiting Dad on weekends. He wasn't happy, but he agreed. I felt relieved that he still cared about me since he wanted to see me more than he wanted Kim to stay over. After that, I only saw Kim for a few hours a month. Dad and I were almost always busy doing something by ourselves, so I didn't get to know her very well.

That happened about a year ago. Things got better between Mom and Dad mostly because after the divorce was finalized, they avoided each other and hardly ever talked to each other.

My Dad must be almost 40 by now, really old. But Kim and Daddy seem to love each other a lot, though I still wish Daddy loved Mom. I guess that Mom still loves Daddy.

I can tell she still feels hurt and angry because she endured so many terrible years and she could never get him to stop drinking.

Now, Kim gets to marry Daddy when he is sober and has a new job managing a small clothing store.

I feel sorry for Mom. She's had a very hard time of it. We could have stayed at Grandpa's. But he died two years ago just after they finally got divorced. He just had a heart attack one day while he was pulling weeds in his garden. He fell over and died and no one was there with him. I was in school and Mom was out looking for a better job.

There were all kinds of serious problems because he didn't leave a will. Grandpa didn't leave us much money. Mom said the state took a lot of that in probate taxes, that is, taxes the state collects from the money someone leaves when they die. If we had kept those taxes, we could have lived on the farm for at least a couple of more years.

After Grandpa died, Mom found a full-time job as a machine operator at the car parts factory to try to save the farm. She took care of a machine that she said did nothing all day but press out different sizes and shapes of superplastic, like parts for bumpers. Any time they needed a different size, shape, or color of a superplastic car part, she had to change the attachments and push buttons on the machine's computer.

She said the job was boring, but it was a job she had to keep. I had learned when I was 10 Mom had dropped out of college not long before I was born. I believe I was the reason why she never completed college. I often feel really guilty about that.

Mom tells me all the time she is doing the best she can for us right now. I know she is, but she has had a very tough time.

My Mom tried as hard as she could to keep the farm, but we lost it because my Dad's small alimony check and her factory job didn't pay enough for her to keep up with the monthly mortgage and the annual property taxes. No way she could afford to keep me at St. Brendan's and Dad was struggling as much as we were.

So we had to move and the bank took back the farm. Last I heard, it was still unsold, sitting there vacant.

Like I said, I love that farm more than any place in the world. Since I was a baby, I had spent summers there with Grandpa. He taught me how to ride a horse, drive a small tractor, plow straight rows, plant seeds correctly, and fertilize and water them in the right amounts so they would thrive.

He was amazing! He grew three crops a year—broccoli in the early spring, corn and beans in mid-summer, and kale and cabbage in the late summer and fall. He even raised tomatoes and lettuce in a small greenhouse throughout the winter. He also had a small orchard with apple, pear, and apricot trees.

The most delicious thing in the world is a fresh apricot pulled perfectly ripe from the tree in late July. You bite into it and the sweet juice dribbles off your lips and onto your hands. The soft flesh melts in your mouth and slides down your throat. Wonderful! I climbed into the trees every July and ate all the apricots I wanted.

I also helped Grandpa sell his vegetables at a little stand by the side of the road. People who had known my Grandpa for years would make special trips from town to visit and buy his vegetables and fruits. They told me his were the best in the area. I felt very proud that my Grandpa could grow from a tiny seed and some black dirt something so delicious and that so many people enjoyed.

After we lost the farm, Mom rented a small rundown house in what we used to call an "iffy" part of town. At first, I felt blown away and depressed. The house needed a "deep clean" of its filthy, moldy vinyl siding, the lawn was mostly bare dirt and weeds. The inside walls were paneled in a godawful fake pine, the kitchen was tiny with old appliances, and the bedrooms were tiny. I had about a foot on each side of my lousy bed to move and only a few feet at the foot for a small desk.

Our neighbors lived in the same kind of houses, but you could tell the owners from the renters. The owners tried to keep the yards up and the outsides clean while the rentals were a lot more like ours. Mom said the landlord was a cheap so-and-so and expected us to take care of everything out of her nearly empty pockets. Not likely.

We had moved at the beginning of summer so I mostly hid out in the house all summer and helped Mom clean the place up. Sometimes, I felt angry and betrayed that I had had to leave both our big house and much worse, my Grandpa's farm.

When school started at the end of an always-hot August, it turned out, though, the kids in my 7th grade class and the school were okay. St. B's had been "lily white" with the occasional minority sprinkled in to make them feel "diverse." Ha!

Compared to St. B's, my school, George Washington Carver Middle, is a United Nations of kids. There are all kinds—blacks, Latinos, Vietnamese, Korean, whites, even real Africans from Nigeria, Ethiopia, and Kenya.

I was told as soon as I enrolled, the school is named after a famous black scientist who invented, or advocated for, hundreds of ways for poor farmers in the south to make more money by growing peanuts and sweet potatoes. Born as a slave during the Civil War, Carver endured serious discrimination as he fought for a college education. But his genius overcame all obstacles, and he became the first African-American—and descendant of slaves— to earn advanced degrees at white colleges and receive accolades—awards—from white institutions.

He is credited with doing more than anyone else to save the peanut industry in the south, improve the lives of farmers who followed his advice, and create thousands of new jobs. He was considered a tremendous asset to the entire country.

St. Brendan's was supposed to be "the" school to go to in our town, even more than the even snootier Briarhurst. Maybe, maybe not. The girls in my class at St. B's were a lot more selfish and snotty than the Carver girls. All the popular girls at St. B's did was hang out in their cliques and gossip about each other, or text each other about which boy liked which girl. Who had just broken up with whom. All kinds of junk.

I certainly wasn't one of the preppies. I wasn't even a geek, a Star Wars junkie, a techie, a gamer, or a skater. I just liked to play sports, so I guess I would have been a jock. But St. B's didn't have any organized girls' teams at my elementary school. I was good at every sport I played at recess or after school on the playground near my house. Mom said Grandpa had been an excellent athlete in high school and college. He played basketball and baseball and could run faster than anybody else on his teams. I guess I got my love for sports and my speed from him.

In elementary school, I always made the boys mad when I outraced them, or outhit them in softball, or won every kickball game at recess. They didn't like me much, and some of the popular girls thought I wasn't really a girl. They spread a rumor I liked girls, but that was stupid. I just wanted to play sports, and my favorite—and best—sport was soccer.

At Carver, I felt a lot happier at first because they have an after-school program with a mixed boys and girls soccer team nicknamed the Redhawks. We play in the spring and the fall in a league against other after-school teams scattered across town in the "iffy" neighborhoods. The other teams call us the "Peanuts" when they want to try to make us mad. The Redhawks never get mad, we get even.

During that fall, I was making good grades and our soccer team was winning. I was one of the best—well, I thought I was the best—player on the team. I felt pretty happy most of the time, even with Mom feeling so tired and so depressed. I really missed Grandpa and I didn't see Dad as often as I would have liked—now that he was sober. But I did my best to shut all that out of my mind.

***

That's how we got to where we were that evening when I had pushed Mom too far about getting a dog—again!

That night, I felt angry at myself because I hadn't meant to push Mom so far. She seemed so mad I was sure she would never let me have a dog.

Sitting on my bed after my fight with Mom, I looked across my room to the picture of Grandpa on my small desk. His round, smiling face always made me feel like he was looking down on me from heaven, if there is such a place. I hope so just so Grandpa can be there when I get there—IF I get there! I love every line on his round face; they look like the longitude and latitude lines on a globe. His pale gray-blue eyes are almost squinched out of sight from his wide smile. His head is bald and his body is pear-shaped. With a white beard and mustache and the right red suit, he would have been the perfect Santa Claus.

Grandpa had promised me that he would buy me a dog on my 12th birthday and keep it for me on the farm. Then he had died just after he had made his promise and just as the worst of the divorce reached a peak.

Now, I'll never have a dog to take to our farm and run in the fields and harass Grandpa's old cow. His old cow Gertie and pony Shelly are long gone. Mom told me she had found good homes for them, but I wasn't sure. I tried not to think about butchers and glue factories; I hang onto my memories of milking Gertie and drinking the milk right out of the pail and pulling myself onto Shelly's saddle and falling off and getting on and falling off until I could stay on by myself.

So many memories raced around in my head, reminding me how wonderful it had been before it became so awful. Now with Kim and the marriage, the nightmare, at least my Mom's, is starting all over again.

I am beginning to get very worried about Mom because she is even more depressed and more upset than she has been since the divorce. She is cranky and snaps at me all the time. I feel bad when I push her buttons when I know I shouldn't. But she just doesn't seem to like being around me much.

I am afraid she blames me for not graduating from college so she could have a much better job and live as well as she used to. She's never said this to me, but like I said, I have heard her complain to her sister about my birth and what it did to her.

All she does is get up early and go to work, come home late and exhausted, throw some dinner together, and go to bed. Day after day, that's all she does. She often works on Saturdays and Sundays too. If she is too wired to sleep, she sits in front of the TV watching whatever blood-and-guts cop or doctor show is on that night. She often falls asleep in front of the TV while I do my homework, or she stays awake way past midnight. She never goes out, she never has any fun, and she never spends much time with me.

All she does is tell me what to do and when to do it: "Get up, eat breakfast, get ready for school, hurry up—you're late, wash the dishes, do your homework, brush your teeth, go to bed." Every day the same thing.

At least now, she calls me "Harry" and not "Henrietta." I hate that name with a passion. It's so…so…uncool. It sounds like I'm somebody's crazy great grandmother who lived 100 years ago!

My Mom named me "Henrietta," over my father's objections!

I was sort of named after my grandpa. His name was Henry Hazzard Stephens, but he had always been called Harry.

I knew that I was named 'Henrietta' after him. I had been called 'Hetty' since I was born. I hated it every time anybody called me "Hetty" or "Henrietta." Yuck, but I couldn't do anything about it—until the day of Grandpa's funeral.

***

I didn't feel anything most of that awful day. I didn't even cry. Mom wouldn't stop sobbing. At the viewing in the funeral home, I hated it when my Mom grabbed my arm and took me to look at Grandpa in a tacky coffin. He didn't look like my Grandpa at all; he looked like some fake, pasty caricature stolen from a creepy wax museum.

After that, I only remember being in a daze. Some of Mom's co-workers from her job came, sat with her, and hugged her. A lot of Grandpa's old friends came, patted me on the head or shoulder like I was a little girl and told me how sorry they felt for Mom and me. They said nice things I couldn't bear to hear. At least, I didn't have to smile and pretend to be grateful. I think I even saw Daddy in the back of the church out of the corner of my eye, but he never came over to me, so I'm not sure.

During the service, I didn't even listen to what the preacher was saying. Lots of people got up to speak about my Grandpa. I guess they said what a great person he was, but I knew that. I didn't need to hear them say it. I just sat there, dressed in an itchy black dress Mom insisted she had to buy for me to wear that dreadful day.

Grandpa would have been happier if they had buried him in his overalls instead of a cheap-looking suit. I would have been happier if I had worn jeans and a T-shirt. I wanted to break a hoe in half and put it in his casket since he loved his garden, but Mom forbade that. She just didn't get what was truly important to Grandpa and me.

After the service, we drove out to the cemetery in our old compact car because we couldn't afford the traditional limousine the funeral home wanted Mom to rent for some outrageous price. They put Grandpa's casket in the ground after the preacher prattled on a little more and said a prayer that didn't mean much to me. The preacher didn't even know my Grandpa. God loves him, I love him, and Mom loves him. There wasn't a lot the preacher, who was obviously reading from some script, could say that meant anything at all.

After we left the cemetery, we returned to our farm with some of Mom's friends and relatives I didn't know. There were tons of food—That's what other people do when somebody dies. They bring food for the get-together after the cemetery and leave some for us to eat. It is a traditional way to show us that they care.

Practically, all the food helped Mom so she didn't have to cook for a few days, but I really had NOT looked forward to eating sweet potato casserole or green bean casserole for a week. Mushroom soup and greasy onion rings on beans?! Who thought of that awful idea?

As people mingled around Grandpa's house, I sat down in a chair out of the way. I wasn't moving. I was hardly thinking. People spoke in a quiet buzz around me.

Suddenly, for some reason I still don't understand, I stood up and announced loudly: "From now on, my name is Harry."

Mom looked at me in shock. She burst into tears and covered her face with her hands. Her friends and relatives stared at me with weird looks and gave little nervous laughs.

I repeated, "From now on, my name is Harry. Don't ever call me 'Hetty' or 'Henrietta' again."

Mom walked over me and hugged me. "Okay, Henri--, eh,

Harry, we'll talk about it later."

"No," I said. "There's nothing to talk about. My name is Harry, not Hetty or Henrietta."

I walked straight out of the living room through all the people to my bedroom at the farm. My bed was covered with people's coats and jackets, so I dumped them out in the hall and shut the door.

Since that day, I have done my best to make everyone call me "Harry." At St. B's, I had to fight some of the boys—no big deals, just a few scuffles. Some of the girls called me names like "lesbo" or "dyke." I didn't care.

At Carver, my new school, the only time "Henrietta" was said formally was the first day of school during roll call. I stood up and told Ms. Andrews, my homeroom teacher, "My name is Harry. You have to change the roll." She looked stunned but said she would consider it. After school, she called my Mom and confirmed that I had to be called "Harry." I felt happy that Mom had stood up for me—for once.

So, except for that time or when my math teacher Mrs. Jackson gets mad at me, everyone at my new school calls me "Harry." Oh yeah, some of the kids tease me, especially Rory, the other "best" soccer player on the Redhawks, and "Peanut, Butter, and Jelly."

That's what I call his trio of groupies. The "PBJs" are Peter, Bu, and Jorge. I'll give the PBJs credit for one thing—they do know how to play hard-nosed soccer.

"Peanut" is a tall, thin African-American the color of a roasted peanut; he is a tough defender who protects our goalie, a tall, awesome Ethiopian girl named Magda.

Magda must have been born to be a soccer goalie because her name means "high tower" and she blocks every shot that comes her way. She's given up only one goal in 15 games. She's taller than I am, about 5 feet 10 inches, and she's only 13. The high school basketball, volleyball, and soccer coaches are already fighting about which elite high school she gets the best scholarship to attend.

"Butter" is a Vietnamese named Bu. He is as slippery as his nickname. He steals the ball from the other attackers before they even know he's there.

"Jelly" is Jorge, who is as bouncy and as funny as his nickname implies. He is our best player at intercepting passes and bouncing them to Rory or me as we attack the other team's goal. Jorge is first-generation Latino. The country his family comes from is kinda vague; he never talks about it and says he doesn't know since he was born here and his parents never talk about their homeland.

The PBJs follow Rory around like a bunch of puppies and do whatever he tells them to do.

They are the core of the team, and thanks to Coach Bill, we have gelled into an awesome team. I wish Grandpa could see me play so he could laugh his deep laugh and take credit for giving me his athletic genes.

I miss Grandpa so much, especially days like today when Mom is so unhappy and Dad is about to marry Kim. Whenever it got bad between Mom and Dad, or I just needed to talk to someone, I could always sit down with Grandpa and talk to him. He always listened and knew just the right thing to say. He'd crack some dumb joke about why the chicken crossed the road—and he always had a different silly answer. Like to get to the corn on the cob on the other side or chase the wayward rooster back home.

Or he'd ask me which came first, the chicken or the egg? He'd always answered, "What difference does it make? I loved fried eggs and fried chicken!"

Or he'd just listen until I finished spilling my guts, usually something about my Mom being so unhappy or the teasing I got at my elementary school St. B's for being a good athlete.

He never tried to tell me what to do. He always said, "You'll know in your heart the right thing to do. When you figure that out, just go do it, and it will turn out right in the end."

That night, I believed with all my heart the best thing in the world for me was to have a dog. Not a fancy purebred like the ones the kids at St. B's used to show off at our silly annual dog show. Instead, a stray or rescue dog that needed somebody to love and care for him and treat him like a real dog instead of a furry pampered prince.

I thought all I had to do was bide my time and wait out my Mom. She'd come around sooner or later. Maybe after she'd calm down after the wedding and I'd started earning some money doing odd jobs around the neighborhood. That was the right thing to do. I knew Grandpa would think so, too.

Chapter 2
I Find the Dog of My Dreams—
for the Wrong Reason

The next morning, only a few months ago—unbelievable!—Mom woke me up at 6 a.m. as always just as she was leaving for her job.

"I'm sorry about last night, Mom. I didn't mean to make you so upset."

"It's not your fault," Mom said. "I'm just really stressed out right now with your father and all. Let's just wait a while and see what happens before we worry about a dog."

"Okay, Mom." I knew better than to even mention the word 'dog' for a while.

After Mom left, I got out of bed and got ready for school. Mom left me a sandwich bag with a ham and cheese sandwich, an apple, and broccoli tops.

Yuck! I hated broccoli then and still do. Usually, I traded them with that funny-looking, round-headed kid, Charles, who actually likes vegetables. I rummaged through the refrigerator and couldn't find any junk food. Mom always wants us to eat "healthy" so she keeps a lot of fresh fruits and vegetables in the fridge.

But I knew she had a stash of something sugary somewhere. I sometimes heard her rummaging through packages in the kitchen late at night. I kept poking around and finally found a bag of cookies at the back of the top shelf of a cabinet. I took only a couple so she wouldn't know I found them.

I strapped on my backpack and walked out the door. I ran down the sidewalk to meet my best friend, Glenda, at the corner of her street like I still do every morning. I'm tall, trim, and athletic to be 12 years old—well, getting close to 13. I'm about 5 feet, 7 inches tall—something else the scrawny, wimpy boys don't like about me.

Compared to me, Glenda looks like an advertisement for some "Save the Starving Children" fund. Glenda is short and scrawny, barely more than four and a half feet tall. She has long, straight, limp black hair.

My hair is wavy and bright reddish-blonde like my Mom's—I always tie it back for games so nobody can pull on it.

Yeah, when the refs aren't looking, both boys and girls in our league pull on the ponytails of the girls or the rasta dreadlocks of the boys stupid enough to wear them long during a game. The tug throws them off balance so they lose the ball. They yell about the pulling, and the coaches complain, but the refs can't do anything if they don't see it.

We play in a tough league. Everybody wants to win and some of the teams come from even rougher neighborhoods than ours, so they don't play by the rules so much. Not that I'm above pulling a ponytail or grabbing a rasta lock here and there if the other team starts it. We want to win as much as they do, and nobody messes with my team and gets away with it.

Glenda doesn't play on the soccer team. She hardly ever gets any exercise and does her best to avoid having any fun at recess at all. She's terrified of getting hit in the face by a dodgeball. She can't shoot a basketball high enough to get near the basket. She runs like a dehydrated duck, waddling on her bony legs, and she wouldn't be caught dead racing.

Lucky for her the school rules say the teachers can't force her to play with the other kids. However, when the teachers try to get her to do something physical, she always says no. She'd rather sit and watch whatever I'm playing. In school and when we walk to or home from school, she usually plods along with a faraway look in her eyes and says little to anybody except me.

A lot of the kids in 7th grade call us "Beavis and Butthead" after the awful, dweeb-to-the-max cartoon characters. This undynamic duo always say and do weird things and have the worst laughs in the world! A lot of the kids think Glenda and I are weird and our friendship is even weirder. I could go after the idiots who call us that, but they're not worth my trouble. We ignore them.

I'm Glenda's best friend because she did two wonderful things for me when no one else did. Like I said, I was new to this neighborhood and I didn't know a soul. On the first day of school at Carver Middle, everybody else ignored me at lunch time. I felt so grateful when Glenda walked up to me and asked if she could sit down.

At the time, I thought she was just being nice to welcome me like that. Now I know it took a lot of courage for her to come over to me because she didn't have any friends either. So, we started having lunch together almost every day.

The biggest thing she did, though, was after my parents' divorce was finalized. I had felt really down and even stayed out of school for a few days. The day I returned, I felt lousy, dreading walking out the door. But Glenda met me on the corner as always and walked with me to school. Even though I lied when she asked me how I was feeling and I said I was feeling okay, she stayed with me and walked with me all the way to my homeroom.

A real friend looks out for you regardless. A real friend just listens and lets you know she cares without saying a word.

Those black days, everybody else, even my soccer team, avoided me like I had the plague. Some kids pointed at me and whispered behind my back, like I couldn't hear them. Rude idiots! Later that night when I complained to Mom, she tried to cover for them; she said maybe they just didn't know what to say or were too embarrassed. She's too nice like that.

That's why Glenda is my best friend. Everybody knows it and nobody teases her or calls her names like I heard they used to. They know I would kick their butts.

That Thursday morning, when Glenda met me at her corner, she looked even moodier and quieter than usual. "Gee, Glenda, what's the matter?"

"Oh, nothing. My father made a lot of noise last night when he came home. I didn't get much sleep, and I'm worried about the algebra test today."

I freaked out! "What algebra test?"

"Gee, Harry, don't you ever pay attention to Mrs. Jackson at all?" Glenda said.

I thought, "Not again. What's the matter with me?" I hadn't even brought my math book home with me.

"If I mess this up," I cried, "my Mom is going to ground me for a year. Quick, Glenda, what's it about?"

"Mrs. Jackson said it would be problem sets on basic formulas. Do you remember any of it?"

"Oh, I don't know. I was so mad at my Mom last night, I forgot about everything and went to sleep. Let's hurry to school so you can show me some of it." I took off down the street and Glenda trailed behind.

***

Mrs. Jackson's math and science classes were the last ones each day, but Glenda's last-minute tutoring during lunch and recess didn't help. After the test, I knew I had flunked. I just stared at the problems, my mind frozen. I had scribbled some quick answers when Mrs. Jackson gave a five-minute warning, but I knew they were wrong.

When Mrs. Jackson took up our papers, she looked at my paper and then looked at me. She frowned her best teacher frown and shook her head.

"Henrietta," Mrs. Jackson said. She still called me Henrietta when she was mad at me. "Please speak with me after school."

"Yes, ma'am," I said. I knew I was in for another lecture about how smart I was and how I could do my math work if I just tried harder.

I hid behind my books the rest of the afternoon and curled up inside my mind. The rest of the class seemed far away. Mrs. Jackson changed subjects and droned on about plane geometry. I didn't hear a word. I wondered, is there a "plain" geometry? This kind of "plane" was more than complicated enough for me.

All I could think about was how much I missed Grandpa, how much I wanted a dog I could raise, and how much fun we could have on my own small farm.

Finally, the last bell rang. As the other kids raced out the door, I stood up, shook myself, and went to face Mrs. Jackson.

"Henrietta, I'm very disappointed in your math quiz," she scolded. "You didn't get any of the problems right. What's the matter, girl? You're smart and I know you can do this work."

"Yes, ma'am," I said. I did my best to look like I felt sorry. "I just forgot everything. I froze up. I don't know why."

"You started off doing well at the first of the year, but now you're doing worse and worse, so I'm going to have to send a note to your mom. Take it to her and bring it back to me tomorrow signed."

I was horrified! I pleaded, "Mrs. Jackson, please don't make me do that. My Mom will ground me forever. I'll do better. Please let me take the test again tomorrow! I promise I'll study all night for it!"

"Henrietta, you know I like you. When you want to, you're one of my best students. I enjoy your sense of humor and your energy. But you've got to learn to channel that energy properly. I'm sorry, but you have to take the note home and bring it back to me."

"Oh, Mrs. Jackson, my mother is having a lot of problems right now, and I really can't add any more. She'll just feel worse, and I don't want to hurt her feelings. Pleaseeee," I begged. I had never begged any teacher before for anything, but this was bad. The dog thing, my Dad's marriage, my Mom's sadness…

"I'm sorry. If your Mom is upset, I'll be happy to meet with her to explain my note and discuss how we can help you improve."

I knew I had lost the battle. I took the note, stuffed it deep inside my book bag and left the school. Glenda was waiting for me on the corner outside.

"What happened? Did she send you to the principal? Did you get detention?"

"No. Much worse. I've got to take this note home to my Mom and bring it back signed. My mom is going to be so disappointed and even madder at me. She's probably going to ground me for a month."

Glenda said, laughing, "Well, you could always run away from home and go to your Dad's house until the heat dies down."

"Yeah, really funny. Like I can walk 50 miles in a few hours, but....wait a minute. That's a thought! I could hang out somewhere for a while. My mom usually goes to bed about 8 o'clock. I could call her and tell her I'm having dinner with you and that I'll be home later. Then, she might be asleep before I get home. Can I come home with you?"

"Well...we can ask my mom," Glenda said, shrugging her shoulders and holding her books even closer to her chest. "But you know she hates last-minute visitors. My Dad, you know…he's home, and he might get upset."

"I don't really have to eat. I just need somewhere to hang out. Tell your mom we want to study together for a test tomorrow. Just for a little while."

"I'll ask, but I'm not sure. My mom doesn't like people to just drop by. You know that."

"I know but this is an emergency. I can't give my Mom that note."

"Harry, putting it off is just going to make it worse. What are you going to tell Mrs. Jackson when you don't bring it back tomorrow?"

"Oh, I thought about that. I'll tell her my Mom was working overtime, so she worked late and had to go work early. I'll tell Mrs. Jackson I missed her, so I'll give it to her Friday night and bring it back Monday. I can think of something else by then."

"How long do you think you can get away with it?" Glenda said. "You've got to show it to her sometime."

"Well, I can get through the weekend. Tomorrow is Friday, and I'm going to my Dad's wedding on Saturday. You know he's getting married again. I'll worry about it Monday."

Glenda shook her head. "Harry, you're nuts! Sometimes I wonder which one of us is Beavis and the other Butthead!"

We reached Glenda's house in a few minutes, but I was out of luck there, too.

Glenda's mom was in a terrible mood. She met us at the door. When Glenda asked if I could come in and study with her, she glared at me and said, "No, Harry can't come in. The house is a mess, I'm going out later, your father's asleep, and I don't want you kids making a bigger mess. You have to give me more warning," she said.

She was dressed in a shapeless, straight dress that hung like a limp sack over her huge body. Her mousy gray hair was rolled up in neon green curlers. She wore dirty pink cotton slippers. Smoke curled from a half-smoked cigarette dangling from her lips; the ash drooped and fell on the floor. She didn't even notice. She didn't look like she was going anywhere soon.

I had never been in Glenda's house though she came over to my place all the time. She had never invited me over before and now I knew why. Her house smelled of stale cigarette smoke, stale beer, and burned grease. From the doorway, I could see trash littering the floors, Styrofoam takeout containers stacked on tray tables, and clothes scattered across what looked like cheap, worn-out furniture.

Glenda's mom was right about one thing: It was a mess.

I didn't say anything about the mess.

"Thank you anyway, Mrs. Babson," I did say, "I'll remember to ask in advance next time. Glenda, I'll meet you tomorrow morning, same time, same place?"

"Sure, but what are you going to do?"

"I don't know, but I'll figure something out."

I walked away slowly and began wandering down the street toward my house. I didn't want to go home and wait for Mom. I dreaded how unhappy Mom was going to be and what she might do to me. Mom wouldn't hit me, of course; she never had. But she would probably ground me, so I'd have to come straight home from school and study all night. Crap, she might even not let me play soccer. That would be unbearable.

The Redhawks had had a great chance to win the championship last fall. I was our best player this year, and there was no way they could win without me. What kind of mess had I gotten myself into and how in the world was I going to get out of it?

Usually, I turn from Glenda's street, Plum Point, onto my own street, Apple Tree Lane. But that evening, I turned onto Horsham Circle. It was the long way home. Since I was usually messing around with Glenda, I never walked this way. I hoped that if I walked slowly enough, Mom might beat me home and go to bed early.

I wished I could have run all 50 miles to Dad's house or called him and asked him to come get me. Like he would do that two nights before the wedding. There was something called a "rehearsal dinner" going on anyway, and Kim's parents and Dad's parents had just arrived in town. Dad's new house would be too crowded as it was.

I had been invited to the dinner, but Mom wouldn't let me go. She said she didn't want it to look like "we" approved of the wedding. The only reason she decided to let me go to the wedding was because Dad's parents called and talked her into it. So, escaping to Dad's wasn't going to work. I knew eventually I would get home and have to face the consequences.

I walked down the street, kicking pebbles like soccer balls. "How could I be so stupid!" I mumbled. "Forgetting a math test. What's wrong with me? My grades are getting worse and worse. I was practically a straight 'A' student, but now I'm lucky to get a C in science or math, and I like them!"

If only Mom and Daddy were still married and Grandpa was still alive, everything would have been fine.

As I wandered slowly down Horsham, I passed a small house on the right side I'd never noticed before. It was even shabbier than ours. A lot of its faded olive green paint had flaked off, exposing rotting wood planks. Most of the windows were cracked or broken. All the broken ones were either stuffed with paper or covered with plastic. The yard was nothing but tall, dead, dirty brown weeds.

A worn gravel driveway, the space between two tire tracks packed with tall weeds, ran about 30 or 40 feet down the left side of the house. At the end, a rusty old Jeep squatted on concrete blocks. Its tires and headlights were missing. It looked like a legless, eyeless creature straight from a horror movie. The empty headlights, staring at me like a skeleton's eye sockets, seemed to follow me as I moved.

And I thought *we* were poor since Mom and Daddy got divorced. How creepy! How could anyone live like that?

As I glanced back at the old jeep just to make sure it really wasn't alive, I noticed a thick rusty chain attached to the front axle. Suddenly it began to creak and move. In the weeds around the Jeep, a dark shape began to emerge. As it staggered to its feet, the shape began to whine, a gut-wrenching, agonizing moan.

It was a dog! At least it might have been a dog. It was the scrawniest, scruffiest, dirtiest, nastiest looking animal I had ever seen.

Chapter 3
Painful Price to Be
A "Good Samaritan"

I stared at the shrunken, quivering creature, half hidden in the tall reedy weeds around the jeep. I thought its coat might be black, but the little hair it had looked filthy and gray. It was about two feet tall and stood shaking on emaciated legs. It stared at me with dull dark eyes. It tried to growl, but the sound came out more like a whimper.

"Oh God! What's happened to that poor dog?!"

I walked up the gravel driveway toward the jeep. As I approached the dog, it whimpered and cowered, tucking its tail between its legs and curling its back end toward its front. As I tiptoed forward, it backed away from me and bared its teeth.

"Take it easy. I won't hurt you," I whispered.

Where the chain bound its leg, all the hair was rubbed off. Oozing sores dripped blood and yellow-green pus from infection. Its back was practically hairless and covered with bright red, scabby scales. I stared at the open wounds, appalled.

"Who would do such a thing to an animal?"

When I was about six feet away from the dog, I squatted down in the weeds.

"It's all right. I want to help you. You're a good dog," I cooed over and over quietly and soothingly.

Slowly, the dog relaxed, but as I inched forward, it shied away. I stopped.

"That's okay. I don't like strangers much either. Take all the time you need to get used to me. I just want to help you." I sat there for a long time; I kept making quiet, calming noises and talking to the terrified dog. I wished I had some food so I could try to feed it or even give it some water.

But just as the dog began to move slowly toward me, the back door with a torn screen flung open, and a tall, scrawny, disheveled, brown-haired man stumbled out.

He screamed, "What the heck do yew think yer're doing, yew little brat! Are yew tryin' to steal my dog?"

He lurched and staggered toward me. I jumped up in terror, and the dog scuttled under the jeep.

"Nooo," I pleaded. "I just wanted to pet it. It's hurt…It's leg…It needs a vet…" I stammered.

"Ain't nothing wrong with that dog. Get away from there, yer stupid…"

As the man came closer, I could see that he seemed even filthier than the dog. His stained denim shirt was full of holes, his work boots were caked with dirt and the leather was cracked, and his blue jeans were spattered with paint and who knows what else.

As he came closer, I wanted to run, but I was too frightened to move.

He loomed over me. I smelled a heavy odor of booze on his foul breath.

"I'll teach yew to mess wit' somebody else's property," he yelled and drew back his hand to hit me.

That was enough. Nobody, especially a creep like this, was

ever going to hit me! Ever!

I dodged to the side as he swung his beefy hand. It just missed the side of my head but whacked my right shoulder.

"Owww," I cried as I tumbled to the ground. I rolled over, got up, grabbed my bag, and ran down the street as fast as I could.

As I ran, I turned to see if the gross jerk was chasing me. He wasn't. He just stood in his yard, cursing and waving his fist at me.

Terrified, I ran all the way home. I flung open the door and screamed for Mom, gasping for air and crying.

"Mom! Mom! A man hit me...for…talking to his dog…All I wanted...It was hurt…Leg bloody and sore…Who would do…that?" I gasped in fear, trying to catch my breath.

Shocked at my screams, Mom ran up to me and hugged me. "What happened? Are you all right? What man? Where were you?"

She held me and stroked my hair. "It's okay now. Tell me what happened."

I calmed down in a few minutes and took a couple of deep breaths. I told Mom the truth about the dog and what I had done at the man's house and what had happened. But I didn't tell her I was walking down Horsham to avoid her so I would not have to give her Mrs. Jackson's note.

"Oh Harry, that man is terrible, and he shouldn't have hit you. But what were you doing in his yard? You know better than that. You were trespassing on his property," Mom said.

"But, Mom, the dog. It's being abused really badly. Its leg is bleeding and infected. It's really sick and needs a vet!" I cried.

"Harry, that may be, but it's his dog, not yours. He can do with it what he wants. But he doesn't have any right to hit children."

Mom wrung her hands, looking at me with a strange, angry frown on her face. "That's right. He doesn't have any right to hit you at all. We'll see about this," she said with more determination in her voice than I had heard in a long time.

She grabbed a sweater and pulled it on as she hurried out the door. "Where does he live, Harry?"

"Halfway down Horsham on the right. The rundown house with the jeep on blocks in the driveway. The dog is chained to it. Mom, wait for me," I said, hurrying to catch up.

"Stay home, Harry. I'll handle this." Mom turned and waved me back to the house.

"No, Mom. I'm coming with you. The dog is in trouble."

"You can't help the dog. This isn't about the dog, Harry."

Mom ran off and didn't look back. I followed but ran from tree to tree and mail box to mail box. I lagged far enough behind so she couldn't see me. She hurried down our street and turned the corner onto Horsham. I ran faster and stayed close enough to help if she needed me.

Mom marched up to the front door streaked with greasy hand prints and stained with splotches of dirt. She banged on it quickly several times.

The door flung open and the tall, scruffy man loomed over my mother.

"What the !@!#! do yew want?" he bellowed.

Mom's eyes got very big. She shrank away as she saw how tall he was and how mean and crazy he looked.

She swayed a bit but steadied herself. "Who do you think you are hitting a child? You could've broken her jaw or knocked her out, you coward!"

The man bent down into her face. "That's what I was trying to do. She was tryin' to steal my dawg. She was trespassin' on my property. And ain't nobody trespassin' on my property and git away wit' it."

I watched Mom wave her hand in front of her face. She must have smelled the sour booze on his breath. She began to step back, her eyes growing wide with panic and fear.

"Just leave my daughter alone," she shouted.

"Yew gist keep her away from my house or I'll have the little @#$&@&@ brat arrested. Yew got that?" he roared.

Mom turned suddenly and bolted to the street. With her head down and tears streaming down her face, she ran past me.

"Oh no," I heard her mumble, "he's worse than Sam." She ran all the way to our house, threw open the door, and ran inside.

When I caught up, Mom was sitting on the worn sofa, her feet drawn up under her, her arms wrapped around her legs, her face buried in her legs. She was sobbing.

She looked up at me. "Harry, stay away from that house and that man. I don't want you to ever walk down Horsham again. Come home any way but that. If you have to, stay at school and call me to come get you."

"Mom, what's the matter? That man is terrible. We should call the police on him. He's hurting that dog, and he hurt me."

Just then, something tiny and black leaped from my shirt and landed on my Mom's hand.

"Oh my god," she screamed. "It's a flea!" She grabbed it between her fingers and squashed it.

"Harry, that dog must be infested with fleas. What else was wrong with it?"

"Its leg was bleeding and oozing pus where the chain had rubbed it raw. It didn't have a lot of hair, and its back was covered in red, flaky scabs."

"Lord, it's covered with mange, too. That's a terrible disease from tiny mites. God knows if you're covered with them. Go take a hot shower right now! Put all your clothes in the washer and wash them in hot water with lots of soap. We can't have fleas and mange in this house. I'll have to buy a flea killer tomorrow and bomb the house. Harry, can't you mind your own business just for once?"

"But Mom, aren't we going to do something? Call the police, the animal control people?" I protested.

"Do as I say—now! We're not going to do anything. Just stay away from that house. You were trespassing and it is his dog. Leave it alone!" she yelled. She jumped off the couch, bolted into her room, and slammed the door.

I slumped down on the sofa, very worried about her. I had not seen her act like this in three years, not since just before she and Dad separated.

Yikes, I remembered the fleas and mites. I ran down to the bathroom, threw my clothes into our small washer, loaded it with soap, turned it on, and jumped into the shower. I didn't want any fleas or mites to infest the house either. I knew from Grandpa how bad fleas could get. Stray cats hung around his barn; though they were great at catching mice, Grandpa complained about their fleas.

As the water pored over me, I washed everything twice and checked my body for fleas. I guessed you can't see the mites.

After I got out of the shower, dried off, and put on my pajamas, I could still hear the sound of Mom's muffled sobs coming through her door.

Now, I thought, I've screwed everything up again. It's my fault that Mom and Dad used to fight so much. Mom yelled that I shouldn't grow up with a drunk as a father, that I needed him to be sober and a good father.

I'd tried to be as good as I could be. I'd never gotten into any trouble in elementary school. I always made As and Bs on my report cards. I was always quiet and stayed out of the way when Daddy was drunk or when he woke up with a lousy hangover. I even learned how to make "Bloody Marys" he could drink so he would feel better after he woke up.

I didn't care if he drank too much. Maybe he couldn't help himself, but Mom had me help her do everything we could to get him to stop drinking. After I learned he was getting drunk almost every day, Mom forbid him to bring any booze into the house. Mom made me help her search every day to make sure he didn't have any hiding places in the house.

Mom even looked up on the Internet all the sneaky places drunks hid their booze—toilet tanks, hidden drawers in desks, behind refrigerators, in hollow books, all kinds of crazy places. That's why he always went out drinking with his pals. Although Mom and Daddy fought what seemed like all the time, he had never hit us like that rotten drunk had just hit me.

Finally, Mom just wore out with all the fighting. We never had enough money to pay the bills on time, though I knew Daddy must have earned a lot of money as store manager.

The month before they separated, she berated him when she found out we didn't have enough money to buy my new uniforms for the fourth grade at St. Brendan's. She was furious since I had grown so much between third and fourth grade she had to let out and mend my worn-out uniforms so I could meet the dress code.

I didn't care; I hated the uniforms with their short plaid skirts and white blouses and white socks and black shoes. I hated my school because the kids were so stuck up and the girls so brainless.

As I sat on my bed in my room, looking for any flea bites, I heard my mom slowly stop sobbing. I hope she fell asleep. I got off the bed, reached into my backpack for my math book, and winced as I felt a sharp pain in my right shoulder.

That jerk! I grumbled, "He better not have hurt my shoulder so that I can't throw the ball in from the sideline at the game."

On an inbounds play, I can throw it farther than anyone on our team. My skill is a real advantage since I can throw it all the way to a player on the other side of the field. Most seventh graders can barely throw it to mid-field. My throws make the other team spread out their defense. It makes gaps that make it easier for us to score. We use the gaps to pass the ball to each other as we run toward their net.

As I took my math book out, an envelope fell out with it. I stared at it in dismay.

"Oh no! The note from Mrs. Jackson. I can't show it to Mom now!"

Chapter 4
Lies and More Lies

"Thank goodness it's Friday," I mumbled as Mom called to wake me up at 6. I had tossed and turned much of the night. My thoughts were a jumbled mess. For what seemed like hours, I worried about the wretched dog and what I could do to help it. I felt petrified about getting in trouble with Mom and Mrs. Jackson. I had no idea when I finally fell asleep, but it seemed only a few minutes ago.

"Harry, get up. Time to go to school!" Mom said through the closed door to my bedroom.

I moved slowly, desperately trying to figure out some way to skip school. I didn't know how I could face Mrs. Jackson, and I knew that Mom was too upset and in too big a hurry this morning to show her the note.

"Hurry up, Harry. I haven't got all day. I can't be late for work, or they'll dock my pay," Mom yelled, knocking on the door several times.

I pulled my favorite soccer shorts off and pulled on my jeans and my Redhawks tee shirt. I gathered my books and put them in my old knapsack. I ran my hands through my messy mop of hair. It didn't help much. It still stuck out in all directions. I didn't bother to look in the mirror and I didn't care.

As I opened the door to the hallway, I heard the phone in the kitchen ring and Mom answer it.

"Hello. Oh. Sam, it's you. I'm fine. Let me get her. Harry! It's for you. It's your father."

I took the phone. "Dad, hello. I'm fine. Yes, the wedding. I remember. It's tomorrow afternoon. Right? OK, you'll pick me up early. When? About 9. Let me ask.

"Mom, Dad said he wants to pick me up tomorrow about 9. Is that okay?"

"Yes, of course. I wouldn't want you to miss the 'big day,'" Mom said sarcastically.

"Dad. That's fine. I'll see you then. Yep, I love you too. Bye."

I hung up the phone. As I turned, Mom looked quickly away, but not before I saw tears in her eyes.

"Mom, if you want me to stay here, I will. It's not that big a deal," I said.

"Oh, don't be silly. Of course, I want you to go. I want you to be the prettiest girl there and have a good time.

"Do I have to wear some dumb dress? I really don't want to."

"Well, you can't wear jeans and a soccer shirt. You have to look nice. Are you ready? Did you brush your teeth?"

"Yeah," I fibbed.

"Let's go."

Ten minutes later, just as Mom dropped me off at school, she cried, "Oh no! You didn't have any breakfast did you, Harry? And I didn't make you any lunch. What am I doing? I can't seem to remember anything these days. I'm so distracted.

"Here, take this money and at least buy a good lunch. See if you can buy a snack this morning. Are there any vending machines?" she said as she took several dollar bills out of her purse and handed them to me.

"It's okay, Mom, really. I'm not hungry any way. Save the money. I'll be okay."

"Don't be foolish. You can't go all day without eating."

"I'll eat some of Glenda's lunch. She doesn't usually eat all of hers. It's no big deal."

"No, you shouldn't ask for other people's food, even if your own mother can't remember to feed you. Take the money and eat a good lunch," she said, stuffing it into my jeans pocket.

As I got out of the car, Mom leaned over and said through the open door, "Remember what I said about staying away from Horsham Circle and that man. He's dangerous, and I don't want you anywhere near him or that dog. Do you understand me?"

"Yes, Mom. I hear you, and I'll walk straight home with Glenda. That jerk scares me, too."

"Good. Now have a great day, and we'll see what we can do about a nice dress when I get home."

After Mom left, I saw Glenda sitting on the steps leading to the school. "You didn't meet me. Where were you? I waited for you for almost half an hour," Glenda complained.

"Oh, I'm really sorry. Something terrible happened yesterday after I left your house, so I stayed up late. I got a late start, then my Dad called about the wedding tomorrow, and Mom insisted on driving me to school."

I told Glenda all about finding the abused dog and how the drunken creep had hit me and threatened my mom.

Glenda looked frightened. "On Horsham Circle? I think I've heard about that guy before. Gees, he might even be somebody my Dad hangs out with. It sounds like he loses it when he drinks too much, like my parents do sometimes. You better stay away from him like your mom said."

"But, Glenda, the dog is in real trouble. It's hurt, and it's scared, and it must be starving. I didn't even see any bowls for food or water by the creepy jeep. How could anybody treat an animal like that?"

"I know it must be horrible," Glenda said, "But you better look out for yourself first or you could get seriously hurt. That jerk might be totally bonkers."

Just then, Rory, followed by the PBJs, walked up to me and joked, "Hi, Hen-rye-etta, I see you're in trouble with Mrs. Jackson again. Now what did you do?"

He was already 13 then. He was lanky with jet black hair and bright blue eyes and a little shorter than I am. He wore a new Team USA soccer shirt and stylish jeans over his slim frame.

The PBJs snickered and laughed at me and Glenda.

"Rory, go away and leave me alone. And take 'Peanut, Butter, and Jelly' with you. I'm not in the mood for your smart mouth today. And my name is Harry!"

"I know, but I like to call you 'Henrietta' because it bugs you," Rory laughed.

"I'm telling you to cut it out," I warned him.

"Yeah, well, geez, what's bothering you? I'm just teasing you."

"None of your business."

"What are friends for if you can't talk to them?"

"Oh yeah, since when have you been my friend? All you do is try to trip me at soccer practice and make me look bad in front of Coach Bill. You make fun of me behind my back in class and get me in trouble with Mrs. Jackson."

"Yeah, well, I'm going to show you who's the best soccer player on our team, and you're just asking for it from Mrs. Jackson," Rory retorted.

"No way! I run circles around you when you don't stick your

fat foot in my way, and Mrs. Jackson would leave me alone if you didn't make so much noise she can hear you. And then she blames me for it."

"Aw, get over it. Are you coming to practice tomorrow? We've got to get ready for the championship game next week!" Rory insisted.

"No, I won't be there. My Dad is getting married again tomorrow and I have to go."

"Remarried? Wow, that was fast. I thought he just got out of the…."

Glenda kicked him in the shin before he could finish.

"Oww! What'd you do that for, squirt?"

"Stop calling her 'squirt' and leave her alone, too. She's a lot smaller than you are, you bully."

"Oh, let's leave 'em alone. They can't take a joke these days. Hen-rye-et-ta," Rory dragged out the name. "Just get ready for the game next week. We've got to win the championship this year."

He ran off with "Peanut, Butter, and Jelly" toward the school door.

"Don't worry about me," I yelled. "You just get out of my way when I kick the winning goal."

They laughed at us. "That'll be the day," Rory yelled back.

They kept running and punching each other as they bounced through the school door.

God, Rory could be such a jerk at exactly the wrong time. And his "PBJ sandwich" of friends were shaped like the cartoon Minions, except each one had two eyes and one big mouth. They followed Rory around like he was some kind of prince.

The school bell rang, and Glenda and I hurried toward our homerooms. The first half of Friday was no big deal. English, history, and art went by too fast, and I didn't pay attention because

I knew I would have to face Mrs. Jackson after lunch and recess.

At lunch and recess, Glenda and I sat by ourselves. I ate part of her sandwich and some carrots. I held onto Mom's money so I could put it back in her purse later. When anybody walked over to us, I scowled at them. They got the message and went away. At recess, I told Glenda I was going to try to sneak into Mrs. Jackson's class with the mob and hope she didn't see me.

Glenda looked at me funny as she asked, "Wh…Oh, Harry, you didn't show your note to your Mom last night, did you?"

"No, of course not! After all that trouble, Mom was crying and frightened and I didn't want to make it all worse. It was terrible as it was."

"What are you going to tell Mrs. Jackson? She's already very upset with you!"

"I hope I can sneak in and she won't see me and forget about it until Monday. Or I can cut class and hide out in the woods behind the playground until the last bell."

"If you cut class and get caught, you'll be suspended. You'd be in even more trouble than you are now. Remember everybody has already seen you in the hallway and at lunch."

"Yeah, lunch—like refried puke. Maybe I can fake getting sick, run to the bathroom, pretend to puke, and go to the nurse's office."

"Or, Harry, you could tell the truth and get it over with a lot faster than the amount of time you spend concocting all these ridiculous tricks to avoid giving your mother that note and face Mrs. Jackson."

"Geez, Glenda, you're not helping me at all! I told you why I can't give Mom that note. There's the wedding tomorrow, and she's got this thing about dressing me up. And the championship game next Saturday—I won't jeopardize playing in that. Worse than that, that poor dog could die any time, and I've got to get it away from that crazy jerk."

Glenda just stared at me and sighed. "Okay, Harry, have it your way." She got up and started walking toward the back door of the school.

"Glenda, wait! I'm sorry." I jumped up and tried to catch up to her. "I'm just so confused right now, trying to please everybody and…"

Just then the bell rang for us to go our next class—Mrs. Jackson's for the rest of the day.

As I got close to her door, I slowed down. It was now or never: Turn and run out the back door, hide in the bathroom, or go into the classroom.

I sighed and told Glenda, "Go ahead. "I'm going to go in with that bunch coming there. Maybe she won't see me."

"No such luck. You know she never misses—or forgets—anything."

Glenda was right, as she usually was about things that I did that got me into trouble. One of these days it might be a good idea if I listened to her—maybe…

As I bent over and tried to sneak into my chair behind the other kids, my tactic didn't work: I am about half a head taller than all the girls except Magda, and I couldn't bend over far enough. I winced as I heard, "Good afternoon, Henrietta. Could I speak with you please?"

As I approached her desk, I suddenly had an inspiration that might distract Mrs. Jackson so she'd forget about the note. It might even help me get back on her good side.

When I reached her desk, I asked before she could speak, "Good afternoon, Mrs. Jackson. Do you know anything about helping injured or abused dogs?"

"What? Abused dogs. Who has an abused dog?"

"Yesterday, I saw a dog that looked like it was hurt bad, and I want to help it if I can."

"Is it a stray?" Mrs. Jackson asked. "If it's near the school, we need to call the animal control department."

Frightened that they would take the dog away, I said quickly, "Oh no. It doesn't live near here. I saw it near my Dad's house."

"Well, you could call the ASPCA. That's the American Society for the Prevention of Cruelty to Animals®, or the American Humane Society®. Both of them have lots of information about how to help abused or injured animals."

"Thank you, Mrs. Jackson. I'll call them when I get home today." I turned quickly and began walking back to my desk, hoping it had worked and I had gotten away with it.

"One moment, young lady. Where's the note I asked you to show your mother and have her sign?"

I turned and smiled nervously, "Ummm. I didn't see her last night or this morning. My mom worked overtime last night, and she had to be in early, so she was gone when I got up and came to school by myself. I left the note for her to read when she wakes up."

"Didn't I see you get out of her car this morning?" Mrs. Jackson asked sternly as she peered down her nose at me.

"Uhh…No, ma'am. I walked to school with Glenda."

Mrs. Jackson looked up and toward the back of the class.

"Glenda."

"Yes, Mrs. Jackson."

"What did you and Harry talk about walking to school this morning?"

"Uh? I didn't…Oh, we talked about some dog she saw yesterday."

"Oh, you did. Uh-huh…"

The teacher turned back and stared at Harry. "You were supposed to bring that note back to me signed today. You could have left it so your Mom found it when she came home last night, couldn't you?"

"Yes, ma'am. I didn't think about that."

"Yes, well, Harry, lately that's been your problem. You are not paying attention in class, you are breaking the rules, and you are defying my instructions. I think you should stay after school today so you can think about it a little more carefully."

"Aww, Mrs. Jackson…".

"No. And you're not going to just sit here in my class, thinking you got away with something. You're going to put your time to good use. I am going to give you a note, and after school, you must go to the library and find information about abused dogs. Since today is Friday, by next Tuesday, I want you to write a three-page essay about abused dogs. You must find and use established facts and figures about the extent of the problem, its causes, and its solutions. You should provide accurate data and include a chart that shows how the problem has gotten better or worse over time. Then, next Friday, you will give the class a two-minute oral report on your findings."

"Oh, okay. Yes, ma'am. That's a good idea. Thank you. I'll learn a lot, and I want to share it with everyone else." Actually, I would rather have all my teeth pulled than stand up in front of the class and talk. At least, writing the report was better than being sent to the principal's office.

I tried to turn again and walk quickly back to my seat.

"Not so fast. I'm going to call your mother this weekend. When can I reach her?"

"Oh, she's working all weekend. A lot of overtime at the factory."

"Henrietta!" Mrs. Jackson said sharply. "When can I call her?"

"Ummm…I guess Saturday morning about 9:15 would be okay."

"Tell her tonight that I'm going to call her tomorrow morning."

"Yes, ma'am."

I dragged back to my chair and slumped down.

"Oh crap," I fretted. "Now what am I going to do?"

I stewed the rest of the afternoon and didn't pay any attention to Mrs. Jackson's math and science lessons. At least I turned in my homework on time. I had to figure out a way to make sure Mom was out of the house Saturday morning, but then I remembered I was leaving with Dad about 9. I hoped he's on time so I can get out of there before Mrs. Jackson calls. I'm certainly not going to tell Mom about the call since she doesn't know about the note.

I probably won't be home from the wedding until late Sunday afternoon. Maybe Mom will have calmed down after a day or so.

After school, as the rest of the class stormed out to catch their buses or walk home with their friends, I got the note from Mrs. Jackson and went to the library.

At the door, Mrs. Reynolds, the librarian, stopped me. "Harry, what are you doing here? I hardly ever see you coming to the library by yourself. I was just about to leave. What's going on?"

"Here's a note from Mrs. Jackson. She wants you to help me find out stuff about abused dogs for a paper I've got to do for next week."

"Well, I have a few minutes. Abused dogs you say? What's that all about? I have two small dachshunds, and I would be very angry if anyone tried to hurt my dogs. Let's start with the library database. It should have lots of information."

For the next 20 minutes, Mrs. Reynolds moved quickly from one page to another, and we found a lot of disturbing information.

"Look here, Harry. Look at these pictures. Some research labs do terrible things to dogs and rabbits just to test lipstick and toothpaste and other simple things. They don't need to do that," Ms. Reynolds said angrily.

"It looks like there are millions of pets that people don't take care of. How can they do that?" I cried.

"That's right. Like children, pets can't protect themselves, but so many people don't care. They treat pets like they were toys and ignore or abuse them and then throw them away when they get tired of them. People ought to do a lot more to help dogs and cats that people abuse. It's terrible," Mrs. Reynolds said.

"You're right, Mrs. Reynolds. I saw a dog that was in terrible shape. It was so thin and so miserable. Its leg was rubbed raw and bleeding."

"Harry, you could call the animal control department and have them come and take the dog away from its owner."

I lied again to protect my Mom. "Uhh...the dog isn't near here. It lives near my Dad's house."

"Oh, perhaps you could ask your Dad to call animal control where he lives."

"I could do that, but I just feel so bad about the poor dog. He didn't ask to be treated like that. He needs someone to take care of him."

"You're right, Harry, but sometimes bad things happen and we don't know why for a while until things sort themselves out." Mrs. Reynolds patted my right shoulder. I almost said, "Ouch," because it still hurt where the jerk hit me, but I just flinched and grunted instead.

"What's the matter? Did I hurt you?" Mrs. Reynolds asked.

"I'm sorry. No, I just wasn't expecting it, so I was surprised. Thank you for your help. It means a lot to me. With this information, I can tell the kids in my class how bad the problem is and encourage them to report stuff to animal control when they see it."

"You're very welcome, Harry. We need a lot more caring people like you in the world. If you'd like, come back Monday morning before class starts and we'll look for more information. These printouts and this list of web sites should keep you busy this weekend," she said.

As Mrs. Reynolds picked up her bags, I left the library and went back to Mrs. Jackson's class.

"What did you learn about the problem, Harry"?

"It's awful, Mrs. Jackson. Did you know that just in this town there have been more than 500 cases of dog abuse in the past five years, but only a handful of the abusers were ever convicted of a crime and none of those jerks were sent to jail? Most of them were given probation or a warning. Some were even given community service to work at the county animal shelter on weekends. That's sounds crazy to me—like putting the fox in the henhouse.

"The police even broke up a dogfighting ring just outside of town a few years ago. More than two dozen men were betting thousands of dollars on which vicious dog would kill the other one first. To make the dogs vicious killers, they beat them, starve them, keep them in tiny pens, taunt them with sharp prods and sticks, and train them to attack other dogs and people. That's just barbaric! How would they like it if they were beaten and starved and constantly taunted and attacked by other people with electric prods? An eye for an eye!

"Worst of all, animal abuse closely relates to child abuse and violence against spouses. And it's almost always men who do it—psychos or criminals with long records of abuse that go back to their childhoods. Most of them were abused themselves when they were kids." I almost shouted at Mrs. Jackson, but she understood how I upset I felt.

"Harry, it is a terrible problem. It always stuns me how cruel people can be to animals and each other. I'm not in the least surprised either by the number of cases in our town or how leniently the courts treat animal abusers. I don't know if I'd go as far as an 'eye for an eye,' but they deserve much worse punishment than they usually get," Mrs. Jackson said.

"I'm glad you found out some great information to share with the class. I look forward to receiving your report. You may go home now."

"Thank you, Mrs. Jackson," and I turned to scurry out the door, hoping our talk had distracted her.

Like Glenda said, no such luck.

Mrs. Jackson called out to me as I reached the classroom door. "Henrietta! Remember to tell your mother I'm going to call her tomorrow morning at 9:15 and give her my note!"

"Yes, ma'am," I said, knowing it was a lie when I said it. I was going to do my best to avoid telling my Mom anything before I left for Daddy's wedding tomorrow morning. Maybe I could call him and see if he can pick me up earlier…

Glenda, usually happy to wait for me, stood outside the school with clenched fists and an angry look.

"You made me lie to Mrs. Jackson. If she ever finds out, I'll be in big trouble. What do you think you were doing? I'm really mad at you!"

"I'm sorry. I didn't know what to do. I just said the first thing that popped into my mind. But you're my best friend. I thought you wouldn't mind helping me."

"Yeah, I am your best friend, but I don't want to lie for you. And I thought you were MY best friend. Friends don't ask friends to lie for them and get them into trouble. You shouldn't take advantage of me like that. It was a terrible thing to do. Leave me out of it," Glenda actually yelled at me. I had never seen her so upset before! She turned and stomped away.

"Glenda, wait!" I caught up with Glenda. "I don't want you to be mad at me, too. My mom, Mrs. Jackson, the dog. Everything is terrible!"

"You should have thought about that before you started doing things that made everybody mad at you," Glenda said as she kept walking away.

I stopped, stung by Glenda's harsh words. But I knew she was right. I have been making everybody mad at me. It was my fault. I just didn't know what to do. I felt so miserable all of the time. I put on this false "happy face" just so people would think I was happy. I just wanted everything to be good again, I just wanted to help that wretched dog, and every time I tried, I seemed to make everything worse.

Grandpa was wrong with his advice—I didn't know in my heart the right thing to do about any of it.

I turned slowly and trudged home. I did make darn sure I avoided Horsham Circle and the dog's house; I certainly didn't need any more trouble today. I hoped that the dog was better off today than it was yesterday, but I knew that I was wrong...I felt angry and helpless and useless.

Chapter 5
The Pre-Wedding Blahs

Friday evening after dinner, Mom and I rushed around my room. Mom was frantic about finding a pretty dress I could wear to the wedding. It had been so long since I had worn a dress, I had outgrown every dress buried deep in my closet. I certainly couldn't have worn the black dress I wore to the funeral; it was all wrong and about three sizes too small anyway.

"Mom, I hate dresses. Why can't I just wear jeans?" I begged.

"For one thing, it would be rude not to dress for a wedding. For another, I don't want your father and his family to think I don't know how to dress you and take care of you. With this wedding, no telling what he's thinking.

"Well, you've just grown too fast. There's nothing here," she said, exasperated. "We'll just have to go to Field-Mart and buy you something."

"But Mom, don't waste the money on a dress that I'm never going to wear again."

"You don't worry about that. I'll just put it on my credit card and pay for it later," Mom said. That was what I was worried about!

We hustled into Mom's little car and drove to Field-Mart. We spent two miserable hours rummaging through dresses and shoes and all kinds of accessories for young girls. All the stuff that I hated.

Mom bought me a new yellow dress with an autumn flower print and a new pair of burgundy dress shoes. We argued whether I should buy heels, panty hose, a new bra, and make-up. With the exception of sports bras, I never wear any of that stuff.

I protested, "Mom, I don't want to wear panty hose. It itches in all the wrong places. I barely need a bra any way. Why can't I wear a sports bra like I always do under my jersey. Heels! I feel like I'm going to keel over and fall flat on my face. I'm so tall already that I'll tower over anybody my age. And makeup will make me look like a Barbie doll on stilts."

"Just this once, young lady, you might try looking like a girl. You might like it. If that Rory you like saw you, he might be impressed."

"Rory? Yuck. He's just a dummy who thinks he can play soccer better than me. No way."

"Well, I'm sure your father will want you to look nice, and I'm sure you want to look nice for him."

"He doesn't seem to care what I wear."

"But this is a special occasion for him and for you."

After what seemed like forever, we compromised. I agreed to wear the dress, a very simple bra, and the panty hose, but I got to wear flats and put on only natural looking makeup. Besides hating all that stuff, I didn't want Mom to put so many extra purchases on her credit card. She already had trouble paying the bill on time sometimes.

At the cash register when we checked out, it was embarrassing because the first card my Mom tried to use didn't work; the clerk told her she had reached her credit limit. Mom turned a bright red as she pulled out another card. When she handed it to the clerk, she turned her eyes toward the ceiling like she was praying this card would work. Fortunately for her, the charges went through. I heard her breath a deep sigh of relief.

I felt even guiltier about buying the clothes because she was overdoing the whole dress-up thing when I would never wear those clothes again. I would probably outgrow them in less than a year, and if I never had to wear another dress, I would be happy.

As we drove home, my mother was quiet, and I felt troubled. "Mom," I said cautiously, "I wish Daddy wasn't getting married again. I didn't see him for so long when he was in rehab. Just as I was getting to know him better, he got together with Kim, and all that trouble started. Now, he's already getting married. And to Kim, too. She looks like she could be my sister. I barely even met her before she stopped coming around most of the time when I visited after you got mad at Dad."

"Well…It wasn't right for her to be there while you were there. They could have done lots of things with you during weekends if they'd wanted to. And your father could have offered to buy you a dress if he'd wanted as well," Mom snapped.

I could tell she was getting upset again, so I stopped complaining and just sat quietly. We drove for a few moments in strained silence.

"Oh, Harry. I'm sorry. I'm just really out of sorts lately. Look, there's a Krum's Kustard. Let's stop and get an ice cream! You love their sprinkle cones."

"I'm not hungry, Mom. It's okay. You've spent enough on me already."

"Oh, live a little. It'll be all right," Mom said, as cheerfully as she could.

Hoping I could at least make Mom feel better about spending the money for the dress, I ate a small cone after we stopped.

When we returned to our house, I took the new clothes to my room and laid them out for the next day. I finished packing my travel backpack with my jeans and sweat shirt for Sunday, and I went to bed.

As I tossed and turned, I thought if I keep the dress and shoes clean, Mom could return them and get her money back. I tried to think about that rather than think about Dad and Kim, the wedding, the wretched dog, Rory and the championship, Mrs. Jackson, and her note and her call. All of it rushed around inside my head. My one good thought was I had managed to avoid telling Mom about Mrs. Jackson's note. Maybe Mrs. Jackson would forget to call, I hoped as I drifted off to sleep.

I was awakened early Saturday morning about 7 by the clattering of pans in the kitchen. "What're you doing, Mom?" I asked, poking my head out my door.

"I'm going to make your favorite breakfast. No telling when they're going to feed you after the wedding. Eggs and bacon and waffles with butter and syrup."

"It sounds good, but you don't have to make such a big deal. I'm not going to starve."

"I know, but I want to do it. So, take a shower and be sure to wash your hair—twice. Get it really clean. Breakfast'll be ready by the time you get done. After breakfast, I'll help you fix your hair."

I did as I was told, and I felt only a little guilty about the enormous amount of food I ate. I was starved. I hadn't told Mom I had saved the money she gave me for lunch Friday and I had not had time to eat before we went shopping. I planned to put the money back in Mom's wallet when she wasn't looking.

"Goodness," Mom said. "You were as hungry this morning as you are after a game. I told you you'd like it."

"Yes, Mom. It was great! Thanks!"

After I dressed in my new outfit, Mom fussed and fussed fixing my hair as I squirmed and fretted for what seemed like an hour. The dress fabric itched. The panty hose itched. The new shoes pinched my toes. She fixed my hair so it looked curlier and thicker than ever.

"I hope none of the other kids from school see me today. I look like a Barbie doll freak."

"Hush, you look beautiful. One of these days, Harry, you're going to realize what a natural beauty you are. You got the best genes from both Grandpa and Gram. He was handsome and she was a great beauty. I'm afraid they skipped a generation with me," Mom said.

She looked sadly across the living room at an old picture of a handsome young man wearing a white suit and a panama hat. He was standing facing the camera with one foot on the running board of a vintage convertible, his arm propped on the window sill. He had a broad smile on his face. Sitting in the car was a beautiful young woman with thick waves of reddish-blonde hair, exactly like mine.

"You've got your grandmother's hair and figure and your grandfather's smile and energy. You're very lucky," Mom said.

"I wish I had known Gram. She died when I was little, didn't she?"

"Yes, when you were just two years old. She had lung cancer. She smoked two packs of cigarettes a day and she wouldn't quit." Tears began welling up in her eyes. She wiped her eyes.

"Well, enough of that. Today should be a happy day for you."

"I don't feel very happy. I just feel itchy, my feet hurt, and I hate my hair," I complained.

"Oh, you'll grow out of this tomboy thing. Pretty soon, you'll want to wear dresses and fix your own hair."

"Not me!"

Mom laughed, "Wait and see what you think a few years from now."

Just then, we heard a car pull up in front of the house. As we opened the door, Daddy, dressed in a dark suit and a white shirt, got out of a shiny red Mustang convertible and walked across our small, bare yard to the door.

"Hello, Sarah. How are you doing?" Daddy asked Mom at the door.

"Hi, Sam. I'm fine. Congratulations. I hope you'll be happy…this time."

"Well…" Daddy stammered. "I hope so for all of our sakes."

I slowly eased out from behind Mom, my head down. I wanted to disappear.

"Henrietta, you look terrific!" Dad exclaimed. "When did this happen?"

"Oh, Mom made me. I hate it. I look like a Barbie doll. And Daddy, call me 'Harry'!"

"Excuse me!" he laughed. "Harry, you look like quite the young lady. Sarah, she looks great."

"No child of mine would be going to your wedding looking like a ragamuffin, Sam."

"Of course not. I'm very proud of her and glad for you. So, Harry ready to go? Why don't you get in the car while I talk to your mother for a minute?"

I took a real look at Dad's new car for the first time as I walked down the front steps and toward it. "Wow, Dad! When did you get this? It's a beaut."

"Oh, it's a couple of years old and got some miles on it. It's just a little wedding present for Kim and me. Glad you like it."

I got into the new car. I felt the plush seats and checked out the controls on what looked like the super sleek panel on the U.S.S. Enterprise in the latest *Star Trek* movie. I pressed the electric door switch and lowered the window so I could listen to Mom and Dad.

On the doorstep, Dad said to Mom, "Look, Sarah. I know we've had a rough time of it. But things are getting better one day at a time. When Kim and I get back in a week, I want us to sit down and talk with you and Harry about helping both of you. Both Kim and I would like Harry to spend more time with us as well."

Mom crossed her arms and frowned. "Why this sudden change of heart, Sam? Feeling guilty? Wanna be a great dad in front of Kim?"

"Now Sarah. Let's not get into all that again, especially today. I'm making a polite request. It's something I've wanted to do for a long time. I just ask for a few minutes to apologize and offer a better way to move forward. We have a great kid, and I want her—and you—to have the best I can provide. In a very real way, I need to do it for me as well as for Harry. You can accept it or not. That's up to you. How about it?"

Mom didn't say anything for a long moment. "Ok, Sam. We'll talk some more when you get back. If you can afford a new car, at least you could afford to help your daughter some more."

"Sure, Sarah. That's part of what I want to talk about. I've got to go. My parents will bring Harry back tomorrow afternoon. I don't want them driving tonight after the party."

Sarah said, "Oh, I thought she might be back tonight. Where are you and Kim going?"

"Just to the Bahamas for a week. We'll be back by next Saturday. I don't want my parents to drive at night, and Kim and I have to catch a 6 a.m. plane. They're staying at my place so Harry will be fine."

"Okay, Sam. Just make sure your parents bring her back here by 3 p.m. tomorrow. She has homework to do."

I didn't have any homework except that report on abused dogs, but I knew Mom wanted me home as soon as she could get me back.

"Thanks very much, Sarah. I wish you the best."

"You, too, Sam."

Dad walked down the front steps and down the driveway by our tiny front yard. It was a far cry from our old house with the landscaped lawn and two-car garage.

Dad got into the car. "So, you like my new wheels?"

"Yeah, it's cool!"

As we reversed out of the driveway, I saw Mom standing on the porch waving goodbye, so I waved goodbye through the open window.

As I waved, I heard the phone ring in the house. Mom turned to go inside and answer it.

I froze and looked at the time on the clock radio. "Oh no!" my mind freaked. "It's 9:15. It must be Mrs. Jackson calling about the note!"

As Dad drove away, I looked back toward my small house with the rickety wood fence that needed painting, the bare front yard, and the filthy vinyl siding. I felt so bad for Mom that we had to live like this, and I prayed that the phone call was a wrong number.

As much as I wished Mrs. Jackson wouldn't call, I knew that it was her calling; Mrs. Jackson was always on time.

I slumped down in the comfortable seat. I felt miserable. I tried to use telepathy to make Daddy drive faster so Mom couldn't burst out the door and stop us. She didn't.

I dreaded the long conversation I was sure they were beginning. I also dreaded the 30 hours until I got home—but who was counting?—and learned what Mrs. Jackson had told Mom and what she was going to do to me. So much for my strategy to help my Mom avoid more sorrow and me to avoid more trouble. Maybe Mom would think about it and see my point of view before I returned.

Chapter 6
Dad's Happy Wedding—
And Mine, Too

Dad chattered happily as we drove along the interstate highway toward his town about 50 miles from my house. I sat quietly, nodding my head and mumbling agreement at the right time.

Finally, Daddy paused and gave me a quizzical look, "What's up, Harry? You're awfully quiet and you look unhappy."

"Oh, nothing." I said. I didn't want to upset him on his wedding day, and I didn't know how he could help me with school, the dog, Mom, being grounded, anything. He was hardly ever around, and when he was, he tried too hard to be the perfect Dad. He always took me places like the zoo, to a movie, or out for hikes. He always did most of the talking like he was trying to impress me or something.

I changed the subject. "Dad, how old is Kim anyway?"

He laughed, "Oh, so that's it. You think she's too young for me."

"Well, she looks like she could be my sister."

"Actually, Kim is 25. I'm only 38, so yes, she's younger, but she's a wonderful person. I really want both of you to get to know each other when we get back from our honeymoon. Remember,

Harry, your mom is 31, so she's younger than me, too."

"Yeah, but Kim just acts so much younger than Mom."

"That's one of the things I love about Kim. She's so full of energy and life. She's great fun, and she's been so wonderful to me for the past three years since the divorce."

"You've known her three years!" I said, surprised.

"Yes, we became friends when I was at the rehab center, and one thing led to another after that."

"She was in the center with you?"

"Oh no, she led one of the recovery meetings there. She's way ahead of me with more than 8 years in the program. But we share the same problem and the same solution, so we have a lot in common. All that attracted us to each other."

"Well, why didn't you come to see us more and let me spend more time with you?"

"Harry, I'm very sorry. I know I should have as things got better. All I can say is that I just wasn't ready. Your Mom and I also had that disagreement about Kim's visits, so that didn't encourage me to spend more time with you. But I told your mom this morning—and it's true—that when Kim and I get back, we want to sit down with you and her and talk about making some good changes."

"What does Kim think about all that?" I asked skeptically. I doubted Kim would be very happy about being more involved in my life. Geez, she probably even wanted to start a family of her own. That would be weird—to have a stepmother who could be my sister and a brother or sister young enough to be my child. They might think they'd be getting a built-in babysitter for the kid, but no way, not me! I hate dirty diapers and screaming kids.

"Harry," Dad interrupted my thoughts. "Kim is the one who insisted that I ask. She feels that I've got to get straight with you and your mother if she and I are going to be happy together. I know she's right."

I was surprised by this change in Dad's attitude toward Mom and me. The divorce had been very tough on my mom. Since the divorce, though both of them tried to keep it from me, I'd heard, through the thin bedroom walls, Mom yelling at him on the phone when he hadn't paid the alimony check on time.

So, if doing something good for Mom was Kim's idea, maybe she wasn't so bad after all. I would wait and see. I kept these thoughts to myself.

I changed the subject again, and we talked about my soccer team and the championship game next Saturday.

"Dad, are you going to get back in time for the game?"

"I don't know. I'd like to but no promises. We're supposed to leave the island about 8 in the morning and get back home by about 2. When's your game?"

"It starts at 3 if the Pee Wee championship before our game doesn't go into overtime. Is that enough time?"

"If we don't have any trouble changing planes in Miami, we might make the second half, so we'll do our best to be there."

"Okay. It'll be fine if you can't be there."

"I really do want to be here to support you. I want to see my star player kick the winning goal, now don't I?"

I blushed and smiled at the compliment.

A few minutes later, we exited the highway, turned onto a back road, and drove by some farms. We soon arrived at a small wooden chapel sitting off the road in a grove of oak and maple trees. In the morning light of a crisp, clear fall day, the leaves blazed in brilliant reds and golden yellows.

"Wow! What a beautiful spot, Dad!"

"You like it? Kim and I really got to know each other here at our AA meetings, and it's the perfect spot for a small wedding with just a few friends and family."

As we got out of Dad's car, his parents, Edgar and Selma, walked up to us in the small gravel parking lot.

"My, my," my short, plump, blue-haired grandmother said. "Who is this? This lovely young lady couldn't be our granddaughter Henrietta?" She gave me a big hug.

"Hi, Grandma. The dress itches, the shoes hurt my feet, and I look like a Barbie doll," I complained as I squirmed under the woman's large arms.

"Now, now. Don't let her tease you, Harry. Come here and give me a hug, too," my razor-thin grandfather said, holding his arms out for me.

Everything about Edgar was thin: his gray hair, his sharp nose, his cheeks. Even in his dark gray suit, his shoulders, his arms, his legs, even his feet in narrow shoes, looked bony.

I turned to face him. "Hi, Pops!" I said as I hugged him. I whispered, "Thanks for calling me Harry. I wish everybody else would." I liked "Pops" Edgar because he seemed to believe that everything was a bit of joke. He teased Grandma Chapman all the time, and he never seemed to take anything too seriously. He always seemed to be happy to see me, on the rare occasions Mom would let me visit them or when they came to visit us. Usually, only around Christmas or Easter.

Since the divorce and Grandpa died, they've wanted me to visit during the summer where they live in a retirement community in Florida, but Mom won't let me. I guess she feels angry with them, too, although I don't understand why. Maybe it's just because they are Dad's parents, and she wants to stay mad at everyone connected with him.

He whispered back, "Oh, give her time, child. Your grandma

always called you Henrietta, and it's hard for her to change an old habit when she's got her mind made up."

"Samuel," my grandmother pronounced, "Kim looks just gorgeous. I'm glad you got here on time. The preacher was getting worried."

"Oh, I wouldn't miss this for the world," Dad laughed.

Just then, a short, young woman with long black hair, dressed in a full length, beige wedding gown came out the door of the church.

Dad cried in mock horror, "Oh no, I'm not supposed to see the bride before the wedding! It's bad luck!"

"Don't be silly, Sam. Come here. We've got a problem and I think I have the perfect solution," Kim said. She turned toward me, "Hello, Harry. I'm so glad you're here. It means so much to both your Dad and me for you to join us. It just wouldn't be the perfect wedding without you."

"Hello, Kim. Uh…thank you. It looks like it's going to be nice. Your dress is beautiful," I said shyly. Her gorgeous wedding dress was obviously expensive, and my cheap Field-Mart dress and shoes looked pitiful next to hers.

"Just give us a minute. I want to talk to your Dad about something."

"Okay."

Dad and Kim turned and walked a few feet away and began whispering to each other. As Kim talked quickly, but quietly, Dad nodded his head a couple of times, frowned once, glanced at me, shrugged his shoulders, and finally gave a big smile.

"Harry, please come here a minute. We want to ask you for a favor."

I felt unsure and a bit nervous as I walked over toward them. What did they want from me? I was just here because Mom let me come.

"Would you do us the honor of being our flower girl?" Kim asked.

"What…Huh? Me a flower girl? That'd be weird. Aren't flower girls like three or four years old? It'd be really embarrassing to walk down the aisle by myself since I'm 12 and so tall. Why do you need a flower girl anyway?"

My Dad jumped in when he shouldn't have. "You're like the lead blocker," he joked. "It'll be easy. Just walk down the aisle, and when you get to the front, just turn left and sit with my mother and father in the front row."

"In front of all those people? I don't know," I said warily.

"It'd be really special if you'd do that for us. We wanted to find a way for you to be in the wedding. But we didn't know how you felt, and we were just too unsure to ask. Now, we've got a problem, and you could help us and participate in the wedding! We really didn't mean to spring this on you. We had asked a daughter of a friend of Kim's, but she's sick and…" Dad explained.

"Oh, so that's it," I said sharply.

"No, that's not 'it,' whatever 'it' is, Harry. I'm sorry. I really am. I've had a hard time figuring out what the right thing to do about the wedding would be. I want you to be here more than anything. I was very worried whether your mom would let you or whether you'd even want to come."

"So, you want me to be a pinch hitter."

"Yes, sort of like that, Harry. You look so nice and…" Kim said.

"But you wouldn't have asked me if I didn't look nice, if I'd shown up in my soccer shorts, right…?"

"Well…" Kim blushed. "Well, no, Harry. That's not it at all. It's just we want you to be in the wedding, and we thought it would be…"

Dad interrupted. "OK, Harry. If you don't want to do it, that's okay. We don't have to have a flower girl. It was just an idea. We thought you might want to help.

"Just go with Grandma and Grandpa and we'll see you after the wedding. I'm sorry if we upset you. We didn't want to do that. C'mon, Kim. The minister will be waiting for us."

As Dad and Kim turned and walked up the small stone steps into the church together, Kim turned back and gave me a small smile and mouthed the words, "It's OK."

My face burned with embarrassment. Why did Dad do that? I was just asking questions. Being a flower girl at my age would just be dumb. And I'd never live it down if Rory or the other guys on the team ever found out.

Standing nearby, my grandparents frowned a bit and sighed because they seemed to have heard everything. Wringing her hands in a lace handkerchief, Grandma said, "Well, Henrietta. Let's go in. Take my arm, Edgar, and help me up the stairs."

I followed my grandparents into the small chapel and sat down in the front row facing a small altar. I looked around and saw that the light inside the chapel was muted. It felt cool and was very quiet. Its walls were paneled in dark walnut. Every few feet, a tall stained glass window made of thousands of tiny pieces of glass in abstract designs was topped with an oval arch shaped like half a football. The filtered light cast shades of dozens of colors blending together. The colors shone in wide, bright lines across 10 old wooden pews divided into five rows. The pews in each row were separated by a deep red carpet. The whole chapel looked like it was loved and cared for by its small congregation.

I felt very relaxed and at peace, the tension draining away.

About 25 people in groups of two or three sat scattered in the pews. Across the aisle from me, I saw another woman, who looked a lot younger than my grandmother. She was dressed in a stylish dark blue 'mother-of-the-bride' dress. It must be Kim's mother as she, too, had long black hair and was just as trim. She looked over at me and smiled, and I saw Kim's smile on her face. No doubt.

I hoped Kim's father was with her. I don't seem to know anybody's parents who aren't divorced or separated, don't drink too much or take drugs, or have died already from alcohol or drugs or both. At Carver Middle, a few kids' fathers, even one kid's mother, had been killed fighting in Iraq or Afghanistan.

It hurts to be what the parents and teachers called "latch key kids" because we have only one parent who's working and is never home when we get home from school. I'm glad I have soccer practice two or three days a week, or I'd be bored out of my skull. The other days I hang around with Glenda after school. When I get home, I catch up on my homework and help my mom with the chores. Otherwise, like so many kids I know, I'd do nothing but watch junk TV or play video games all afternoon until their moms or dads came home.

Yet, Dad was getting married again to a pretty young woman while Mom, who looked so pretty in the old pictures I had seen, stayed angry and depressed all the time.

It just didn't seem fair. Dad and Kim seem to love each other, and Kim seems okay. I hoped he got it right the second time. But the divorce still hurt Mom and me like the devil, living in that cruddy house and just scraping by every month. My calm feeling withered as I let my complaints take over my thinking.

Curious about the type of people who were invited, I turned to look around the church; I didn't recognize any of the other people. I wondered if any of Dad's old "friends" would be there. I hoped not because they had caused Mom and me so much trouble when

Dad and she were still married. They were the ones who used to bring Dad home drunk almost every night and drag him to the door or leave him in the yard. They didn't seem like very good friends to me; they seemed more like selfish bums.

A few moments later, an organ hidden in the far corner behind the altar began to play a familiar tune. A door to the right opened, and Dad walked in, looking solemn and nervous, with another man about his age. Sam looked at his parents and me, smiled a nervous smile, and looked back toward the preacher.

The music changed and became what I thought was probably the famous "wedding march." Everyone stood up and turned to face the door of the chapel. Holding an older man's arm, obviously her father, Kim smiled radiantly beneath a sheer veil, as she walked down the aisle looking from side to side and nodding at her friends.

As she passed the front row, she looked down at me, smiled and winked.

I was surprised and felt a little guilty. Maybe carrying a bunch of flowers down the aisle for a few seconds wouldn't have been so bad after all.

The ceremony was over before I knew it. The minister—I guess it was, he was only wearing a suit and not a collar or a robe—said all the stuff they usually say at weddings. I watched Dad take Kim's hand and turn toward the minister. He spoke the words I had heard many times in movies and on TV "about until death do you part" and all that.

I wasn't very convinced. If the words meant what they said, then why did Mom and Dad ever get divorced?

Then, in a surprise to me, Dad walked up to the altar, looked at Kim, and said in a quavering voice: "Kim. You are a miracle. You have restored my soul, my belief, my life. I will do all I can to repay your faith and trust, and I give thanks every day because God brought you into my life. I am the luckiest man alive that someone as wonderful as you could ever fall in love with someone like me. I love you."

I saw tears well up in my grandmother's eyes, and my grandfather wiped his eyes with a handkerchief. Behind me, I heard a few sniffles and sobs. I felt strange—very happy and very sad at the same time.

Dad stepped aside and Kim walked to the altar. She looked at him and said, "Sam. I am so grateful that God would bring to me someone with your courage, your joy, your passion, your incredible capacity to love. I do love you, and I promise to love you with all my heart and all my soul."

I swallowed hard, and a tear, the first one I had felt since Grandpa had died, trickled down my check. I didn't know why. I should have felt mad at Dad for leaving us and getting married again so soon. Instead, I just felt happy for him and for Kim. Maybe they would have true love if they stayed sober. That seemed to be the trick.

After they spoke, the minister declared them husband and wife and the ceremony ended. Dad gave Kim a very serious kiss and grinned at her like a happy maniac. Then, they turned toward us and to the sound of the organ, they sailed down the aisle arm in arm with wide smiles and out the door.

Outside in the churchyard, Dad and Kim were waiting to shake hands and hug everyone.

As I came into the yard, I shuffled over to them and mumbled, "I'm sorry, Dad. I didn't want to do anything to ruin your day."

"No big deal. We shouldn't have put you on the spot. It was a lot to ask without notice. Our fault. Just forget about it, and just be as happy for us as we are," Dad said and gave me a big hug.

"Can I get in on this, too?" Kim asked.

"Sure," I mumbled. I let them pull me in for a three-way hug. It felt so good to be hugged that way again. I had forgotten how it felt to be safe and cared for.

After everyone had shaken hands, exchanged hugs, and were standing around the churchyard talking, Dad announced that everyone should walk over to the small church hall for the reception. Dad and Kim each took one of my hands and walked with me. Maybe that's how we could have walked down the aisle together; that would have been awesome!

Inside the hall were a few small tables with what they call "finger food"—sliced veggies and dip—and some cookies, bottles of soda, and a full punch bowl. A few chairs lined the walls. Looking around, I realized that it wasn't exactly the fancy party that Mom expected.

I left Dad and Kim when friends came up to talk to them. I walked toward my grandparents who were talking with the couple who appeared to be Kim's parents. I stopped a few feet behind them and listened to what my grandmother said.

"I never thought I'd see the day this would happen. It's a real miracle. My Sam was so sick and so crazy. That boy was always a handful, always wild, and we did all we could to calm him down, but nothing seemed to help. Your Kim sure has brought out the best in him."

"They're good for each other, Selma. Our Kim had plenty of problems of her own. We're just so thankful that she got help in her freshman year in college. Both of them seem dedicated to staying sober and out of trouble," Kim's mother replied.

"Well, I prayed for him all the time, and somebody up there must have been listening. We thought for sure Sam was going to die before he got taken to that rehab center."

I felt shocked. My father, dying? I remembered that my Mom cried a lot when Dad didn't come home at night. I remembered the "dad swimming in the yard" incident. And one time, he brought his "friends," Buck and Clinton, home and the three of them had drunk far too much and wrecked the living room.

I sat down quietly in the nearest chair, as I began to understand the truth about what my Dad had been like before we left and why my Mom couldn't endure any more of his craziness.

I looked around the room and I didn't see any of Dad's old "friends." Thank God! Instead, I saw friendly, well-dressed, happy people; a few even looked quite distinguished.

A few minutes later, Dad's best man, the friend who had stood at the altar with him, picked up a tall, thin glass, pinged a fork against it several times, saying, "Attention please. Time for the best man's toast. Everyone, pick up your glasses."

Everyone picked up from the nearest table a plastic cup that looked like a champagne glass. Each was filled with a sparkling, gold-tinged liquid.

The friend said, "To Sam and Kim. A toast to their love, their faith in a Higher Power, their mutual trust, and their 12 Step Way of Life. May they have a lifetime of joy together." Pausing, he turned toward me and said, "And may they have children as lovely, as smart, and as talented as Sam's daughter, Harry. I give you Sam and Kim, Mr. and Mrs. Chapman."

"To Sam and Kim!" everyone roared and drank from their glasses.

As I sipped—I knew I wasn't supposed to drink alcohol, but the drink wasn't champagne like I expected! It was sparkling apple cider!

My grandfather Edgar was surprised, too. "Ma, what is this? This ain't champagne."

"Of course not, Edgar," my grandmother admonished him. "They're not serving any liquor here. Ain't liquor caused enough trouble in this family for long enough? Now hush and be polite."

Someone turned on a CD player and put on some dance music. Someone else called out, "Dance with your bride, Sam, or do you have two left feet?"

Sam said, laughing, "We'll see who has two left feet." He swept Kim into his arms and danced lightly across the floor. As they turned, he smiled broadly toward the man who had joked with him.

As they circled the floor and came close to my table, they slowed and Dad said, "Harry, come on. Let's dance."

"I don't know how!"

"Don't worry. I do. Just follow my lead."

Kim said, smiling at her, "Come on. Our first dance won't be the same unless you join us."

I felt a rush of joy well up inside me, but I wasn't going to let them know it. I moved slowly out of my chair, but my father took my right arm and swept me onto the floor. The three of us twirled and swirled until we were out of breath. I never knew my Dad was such a good dancer and Kim felt as light as a feather. I don't know how Dad knew how to move both of us around in time with the music, but he did. It felt great!

After *our* first dance, Dad and Kim brought me to my grandparents' table. Edgar danced with Kim and Dad danced with his mother. Then, they traded partners and danced with Kim's mom and her father for a while longer.

Later, after they moved from table to table to speak with their friends, Dad and Kim came back to our table. He said to me, "After the party, we're leaving on a plane tonight. I think I told you that you're staying tonight with Grandma and Pops. I don't want them driving at night. They'll take you home tomorrow afternoon by 3.

Right?"

"Okay with me," I said. Thank goodness! I didn't have to face my mother until tomorrow afternoon. Maybe by then, she would have calmed down about Mrs. Jackson's call.

Chapter 7
Serious Trouble

She hadn't.

Sunday afternoon at precisely 3 p.m., my grandparents' car pulled in front of our small house. My mother practically ran out the door and down the steps and stopped. Her lips were pursed sharply together. She was frowning her deepest frown. When she got to the driveway, she pressed her hands firmly against her hips. Very bad signs.

The car pulled up next to her and stopped. Pops rolled down the window. "Hello, Sarah. It's nice to see you. Harry has sure grown up during the last two years. We hear she's quite a soccer player," he said.

"Uh, thank you. It's nice to see you, too. I hope you're both doing well. Thanks for bringing Harry home today. I don't mean to be rude, but Harry and I need to talk about something *right now.* Thanks again," Mom said as she jerked open the back door.

I grabbed my backpack and got out of the car. Mom said sharply, "Get into the house. I want to talk with you, Henrietta!" I ran across the bare lawn, up the rickety steps, and into the house. I knew I was in serious trouble and feared the worst—in fact, it was much worse than I thought it could be.

As I ran toward the house, Mom turned and began walking away from the car. Grandma Selma called after her, "Is there anything wrong, Sarah?"

"No, just a problem with school work. I'll handle it," Mom said as she climbed the stairs, entered the house, and slammed the door.

As my grandparents drove away, Mom turned toward me. She was furious, her eyes blazing and her hands clinched.

"Henrietta! Do you know who called me Saturday morning just as you snuck off to your father's wedding? Of course you do, 'cause you knew she was going to call and you didn't tell me, did you?"

"Mom…" I tried to interrupt.

"Don't 'mom' me, Henrietta. Mrs. Jackson told me that she sent a note home with you about your grades and your homework on Thursday. I was very embarrassed when she called and wanted to talk to me about it. I felt like an idiot on the phone with her.

"I found that note at the bottom of your book bag where you had hidden it. What's the matter with you? Don't you know better than to not show me notes from your teacher? I'm your mother, and I'm responsible for you. Don't you ever do that again! Do you understand me?"

"Yes, Mom. I'm sorry."

"Well, sorry isn't good enough. In fact, you're grounded for the next two weeks. You're going to go to school and come straight home, and you're not going to watch television. You're going to catch up on your studying and bring your grades back up to where they belong."

I was horrified. "Mom, what about soccer practice? I can't miss that! We've got the championship game next Saturday!"

"Well, you can forget that. You're not playing. By grounded, I mean grounded. Maybe that way you'll learn your lesson."

"No! I have to play! I'm the best player on the team. They'll lose without me. If I don't show up, everybody will hate me!" I screamed.

"If they hate you because you can't play a stupid game, they're not very good friends anyway, now are they?" she retorted.

"Mom, please, please. I'll do anything," I begged. "You can ground me for two months after the game, for the rest of my life. I'll wash the dishes every night for a year. I'll do the laundry every week, I'll take out the garbage. Please!"

"No. You heard what I said, and I mean it. Now go to your room and do your homework for tomorrow. Your grades in school are a lot more important than any game, and I won't tolerate your behavior and your deceit anymore," Mom snapped sharply.

"Tomorrow at school, Mrs. Jackson is putting you on a contract. You have to bring it home every night. I'll look at what you have to do and sign it after you've done it."

"Mooommm…a contract! Only the dumb kids have contracts. That'll make me look stupid in front of everybody else. Grounded and a contract, that's really mean!"

"Well, since you've failed your last two math tests, your best subject, and you haven't turned in your math homework on time for weeks, maybe you better think again about the definition of 'dumb.'"

Screaming at the top of my lungs, I ran down the narrow hall my room and slammed the door so hard that the whole house shook violently.

"Slam that door again, young lady, and you'll be grounded for a month!" Mom yelled through my door. I heard her slump into one of the creaky metal dining chairs. She began to cry, mumbling, 'What have I done wrong?"

I threw myself on the bed. I was angrier than I had ever been in my life. I refused to cry, I wasn't going to let my mother—anybody—see me cry. I decided I would never beg or plead with her for anything ever again.

I jumped up and down on my bed, almost breaking the thin slats holding the mattress up, thinking of horrible things I wanted to do to Mrs. Jackson and to my mother.

I could accept the grounding, I admitted, because I was wrong to avoid showing her the note and not telling her Mrs. Jackson was going to call. One serious mistake on top of another. But to not let me play in the championship game, the one chance I had ever had to be a real winner, that was just plain vindictive.

The game was so important to me, more than anyone knows! I was the best wing striker on the team, maybe the best in the league. I'd scored more than twice as many goals as anybody else in the league, even that jerk Rory. The Redhawks couldn't win without me. Coach Bill told me I was going to be on the All-Star team.

Mom had ruined all of it. Just because she was mad at me, mad at Dad, mad at the whole world, and too scared to stand up to that stupid drunk. She was taking it out on me. I knew it—she's just like all the other adults. It's not fair! It's not right!

Nobody—not Mom, not my teachers, nobody!—even cares about that poor, abused dog. They stand by and watch bad things happen because "they don't want to get involved." They're either afraid or uncaring or selfish. But since they're the "parents," they can take it out on their kids and tell us what to do and punish us any way they want.

All the adults want is for me to obey their stupid rules. Just because they're older than me, they think they know everything. They have no idea what's really important. Being true to your team, helping your team win, being the best you can be, saving abused animals—those were—and are—right and true.

Mom wouldn't do the right thing and help that poor dog. She wouldn't do the right thing and let me play in the championship. I told her I'd do anything she wanted me to do if she'd let me play and help the dog. So I missed a few dumb assignments that I could do in my sleep! They don't mean much compared to the suffering of that poor dog.

Mrs. Jackson was even worse for giving me that stupid note and not letting me retake the test and catch up on my work. Worst of all, she didn't have to call my Mom and make a bad situation so much worse.

Why wouldn't they listen to me? They only cared about their stupid rules and punishments, I groused. Grounding me for the championship and putting me on a contract just to embarrass me in front of the whole class. That was just spiteful.

Who cared about their silly rules when a life is at stake, when my future was on the line? They sure as heck acted like the rules were all that counted when so much more was much more important, I fumed!

Mom was even more miserable because I went to the wedding and Dad and Kim were happy. She hadn't even had a date since they got divorced. Her constant misery wasn't my fault.

Crap, I groaned, the whole school will know about my punishment within minutes. I was glad we couldn't afford a cellphone or a computer. Mom had a cheap phone only for emergencies. I knew some moron was going try to embarrass me; they'd put up on Mebook and EgoGram that I wasn't playing and was on a contract. I hate the "social media"! It could be used for so much good, but most of it was idiots and morons spouting off some political nonsense or invading people's lives.

When the Wasps found out I wasn't playing—in like two

minutes, their coach would change their entire game plan to double team Rory and attack our goal every time they got the ball. God, I was so afraid we'd get massacred!

I sat on my bed, fuming and beating on the pillows for an hour. Finally, I felt exhausted and stopped. As I calmed down, I began to think there must be a way to get back on Mom's good side, even if I could only convince her to trade just this Saturday for months of being grounded. I had to find ways to get back on Mom's good side. Just maybe, if I was good all week and I did my homework perfectly, she would let me play Saturday. I knew I didn't really need to practice. We'd been playing for three months and had already beaten the Wasps once.

I figured I better begin with my homework, so I dug into my book bag looking for my homework assignments. I couldn't find them so I called out the door, "Mom, did you see my homework assignment when you looked in my bag?"

Mom walked down the hall to my door. She didn't knock and I didn't open it. Through the door, she said, "No, I didn't. It wasn't with the envelope the note was in. Don't tell me you forgot that, too!"

"I'll look again." I tossed everything out of the book bag, and tossed everything around my room, threw the covers off my bed, looked in the trash, scattered everything on my small desk, and looked under the bed and in the closet. But I couldn't find it anywhere. Darn it! Another mistake.

"I can't find it. Can I call Glenda? She should have it. I could go to her house and copy it from her," I said through the door.

"I said you were grounded. You're not going anywhere. But you can call Glenda and see if she can bring it over here."

I came out of my room and went to the kitchen, deliberately avoiding looking at Mom as I passed her in the hall. I called Glenda from our home phone as Mom watched and listened over my shoulder. Geez, it was going to be so annoying if Mom planned to follow me around like a hawk looking for a mouse to pounce on. The call rang through and Glenda answered.

"Hi, Glenda? Hi, it's Harry. Yes, the wedding was nice. But,….um, do you have the homework assignment for tomorrow? Ok, I'll wait."

In a moment, Glenda came back to the phone and told me she found it. I said, "Oh, great! Can you bring it to me? I really need to find out what I've got to do by tomorrow."

Glenda was reluctant, but I suggested, "Well, ask your mother."

I waited another minute while she put down the phone. I could barely hear what they said in the background, but it didn't sound positive. I could hear her mom mumble and complain before Glenda came back to the phone.

Glenda said, "She won't let me bring it to you."

"Oh, Glenda, it's really important. My mom won't let me leave the house…Oh, it's a long story, the note and Mrs. Jackson. You know. I'm grounded and Mom is being really mean about it. Please ask her again."

"Oh, grounded…I see…That's bad…Let me ask again," Glenda said. It didn't work. Glenda's mom was in one of her colossal bad moods. It's a wonder she was even awake by Sunday evening, considering how much she usually drinks between Saturday morning and Sunday afternoon. If Glenda had to wake her up, no wonder she had snapped at Glenda and refused.

I put my hand over the phone and said, "Mom, Glenda's mother is…um…not feeling well and she doesn't want Glenda to go out. You know what I mean. So, can I go over there and get it?"

Mom replied, "No, I don't know what you mean, 'her mother's not feeling well.'"

"You know…She's like Dad used to be sometimes on Sunday afternoon."

"Oh Lord, not her, too," Mom said wearily. She thought for a moment and said, "Well, I'm not going to waste gas by driving you two blocks. You have 15 minutes to run over there and get back here."

"OK. Thanks, Mom! That's really nice of you," I said, beginning to try to get my "good daughter" status back one compliment at a time.

I took my hand off the receiver and said to Glenda, "My mom says I can come over and get it from you. I'll be there in a few minutes."

I fled out the front door before my mother could change her mind.

I don't know why I did what I did next because the shortest route to Glenda's house was along my street, not Horsham Circle where the abused dog lived. That's not true—I felt very angry and rebelled against what Mom told me to do. I thought I could get away with it.

I raced down the street anyway in the late afternoon sun. I did not slow down at the dog's house, but I did glance over as I ran by. The ruined jeep was still covered with weeds, and I saw the chain was still secured tightly to the bumper. I thought I saw the large black lump hidden in the weeds beside the jeep.

When I reached Glenda's house out of breath, I quickly explained to her what had happened and how I was grounded for two weeks. I told her I was supposed to miss the championship next Saturday, but I said I was going to do everything I could to convince my Mom to let me play.

"Oh Harry, what did you hide the note for? Mrs. Jackson's not that bad. She wanted to help you," Glenda said as she gave the homework assignment to me.

"Well, I forgot about it with the wedding and shopping and all."

"C'mon Harry. You never forget anything. You just didn't want to show it to your mom. Now it's a lot worse than it would have been."

"Yeah, well, thanks for backing me up. Everybody at school is going to think I'm stupid when I go on a contract, and everybody is going to hate me when the Redhawks lose the championship."

"It's your own fault," Glenda said crossly. "You're always getting into trouble for no good reason. Why are you your own worst enemy all the time?"

Behind them, Glenda's mom called out, "Who's at the door? Tell 'em we ain't buying nuttin'. Them coming here on Sunday to sell us something. Ain't they got no manners."

"Mother, it's just Harry. She came over to pick up our homework paper."

"Well, tell her to get along. It's time you was cooking dinner. I ain't got the strength today."

"Sorry, Glenda. I'll see you tomorrow at school. I don't know if Mom is going to let me walk or make me ride with her. I'll call you if I am walking so we can go together."

I ran back down Horsham toward my house. This time, from my fear for the dog? My compassion? My rebellion? My rage that no one but me cared? For whatever reason, I slowed at the dog's house, looking more carefully toward the lump in the weeds. I stopped and looked for the owner's beat-up truck. There was nothing in the driveway, on the street, or in the backyard except the ghost-eyed jeep on blocks.

As I strained to see, I thought I heard a whimper. I was sure I heard the dog whimpering and groaning. I was very worried; I knew the dog was dying. I thought I might have a minute or two to just check on the dog. So, with my fingers crossed that the man wasn't home or couldn't hear me, I quietly and quickly ran up the gravel driveway to the jeep and kneeled into the weeds.

The dog was even worse than before. Now, its chained leg looked badly swollen, twice its normal size. The dog's back had even more bare spots where more hair had fallen off, and the bare skin was covered with deep red patches that looked like they had been burned. Surrounding and under the dog, I could see dog droppings and I smelled the stench of dog urine and decaying flesh.

"Oh…this is so horrible." I reached over to pat the dog's head, and as I touched it, the dog rose its head just a bit. Then, its head dropped back into the weeds.

"You poor creature. How could anybody do this to you?" I murmured, as I stroked its head.

I sat there whispering to the dog for just for a few moments, but my quiet words and calm strokes were interrupted as a loud truck came roaring down the street and turned into the driveway.

I leaped up, and as the truck screeched to a stop, I ran as fast as I could across the backyard. I darted between the man's house and the neighbor's house. Behind me, I heard a harsh yell, "Git out of my yard and stay away from my dog, or I'll shoot yew! If yew don't believe me, try me one more time, you stupid little…."

Chapter 8
Live and Let Die

I ran into our yard and looked up as I got to the steps, Mom was standing there with her arms crossed and an angry frown.

"Where have you been? I told you 15 minutes. You've been gone 20 minutes. Why do you keep pushing me like this, Henrietta? Are you deliberately trying to get into even more trouble? "What's the matter with you? Why are you dirty and what's that smell?

"Mom. That's why I'm late," I lied. "On the way back, I was running, and I tripped on a tree root in the sidewalk. I fell and had to brush myself off."

"You smell like you fell into something really bad."

"It could have been dog poop. I'm not sure," I said. I hurried through the door and toward the bathroom so Mom couldn't ask any more questions. "I'll go get cleaned up."

She yelled after me, "How did you fall into dog poop? You didn't go down Horsham to see that dog, did you?"

I yelled back, "I don't know what it is. No, I didn't go that way. You told me not to."

"Did you get that homework assignment?"

"Yes, it's in my pocket."

"After you take a shower, we'll have dinner and you can do your homework."

After I showered, we ate dinner silently, neither of us willing to speak first. I wanted to avoid my Mom's angry, suspicious, disappointed look. I hate it when she looks at me like that.

At dinner, I stared down at my plate and picked at my food, although Mom had made our "special" Sunday lasagna. I just felt paralyzed, my heart ached, my head throbbed, and my chest felt like a claw was squeezing it.

I knew I had let Mom down again. I didn't understand why I kept lying and making Mom feel angry and sad. I believed I had let Mom down so much that I would never feel good again.

When I finished, I did my best to be polite, picking up Mom's plate and carrying our dishes to the kitchen sink. "I'll wash dishes, Mom. Why don't you rest and watch TV?" I said. I knew I was going to have to make an extraordinary effort to do more than my share of chores this week if I had any chance of playing Saturday.

"Thank you, Henrietta. After you're done, catch up on your math homework. I also want you to ask Mrs. Jackson to give you a make-up test by Friday so you can bring your grades up. No radio, no video games."

I began to protest, "Moth…er…!" But I stopped to avoid irritating her even more. "Yes, ma'am," I said meekly.

Suddenly, there was a loud banging on our front door. Startled, I turned from the sink to face the door as Mom quickly moved across the small room and opened the door. It was the huge, scruffy, drunken man who owned the dog. He looked furious.

"I thought I told yew to keep yer brat away from my dog!" he bellowed. He loomed over her and stared at her with bloodshot eyes. Even from the kitchen, I could see that he was wobbling on his feet with his fists clenched and his face beet red.

"What are you talking about?" Mom asked, taking several steps back away from the drunken sot.

"I saw yer brat runnin' from my driveway not an hour ago. Now, what are yew going to do 'bout it, or am I gonna have do something about it myself?"

"Mom!" I cried as I cowered in the kitchen. "He said he would shoot me!"

"I ain't gonna shoot nobody right now, but if yer girl trespasses on my property agin, I'm gonna have her arrested and put in juvenile hall. Do yew hear me?"

Mom wrapped her arms tightly across her chest and looked down at her feet. Mom said feebly, "I'm very sorry. You're right. I had no idea she had been in your yard this afternoon. I told her to not ever go down your street or stop at your house ever again. We don't want any trouble, and she's not ever going to bother you or your dog or cause you any trouble ever again. I promise you that."

"Well, yew damned well better make sure because next time, I'll make more trouble than yew'd know what to do wit'!" the man spat out. Mom and I watched as he turned and staggered down the steps, lurched down the driveway, and lumbered down the sidewalk back toward Horsham.

Once inside, Mom flew into a rage. "How dare you stop at that house again! You know better than anybody that man is dangerous. And how dare you disobey and lie to me again, right after you lied to me before! You have no respect for me and my rules, Harry, and you're going to learn some respect right now."

"But Mom, the dog is dying. It's lost most of its hair and it's got terrible scaly things all over its back and its leg is really swollen now. It's infected real bad," I pleaded.

"So, you were there, disobeying me twice, doing exactly what

I'd told you not to do. Is that right?"

"Yes, but…"

"No 'yes buts.' Did you or didn't you?"

"I did, but…"

"I told you before the dog has mange. That's very infectious. You could catch it, too. Lord, am I glad you took a shower as soon as you got home!

"Now, I don't want to hear any more excuses—ever. For disobeying me again, just like you asked, you now are grounded for two months. Unless you start minding me, minding your own business, and pulling your grades up at school, you're not playing basketball this winter or soccer next spring."

"Oh!!!" I screamed. "You don't care about me! You wouldn't help me if that terrible man did try to shoot me. You'd let him hurt me. You hate me because I went to the wedding! You hate me because Dad is happy and in love and you're miserable! All you care about is feeling sorry for yourself and making me pay for it. You don't care about me and you don't care that dog is going to die!"

"Be quiet, Harry!" Mom yelled back. "I've had enough! Now get in your room and do your homework, or it's going to get worse for you."

I flew to my room and slammed the door again.

Mom yelled, "Now you're grounded for three months. Do it again and it'll be four months."

I grabbed the door handle; I wanted to slam the door so hard it broke off its hinges, but I stopped. Three months was enough, but I was seething.

No championship! No basketball! No spring soccer! Grounded for three months! It might as well be the rest of my life! I was frantic! When the team found out, they were going to hate me forever!

I felt even more outraged when I remembered that I had to make a fool of myself in front of the class tomorrow. I had to get that blasted contract from Mrs. Jackson and look like one of the idiots who failed everything. And ask her for more math homework! Nobody, not even the class 'brains,' ever asks for more homework!

I fumed and my face was hot. Mom is awful. She just doesn't understand. She doesn't care about me, or she would have gotten me a dog a long time ago. Or she would help me take that poor dog away from that horrible drunk. She would let me play in the championship. And she never, ever would have divorced Daddy. She would have stayed with him and helped him get sober. 'Til death do you part' was such a pile of crap. 'Til you get too angry or too selfish' is more like it.

I practically threw the answers to my homework onto notepaper. I knew the answers easily enough. Why do I have to get a good grade to prove that I know it? What are grades anyway? Just a dumb excuse for the teachers to give you something to do rather than enjoy what you like to do.

After I finished my homework, I went to bed but couldn't sleep. I clenched the covers around me with my fists tightly balled under my chin. I tried to think about how I could change my mom's mind, but I knew she was so infuriated that she wouldn't back down. I stayed awake all night, confused ideas cluttering my mind.

What could I do? Maybe Daddy would let me live with Kim and him? Unlikely. They wouldn't be back for a week, and he would have to fight with Mom in court to get full custody of me—like I was some piece of property or a slave they were fighting over. I doubted Dad and Kim would want a lying teenager living with them anyway after Mom told them what I had done.

Maybe I could run away? Where to? Grandpa's farm, but he's

not there anymore.

Running away could get me into serious trouble anyway. I'd heard rumors about what happened to a couple of 9th grade girls. I heard they ran away because their parents told them to break up with their skanky high school boyfriends. They thought their boyfriends would take care of them. The boyfriends supposedly dumped them out of their car in a slum downtown in the middle of the night.

I heard the girls have not been seen since. The rumors are they were kidnapped and shipped overseas to be slaves for some Arab creep, or pimps scooped them off the street and forced them to take heroin and sell their bodies. Unbelievably scary!

I kept thinking about the battered dog. How all really I wanted to do was to help the dog and take care of it. I'd even give up the soccer championship to do that.

It's a terrible world that considers dogs and cats, and even gorillas and chimpanzees, to be somebody's property. Property that an owner like that drunk could do with as he likes. There are laws against abusing animals, but somebody has to be willing to enforce the law and stand up for the animals. In this part of town, people take their property rights seriously, probably because they have so little property to protect. They're not about to challenge a drunk over how he treats his dog when most people in this part of town think a pet is their property.

"Live and let die" seems to be my neighborhood's motto.

Chapter 9
The Second Worst Day—I Thought

That Monday was the second worst day of my life, or so I imagined at the time. In the morning, Mom hardly spoke to me at breakfast and drove me to school. All she said as she dropped me off was, "Go straight home after school. I'm going to call you at 4 o'clock, and if you don't answer the phone on the first ring…well, just be there."

As I dragged slowly toward the door, Glenda plodded up behind me. "Where were you? I waited and waited and you never came by to get me. What's the matter with you? Don't you ever think of anybody but yourself?" She stormed past me in a huff.

I stopped and stared at the back of Glenda's head, mouth open and speechless. "But, but…wait, Glenda, I can explain…" I cried.

Glenda ignored me and kept walking.

As the final warning bell rang, I walked slowly to my homeroom, my head down and my shoulders slumped. I didn't want anyone to notice me, and I didn't speak to anyone. I got through the first half of the day by hiding behind my textbooks and not raising my hand to answer any questions. My history and English teachers gave me some odd looks but didn't call on me. I snuck along the sides of the hallways, ducking and changing directions when I saw Glenda or Rory and his PBJs or anyone else on the Redhawks.

During the lunch period, I remembered Mom hadn't given me any money or made me lunch—again, so I went to the library to hide out and research how to take care of dogs. Mrs. Reynolds came over to me and asked me how my report on abused dogs was coming along. I lied to her that it was fine and left it at that. She tried to make conversation, but I turned away from her to look at the computer. She hesitated like she was going to say something else, then walked away and left me alone for the rest of the period.

But in P.E., I had to go outside since I didn't have a note to be in the library. Glenda avoided me and walked all the way to the other side of the field to sit and watch the other girls pretend to play kickball as they gathered in their cliques and gossiped about their weekends.

Of course, Rory and his PBJs ran up to me to taunt me as soon as I walked outside. "Are the wedding bells still ringing in your ears, Hand-dry-etta? Coach Bill was really unhappy that you missed practice without telling him about the wedding," Rory said.

I snapped, "I don't care what Coach Bill thinks. I don't need to practice with you bozos anyway. Just get me the ball and get out of the way."

"That's right," Rory snapped back. "You're the queen of the team, and we're just your minions."

"No, the PBJs are *your* minions." I pointed at Peanut, Butter, and Jelly. "They're the one-eyed yellow clowns that can't speak English and stumble around getting in everybody's way."

"Heck with you, jerkwad," Rory spluttered. "I'd rather play with Pete, Bu, and Jorge any day of the week than with you, you conceited, selfish…"

"Who wants to play with you jerks anyway? All you do is give me a hard time and treat me like dirt. Why should I help you win something you don't deserve? I think I'll go ask the football coach if I can borrow five tackling dummies and put them on the field with me Saturday. At least they'd move faster than the rest of you. Then, the Wasps would have to dodge something so I could beat them to the goal and score."

"That's it! Shut your face!" Rory yelled. His face got redder than I had ever seen it. He balled his fists, and I thought he was going to try to hit me. If he had done that, I'd have hit him back and kicked him where it would've really hurt.

Instead, he just stared at me, his eyes blazing and his fists clinched at his side. "My Dad taught me to never hit a girl, whether she thought she was one or not. Since you think you're so much better than we are, maybe you're not a girl, and I can make an exception this time."

He lurched toward me, but Peter and Bu grabbed him and dragged him away. "Don't do that, man," Peter said. "She ain't worth it. She's just like the rest of them. Miss High and Mighty thinks she's better than us because she's slummin' in our 'hood.'"

The PBJs pushed Rory away, and he snarled at me, "You better not show up for the game Saturday. We don't want you, and we don't need you. We'll show you we—the team—can win without you, Miss Hang-Out-To-Dry-etta."

They turned and ran toward my—well, their—other starters on the Redhawks, Keysha and Magda. They had been standing about 50 yards away, staring at us.

I ran the other way toward the woods next to the ballfield. I hid along the edge of the trees. Everybody ignored me until I heard the bell ring for the next class. Mrs. Jackson's class. Crap!

I did my best to sneak into Mrs. Jackson's class without her seeing me, but she must have a video camera in the top of her head. As I slid into my seat, Mrs. Jackson looked up from the papers on her desk. She looked directly at me and said tersely, "Henrietta, please come to the desk."

She beckoned me, curling her index finger and looking down her nose through her glasses. I flinched because it was Mrs. Jackson's look we most feared.

"Yes, ma'am," I said quietly. I dreaded what was coming next as I got up and walked slowly to the front of the class.

My face and ears burned as the whole class watched me. Rory and the PBJs snickered, and he whispered as I went by, "Oh, how the Miss High-and-Mighty does fall."

Mrs. Jackson tried to whisper. But the anxiety in her voice carried the sound so that the other students, who were leaning forward in their desks, could hear what she said.

"I assume you have spoken with your mother about our talk on Saturday morning. I am very, very disappointed that you did not inform her in advance that I was going to call. It was quite unpleasant to have to explain the whole situation to her.

"Your mother was very polite and understanding of your need to pay closer attention to your work. We agreed that you should go on a daily contract that you will receive from me every afternoon. You will take it home and have her sign it and bring it back to me every morning. Is that clear?"

At the back of the room, Rory let out a quick laugh, but stopped when Mrs. Jackson gave him a stern look and said, "Rory, is something funny? If so, would you like you to share it with the rest of the class?"

"No, ma'am. I'm sorry," Rory said as he faked his best humble apology.

She gave him a look and turned back to me. "Do you

understand?"

I leaned toward her and whispered so she could barely hear me. "Mrs. Jackson, please don't make me do this. I'll do the work. I promise."

I glanced around to make sure no one could hear me. "Only the dumb kids go on contracts. You know I'm smart, pleaasseee."

Mrs. Jackson said stiffly as she sat straight up and looked me in the eye. "Unfortunately, most of the so-called dumb kids turn their work in on time. And right now, they are making better grades than you are. You need some order and discipline in your life. I've given you several chances, and since I don't know what else to do, I'm going to stick to my word. You go on a homework contract as of this afternoon. Pick it up at the end of the day. Now return to your seat and pay attention."

I hurried down the aisle and slid into me desk. I hunched down, trying to hide from everyone's stares and avoid hearing their comments. Rory smirked and mouthed the words "Miss Dumb and Dumber."

Keysha, who sat to my right, whispered, "So now who's the dumbest one, Miss Smart Aleck Preppy…!" I knew that Keysha, our—well, now their—best mid-fielder, had struggled with math and writing for years. Sometimes I had teased her when she made simple mistakes like swapping the numbers in math problems or adding them backward.

I slunk even more down in my seat until only my eyes and forehead peered over the desk. My face burned and I felt ashamed. I did my best to pay attention. I answered Mrs. Jackson's questions when she asked me, but I never volunteered. I did my best to say as little as possible the rest of the day.

When the final bell rang, I got the contract from Mrs. Jackson, and I tried to scoot out of the building and run home. But Rory and the PBJs caught up with me. They were merciless. "So, Hair-less-etta, you got yourself in a lot of trouble this time, didn't you? About time for Miss Teacher's Pet to get what she deserves," Rory jeered.

The four of them danced around me as I scurried down the sidewalk. They teased and goaded, trying their best to get me to fight back, but I never looked at them and never said a word. Finally, they stopped running circles around me.

"Geez, Hair-less-etta has lost it," Rory said to my back as I kept moving. "C'mon guys, we've got to go to practice for Saturday so Miss Contract USA can go do her homework and get her Mommy to sign her certificate of stupidity."

As they ran the other way, I stopped and glanced back over my shoulder just as Rory looked at me and shook his head. I felt so alone and so angry. I had botched with Mom my only chance to play Saturday. Now, I had ruined any chance my team would ever want to play with me again.

I saw Glenda loping down the sidewalk toward me and waited for her to catch up. She said, "I'm sorry I snapped at you this morning. My mom and dad…well, you know. It was a bad morning."

I said, "I know. Dad used to get like that, too. It's no big deal. I asked for it. I should have called you."

Glenda tried to put her arm around me, but I shrugged her away.

Glenda just looked at me with what I hoped was concern and not pity. I couldn't stand that, but it was just that—pity.

Something inside me, some dammed up emotion just broke. I poured out the whole story—the note, the dog, the confrontations with the crazy drunk, the wedding, Mom's fear and anger, Mrs. Jackson's contract, Mom grounding me for three months, and Mom not letting me play Saturday.

"Everything is awful. I've never felt so bad. That poor dog is dying and nobody wants to help it. That jerk could kill me and hurt my mom. Mom is more miserable than ever. I let the team down and now they hate me. I treated you badly and you're my best friend," I wailed.

Glenda just looked at me. Finally, she said, "I'm really sorry. I don't know what to do. Is there anything I can do to help?"

"No. There's nothing anybody can do. I just have to figure out a way to straighten out this mess."

I glanced at my watch; it was 10 minutes til 4. "I've got to get home. Mom is going to call at 4, and if I don't answer the phone, I'll be grounded for the rest of my life. I'll see you tomorrow—oh, Mom is driving me now so I can't meet you." At least I hadn't made that mistake again. I ran down the sidewalk.

As I ran, I looked back. I saw Glenda had wobbled the other way down the sidewalk and was talking to Rory. "Oh, darn it. She'll go and blab the whole mess. Just what I need, more trouble."

More trouble was what I got.

I made it home as the phone began to ring. I talked to Mom to assure her I was home and I had the first contract with me. She said she would be home by 7 and asked me to warm up the leftover lasagna and make a salad.

Mom came in a little after seven, and I had the table set, the salads served and the lasagna warming in the oven. She thanked me and we had just begun to eat.

The phone rang and Mom got up and answered it before I could reach it. It was Coach Bill. I couldn't hear what Coach said on the other end of the line, but I could hear Mom's direct answers plain and clear.

"Hello, Coach. This is Ms. Chapman. Uh-huh. Uh-huh…

"Yes, she is grounded. No, she is not going to play Saturday…

"No, she did not tell me the truth and disobeyed my orders several times and she must suffer the consequences. I'm very sorry that you're losing your best player, but she is my daughter and I decide what is best for her…"

It went on like that for 15 minutes until Mom became very annoyed. Finally, she said angrily, "This conversation is over. My final answer is no. She will not play in that game. If you call me again, I will call the Recreation Director to complain about your harassment. I will ask the Director why you—and he—appear to think winning a stupid game is more important than my daughter knowing how to tell the truth! Goodbye!"

She slammed the phone down.

"Harry!" she snapped at me. "Did you ask your coach to call me and twist my arm so you can play?"

"No, Mom. I promise. Glenda told Rory and I guess he told Coach during practice."

"Well, it's none of anybody else's business, young lady."

"I know, Mom. I wouldn't tell anybody."

Coach's call was just the beginning. His call was probably the nicest one. For the next three hours, the phone rang continuously with parents calling and arguing with my mom.

I hid in my bedroom, but left the door cracked open so I could hear what my Mom said. I sat on the bed and rocked back and forth with my arms wrapped around my knees pulled tightly into my chest. I listened to Mom's direct and often angry defense of her actions to discipline me.

About 11 p.m., long after both of us should have been asleep, Mom took the phone off the hook and walked wearily into my room. She sat down on the edge of my bed, leaned on one arm and shook her head.

"Harry, what in the world is so important about a soccer game, especially for 7th graders? I can't believe these crazy people. They threatened to call Social Services on me. They called me an unfit mother. They cursed me with words I haven't heard in a long time. They threatened to run me out of town. They even threatened to attack me. What has gotten into these people? Is winning a silly children's game all they have for a life?

"I know you are very mad at me right now, Harry. But you know who is responsible for this. You lied to me not once but many times. You disobeyed me and put both of us in physical danger from that madman who owns that stupid dog.

"I know you're upset right now about your Dad getting remarried, and neither of us has been the same since Grandpa died. Sometimes, it just seems too much for me to bear," Mom lamented.

I didn't know what to say. I thought playing in the game was about the most important thing in the world, besides helping the dog, but I couldn't say that, or Mom would have gotten even madder at me. She just didn't understand what was valuable to me.

Instead, I looked at her and said, "Yes, Mom. It's all my fault."

"Well, I'm sorry, too, honey, but that's just the way it's going to be. It doesn't mean I don't love you. It's because I do." Mom stood up and went to the door. "Now, try to get some sleep. It's only Monday. Lord knows what the rest of the week will be like, but I'm definitely going to change our phone number tomorrow."

I watched Mom leave, rolled over on my side, and curled up in a ball. I lay there for what seemed like hours. I felt ashamed I lied to Mom; I had never done that before, and now it felt like every other word I said to her was a lie.

I felt angry at myself because I'd been screwing up my school work. I don't know why, but nothing at school means anything to me. The work is easy, and I could do it, but it doesn't seem worth the trouble.

I felt sad for my mom; she is so depressed, overworked, exhausted, and miserable all the time, and I was just making it worse and worse.

But she was wrong about how I felt about the wedding. I was happy for my Dad and Kim; I hated to see Mom feel so bitter and resentful about their happiness. I felt torn between Mom and Dad. I love them both so much. Their divorce ripped apart something inside me, and I didn't know how to heal it.

I felt appalled that no one cared about helping the dog, that my Mom, the kids at school, even Glenda don't seem to think they should do anything since the dog is that drunk's "property."

That's moronic. Obviously, an animal suffers pain when you abuse it and feels joy when you treat it well. You just have to see a dog's smiling face and wagging tail when you give it a treat or rub its stomach to know it has feelings like we do.

I hated Mrs. Jackson and mom for putting me on that rotten contract and treating me like I am stupid! Oh, crap! My homework! I reached off the bed to get my book bag. I pulled out my books and notebooks, and on top I saw the contract.

Double crap! The contract! With all the nasty phone calls, Mom hadn't seen it or signed it. I tip-toed down the hall and put it on the kitchen table so she could see it and sign it in the morning.

She would insist on checking my homework, too, so when I got back to my room, I opened my math textbook and went to work. I don't know how long I worked, but I completed all my assignments for all my classes. I knew they were perfect or close enough to it. Finally, I lay down to go to sleep, and as I began to doze, I heard the alarm in my mom's room ring.

Triple crap! I had stayed up all night.

"Harry, wake up. It's time to get ready for school." I was ready alright. I just didn't know how I was going to bear it.

Chapter 10
The Biggest Loser

The rest of the week became steadily worse. Every morning, Mom dropped me off at school. Every afternoon, I had to be home by 4 p.m. for her check-up call. Every day, Rory and the PBJs ignored me and refused to speak to me. Magda, Keysha, and the rest of the team made fun of me whenever Mrs. Jackson's back was turned, or we were at P.E. or lunch.

I was called every nasty variation of "Henrietta" I had ever heard and even some new ones, like "Henry-Hate-Her" or "Henry-Not-So-High-and-Mighty" or "Harry Chapped Lips."

Seventh graders can be vicious twits when they feel like it, and boy, did they feel like it. They'd been waiting months for me, the smart, athletic, new girl in town, to screw up so they could bring me down.

At the beginning of Mrs. Jackson's class, I felt humiliated when I had to walk up to her desk and give her the contract Mom had signed the night before. Then, at the end of every class, I had to go back to Mrs. Jackson's desk and pick up that day's contract while the whole class snickered.

Even Glenda avoided me most of the time; on the good side, maybe she just didn't know what to say to me. On the bad side, maybe she just didn't want to be seen with the biggest loser in 7th grade. When she did offer to talk to me, I usually refused to talk to her, just out of spite more than anything else.

I couldn't do anything about any of it. I just took it. I didn't respond to their jibes and stayed away from everybody as much as I could. I got home by 4 p.m. every day to get Mom's call. I prepared an easy dinner like macaroni and cheese and a salad before Mom got home, washed dishes without being asked, did my homework, and went to bed on time.

Mom and I hardly said a word to each other. I wasn't going to start and she didn't seem to want to ask. It felt like living in a convent where the nuns don't like each other but can't say anything because they took a vow of silence. But I sure could show it by keeping a perpetual frown on my face, slightly slamming doors, and giving her the silent treatment.

Thursday afternoon, though, I was shaken from my constant misery into something close to despair. When I brought the contract to Mrs. Jackson, she said, "Harry, have you prepared your oral report on abused animals so you can present it to the class tomorrow?"

"What!" I exclaimed. "Oh, no. Please Mrs. Jackson, I can't do that now. I forgot all about it."

"That was part of our agreement. You've made good grades and turned all your homework in on time this week, so I'll let you go to the library. I know you spoke with Mrs. Reynolds twice and you gathered some good information. I'm sure all you need to do is fill in the details. Just practice tonight, stand in front of the class tomorrow, and tell them about abused animals for two minutes. Don't you care about this?"

"Yes, Mrs. Jackson, I really do, but the guys…They hate me right now. They'll laugh at me and make fun of me or worse."

"Of course not. Not while I'm here. Harry, they don't hate you. Some of them are acting mean because they think they are getting even, some are jealous of how smart and talented you are, and some of them are just joining in because they always follow the crowd."

"I just wish they'd leave me alone. Getting picked on all the time feels so lousy. I can't face them right now," I complained.

"Yes, it does hurt. That's an unfortunate part of life. Standing up to them and giving your report tomorrow will show them that you are bigger and better than their teasing," she replied as firmly as always.

"Please, Mrs. Jackson. Do I have to? Can't I wait until next week—after the game is over?"

"No, we agreed on tomorrow. Get ready to give your report first thing tomorrow afternoon. Remember this: What they think or say is not important. Only two things are important. First, we have an agreement and I expect you to keep your end of the bargain. Second, the abused animals. Don't you think it's important for other kids to know about this so they can help stop it, too?"

"Yes, ma'am, they need to know, but I don't think they'll listen to me right now."

"So, you'll have to get their attention in a positive way and convince them to listen to you. Now here's a note, so go to the library, but be back in time for the final bell."

I slunk back to my desk and picked up my notebooks and a pen. Glenda quietly passed me a note: "What's up?"

I quickly wrote back, "I forgot I have to give a report on abused dogs tomorrow. It'll be terrible. I have to go to the library."

I spent the rest of the last period with Mrs. Reynolds. "Harry, I know you've got to give your report tomorrow," she said. "I found some more good information on the Web and in some books about animal care."

As I surfed the databases and web sites on the library computer, I asked, "Mrs. Reynolds, what happens to most of these abused animals? Does anyone save them and find them good homes? Do most of them die?"

"I don't know off hand. What does the information tell you?"

"It looks really bad. The Humane Society site says that of the thousands and thousands of abused animals, only a couple of thousand are reported each year. Most just appear to die in lots of pain and misery. Nothing at all seems to happen to most their owners. That's just terrible!

"Shouldn't those people be punished for hurting their animals? They should go to jail, or they should be treated just like they've treated their animals. How'd they like it if they were tied outside in the rain to an old car and never given any food or water?" I exclaimed, angry at a world that allowed such abuse and refused to punish the abusers.

"Well, Harry, do you think that kind of an eye-for-an-eye revenge is going to help either the abused pet to heal and live in a better home, or the owner to learn from his mistakes?" Mrs. Reynolds asked.

"I don't know, and I don't care. Anybody who treats an animal that way should be punished," I said harshly.

I was shocked and infuriated as I read the cruel facts and reviewed the graphic photos on the web sites. One dog in the photos on the web even looked like the poor dog tied to the jeep on Horsham Circle.

As awful as it seems, being beaten, starved, burned, left outside in sub-zero temperatures, or left without water or given filthy water is "good" treatment compared to the number of newborn puppies and kittens who are just thrown into rivers and lakes to drown. Or maybe the drowned newborns are the lucky ones; at least they don't have to suffer for long...

The web sites stated that most animal shelters are overwhelmed by the number of abandoned pets. They euthanize the older, sicker animals that are not adopted within a certain time, sometimes as little as 15 days.

Only the "always live" shelters never put any animal to sleep, and they constantly need more money to keep their strays alive. When they reach their limits, they have to turn animals away. The rejected animals are then taken to the local public animal shelter, or their owners just abandon them or kill them. The public shelters try to adopt them out, but only the young, cute puppies and kittens usually get adopted.

I told Mrs. Reynolds, "Animal abuse is a lot worse than I thought. Many of the people—men and women—who abuse animals tend to be criminals with a history of both being abused and abusing animals when they were children. And the crazies, like that guy who's killing that poor black dog, tend to be alcoholics or drug addicts. Occasionally, they are what—how do you pronounce it—psy-cho-paths. People with no conscience who like to hurt people and animals."

I felt so frustrated that this time, I told her the truth—I needed the practice.

"I have to tell you the truth. I don't have a dog, and I want one more than anything, but Mom won't let me have one. Then, last week, I saw this starving, injured, mangy dog shackled to a jeep without food and water near where I live. I want to help it, but the owner is a crazy drunk. He threatened my Mom and me and told us to leave the dog alone. My Mom won't let me report him to Animal Control because she's afraid he'll retaliate against us."

"Oh, Harry, I'm so sorry," Mrs. Reynolds said. "If the man is dangerous, that's a very good reason to stay away from him. You could get hurt badly by somebody like that. Years ago, when I was about your age, I remember that we had just gotten a kitten, but my dad got mad at it for messing on the rug. He screamed and kicked at it.

"A few days later, when my sisters and I came home from school, the kitten was gone and never came back. My parents said it had run away, but I'm not so sure that's what happened. I wouldn't blame it if it did. We never asked to have dog or a cat again. So, I do understand how you feel."

"But Mrs. Reynolds, who's going to help these thousands and thousands of poor animals? I can't help all of the animals in the world, but I could help that black dog. It looks so bad and it's in so much pain."

"Harry, I know you want to help. That's a very wonderful and noble desire, but I hear you have been having trouble lately. So, doesn't it seem better if you do your best to improve things in school and at home first?"

I lost my temper. I cut her off, and whispered fiercely, "I know all the kids hate me. I don't care about any of them. They're all stupid and mean and jealous. So, heck with them. But I do care about that dog, it needs help or it's going to die soon, and no one else beside me cares at all."

"I'm sorry you feel that way, Harry. I'm just trying to help you understand that you can't help others, even an abused dog, until you help yourself," Mrs. Reynolds said gently.

"I'm sorry for snapping at you, Mrs. Reynolds. I know you are trying to help me, and I appreciate it. But didn't somebody famous say something like all evil needs to win is for good people to do nothing?

"I have been listening in history class, Mrs. Reynolds," I

grinned at her. "Well, it's up to me to do something about that dog."

"Harry, that is a good summary of great quotes from Edmund Burke, an Anglo-Irish philosopher," Mrs. Reynolds complimented me. "He said two similar things about evil and tyranny: 'The only thing necessary for the triumph of evil is for good men to do nothing,' and 'All tyranny needs to gain a foothold is for people of good conscience to remain silent.'

"Harry, I don't want you to remain silent or do nothing. The difference is you have to choose the right things to say to the right people and the right actions to take. You have to do both at the right time so they will listen and rally around your ideas.

"Why don't you discuss what you can do with your Mom? I'm sure she would have some good ideas. And your report tomorrow is a great start in learning to speak up for what you believe," Mrs. Reynolds suggested.

I could tell she just didn't get how desperate the situation was. I felt very frustrated with all the so-called "sensible" advice from grown-ups. Rather than argue with her anymore, I thanked her politely and returned to Mrs. Jackson's class.

She asked me if I had found enough good information for my talk, and I said I had. I thought I had too much information, but I was prepared to tell the entire class how bad the situation was and tell them what they could do about it.

After school, Glenda came up to me for the first time all week as I headed home.

"How are you doing?" she asked hesitantly.

"Oh, I'm just peachy." I said sarcastically. "I've got to give a 2-minute oral report to a class full of people who hate me and could care less about abused pets. Mom hasn't spoken to me all week. The Redhawks are treating me like I'm a traitor. And nobody understands or cares about that poor dog; they're just as happy to ignore it and let it die. In fact, I haven't been by there all week. I think I'll run by there now to see how it's doing."

"Harry!" Glenda cried.

"You keep your mouth shut if you want to stay my friend. Don't say anything to anybody. Promise?!"

"No, I won't promise. You're making a big mistake," Glenda pleaded.

I grabbed her left arm, squeezed it tightly, and looked her straight in the eyes. "Promise! Promise and cross your heart, hope to die."

"Oww! That hurts!" she yelped, pulling away. "Okay, okay, I promise—cross my heart, hope to die." She crossed her heart with her right hand.

I let her arm go. "Good. You're a real friend."

I left Glenda and ran to the corner of Horsham Circle. I stopped at the corner and peered carefully down the street to the rundown house and yard where the dog was. I didn't see the man's truck anywhere, so I walked casually down the street to the gravel driveway.

I looked toward the beat-up jeep covered with weeds and saw the dog, little more than a black lump, huddled by the axle to which it was chained.

Glancing up and down the street, I didn't see or hear any cars or trucks coming, so I took a short step or two up the drive. I knelt down and whistled softly.

The dog's ears flicked a little and it raised its head slightly. "Hello, boy. It's going to be okay," I whispered. "One way or the other, I'm going to get you out of this mess and take care of you."

I spoke softly to the dog for a few moments, and it looked at me with the saddest, most hopeless eyes I could imagine. I sighed and felt so miserable for the dog and so angry at my Mom and all of the selfish kids and adults.

I gripped my fists tightly and noticed my watch. "Oh darn it, it's almost four." I jumped up with one more look at the dog and ran home. As I ran through our gate, I heard our telephone ringing. I quickly fumbled with the house key, opened the door, sprinted into the house, and grabbed the phone.

"Hello!" I cried out of breath.

"Harry, is that you? Where have you been?" Mom irritably. "The phone's been ringing at least a dozen times."

"I was out in the yard talking to Glenda and I didn't hear it until a second ago."

"I thought I told you couldn't have any visitors."

"Well, she wasn't visiting. She just walked me home from school and we were talking. I had trouble with the key opening the door after the phone started ringing."

"Don't get cute with me. Has she left?"

"Yes, she did."

"Well, do your homework and set the table for dinner. I'll be home about 6. And no TV."

"Yes, ma'am," I said as she hung up the phone.

I breathed deeply. "Wow, that was close."

That evening, I figured I knew enough about abused dogs so I didn't have to practice for the stupid oral report. After I finished my homework, I spent most of my time in my room worrying about the poor black dog and daydreaming what it would be like to have it for my own. I saw myself cleaning and brushing it, feeding it good food, and giving it treats like doggie biscuits. Most of all, I imagined running and playing with it in the open fields at Grandpa's farm. I knew that one day, I would own that farm again and live there as happy as I was when Grandpa was still alive.

The next day, "TGI Friday" morning at breakfast, I skimmed the pages about abused dogs I had printed off the web. I only knew that what I wanted to tell everyone was that lots of disgusting people hurt their dogs and cats and either abuse them, abandon them, or kill them because their pets "belong" to them. The more I thought about pets as property the more angry I became about the abused black dog at that crazy man's house.

"Harry, what are you reading about?" Mom asked me.

"Oh, I've got to give a dumb oral report today about pets," I said, pulling the papers closer so Mom couldn't see them.

My Mom came around the table, looked over my shoulder, and saw the gross photos. "What's happened to those animals, Harry? Does this report have anything to do with that dog you saw?"

"No, ma'am, not directly," I said evasively. "I told Mrs. Jackson about the dog, and she told me to do a report about abused animals to make up for that homework I missed."

"You still aren't thinking about trying to help that dog over there, are you? If you are, forget about it. It's not your dog and that man is dangerous," Mom warned me.

"No, mom, I'm not," I lied. "I'm just doing what Mrs. Jackson told me to do."

"Alright but be smart about this. Let's go, I'm going to be late for work."

At school, right after P.E. and my math class started, Mrs. Jackson called me to the front of the class. "Now class, Harry is going to give us a brief report on abused pets and what we can do to help them."

Shivering with fear, I stood up and moved toward the front of the class. My ears burned and my face turned bright red as Rory snickered behind her back. "Hey, teacher's pet. Are you abused these days?"

Everybody around him started snickering and stifling bursts of laughter.

"That's enough! Be quiet! If I hear any more outbursts, the entire class will stay after school on Monday," Mrs. Jackson said sharply. "Go ahead Harry."

"Well…," I stammered. "Uh, uh…millions of people don't take care of their pets—dogs and cats, even snakes and iguanas. They don't feed them right, they don't take them to the vet when they get sick, they don't keep their pens clean. Some people are really mean and punch and kick their dogs and cats, even throw them around and burn them or pour hot water on them…"

Rory raised his hand and interrupted me, "Who cares? My father says we've got too many dogs and cats any way. He says we need to get rid of most of them so they stop eating all the food."

"Rory, your Dad is stupid and if you agree with him, you're stupid, too," I spat out, furious at Rory's attitude.

"Yeah, well, look who's calling who stupid. At least I'm not on a dummy contract," Rory yelled back.

Mrs. Jackson interrupted, "Stop it, both of you! Rory, your question was insensitive and ignorant at best, and Harry, your response was rude. Harry, don't you have some information that answers the intent behind Rory's question? It's an important one because many people don't seem to care."

"Well, uh…I think pets have feelings like people. We know it's wrong for parents to hurt their kids," I said. "Pets are just like kids in a lot of ways. Children's parents have to feed them and take care of them because they can't do it for themselves. So, our pets need us, and we're supposed to help them grow strong and healthy. Even some animals like orangutans do that better than many human parents."

"Well put," Mrs. Jackson said.

Just then, Keysha raised her hand and said, "But my uncle said that a pet is just property and we can do with it whatever we want to do. You ain't supposed to mess with other people's property if it belongs to them."

Mrs. Jackson corrected, "Aren't, not 'ain't,' Keysha. Harry, what do you have to say to her argument? A lot of people agree with her, too."

"Mrs. Reynolds showed me that there are laws against hurting animals, and if you do, you can go to jail. And I think you should go to jail," I said sharply.

My voice rose as I yelled, "I really think that if you hurt an animal, you should be hurt the same way you hurt the animal. It you tie a dog to a truck and starve it and beat it, you should be tied to a truck and starved and beaten. Let's see how you like it!"

I stood at the front of the class with my hands on my hips, my jaw jutting out, and my eyes glowering at the class, as I dared them to disagree with me.

My tough stance set the whole class to hooting and hollering. "You're crazy!" "That's mean and stupid!" "You can't treat people like that!" 'What a jerk!" The PBJs threw paper wads, and Keysha and Magda booed and yelled, "Sit down!"

Mrs. Jackson jumped out of her chair and banged on her desk with a long ruler. "Cut it out this instant! All of you, sit down and be quiet! Everyone will stay after school on Monday and write an essay about why we have an obligation to care for animals properly! I will not tolerate this behavior!"

"Harry, that's quite enough. Return to your seat. I was expecting more information and less 'inflammation' from your report," she said sternly.

Seething with anger, my face felt as hot as a roaring campfire.

I plopped into my seat and folded my arms tightly across my chest.

Behind me, Rory whispered fiercely. "Now, you've really gone and done it. We have to stay after school because of your dumb report. You aren't playing tomorrow. You really can't do anything right, can you, Hen-ri-Ate-A," he mocked.

I jerked around, "I don't care what you think. You're just a...."

"Harry, turn around and pay attention...right now," Mrs. Jackson said.

"But, Rory started it..." I pleaded.

"I don't care who started it. Now, both you and Rory can stay after school today and learn some respect, and that's the end of it," Mrs. Jackson said.

"But Mrs. Jackson," I pleaded, "my mom says I have to be home by 4. She's going to call me, and if I'm not there, I'll be grounded for the rest of my life."

"I'll call her and let her know you'll be late today," she said.

"Oh, no, please don't do that. I'll just get into even more trouble."

"That's unfortunate, but both of you have to stay after school. I'll explain the situation to your mother. Now open your math books and let's see if we can make something out of the rest of this day."

Both Rory and I stayed after school for 30 minutes. Placed in different corners of the room, we had to write an essay on how to behave in class while Mrs. Jackson sat at her desk.

At the end of the half hour, Mrs. Jackson said, "Both of you may go, but stay away from each other. Cool off over the weekend and come back Monday with a better attitude. You two used to be friends, I thought.

"Harry, I did speak with your mother. I explained to her that you had acted inappropriately in class but that you were passionate about a good cause. I told her how much you cared about abused animals, and she seemed unhappy but not too upset."

"Oh, Mrs. Jackson, I wish you hadn't said that," I said, "She's already upset enough."

"Well, Harry, I did the best I could to explain. I'm sure your mom will be understanding."

Rory didn't say anything to me when he left. He didn't even look at me. I don't know if I could have wished him "Good Luck" on the championship anyway, so it was just as well.

Of course, Glenda hadn't waited for me, so I walked slowly home, feeling angry, sad, and lost. At least I didn't have to run home to answer the phone today, so I took the long way past the dog's house—just to check.

This time, the man's truck was in the driveway, so I hurriedly crossed the street and ran by the house and all the way home. I didn't need any more trouble today, but I did catch a glimpse of the dog, still mostly hidden by the high weeds around the rusting wreck he was chained to. How was he even still alive?

At 6 o'clock when Mom arrived home, she looked at me sitting in a chair at the wobbly dining room table with my head down doing my homework for the weekend.

"What am I going to do with you, Harry? I hear your report caused quite a commotion in your class. Can't you control your temper? You're just like your father, and his terrible temper got him into a lot of trouble. If you don't watch out, yours is going to get you into more trouble than you can handle, too."

I mumbled, "Yes, Mom. I know you don't want me to be like Dad. I don't want to cause you any more trouble."

Mom sat down at the table and put her right hand to her forehead. "Well, let's just get something to eat. Thank goodness tomorrow is Saturday. Maybe the weekend will do both of us some good."

I jerked up, "Saturday! The game! Dad said he was going to try to get back from his honeymoon to go to it. Mom, I've got to call him and tell him not to go!"

"Harry, I have no way to get in touch with him. I'll call Rory's mom and ask her to tell him to call me if he manages to get back for the game. But I doubt if he'll really make that big an effort. He never used to go to your games anyway."

"But he promised he would do his best, Mom, and if he shows up and I'm not playing…"

"Well, just because your father *might* show up, which I doubt, is no reason for me to change my mind and let you play. You're not going to play, do you understand?" she said hotly.

"I'm not trying to play. I don't want to play with those jerks anyway. They've been mean to me all week. I just want to warn Dad so he doesn't go."

"Well, I have no idea where he is, except somewhere in the Bahamas. Just let it alone, Harry."

With that, I stopped talking, fuming that Mom didn't trust my Dad to keep his promise and worrying that maybe he wouldn't even remember he said he would make it back. Why should he? He was having a great time on his honeymoon, sitting on the beach with Kim and drinking fruit juice smoothies instead of margaritas—I fervently hoped.

Chapter 11
The Miracle I Missed, The Mess I Made

I spent all of Saturday morning sitting in my room. I zoned out and dozed on and off to avoid thinking about the game or the dog. At lunch, I munched on a bologna sandwich and chips, without saying anything to my Mom.

Then she said with a false cheery sound in her voice, "Harry, why don't you go to the game and cheer for your team? That'll show them you have team spirit, and when they win, you can celebrate with them."

I mumbled, "Remember, you grounded me and I can't leave the house."

Mom sighed, "Well, I'm willing to make this one exception."

"If you are willing to let me go watch, why won't you let me play?"

"You know why you can't play. I was just trying to help you with how your team feels about you."

"Well, I don't care what they think. Why should I go cheer for a bunch of jerks who've been making fun of me and yelling at me all week? I don't want to go and see them lose. If I were there, they'd blame me for not playing and for distracting them from the game. Anyway, I don't see how they can win. The Wasps are really tough, and I was the only player on our team faster than their best guys."

"Sitting here moping around just lets them have their way," Mom coaxed. "If you go and cheer for them, you'll show them you're a bigger, better person than they are."

Mom had a real thing about showing your tormentors you're a "bigger, better person" than they are. Ummmm....NOT! Especially if that means they can take advantage of you or torment you without you or someone defending you.

"Maybe I'm not and maybe I don't care," I retorted. "Anyway, it's all your fault. You didn't have to ground me this week. You could have let me practice and play. You did it because I went to Dad's wedding and I think Kim is nice. You're mean and awful," I screamed, jumping up and running to my room. I slammed the door and fell onto my bed with my fists clinched.

I gritted my teeth and hissed, "I'm not going to cry. She can't make me cry. Crying is for wimps." I sat there, taking deep breaths to calm down, but I couldn't. I felt enraged at Mom for making such a stupid suggestion. Go to the game and watch them lose when I knew I could help them win. Right! Coach Bill would give me dirty looks, the other parents would whisper nasty things just loud enough for me to hear them, and the team would stare at me and wonder what the heck I was doing there.

I checked the clock on my bedside table. It was almost 3. The game would be starting any minute. I could see the Wasps running up and down the field, running circles around Rory and the PBJs, getting by Keysha with head fakes, and juking Magda at the goal. I knew how good they were and how they would attack us as soon as they saw I wasn't playing. I knew my—well, the Redhawks would lose big and they would hate me even more. Our only loss of the season happened in the third game because I twisted my ankle in the first half and couldn't play in the second.

I felt exhausted from my anger and worry, so I lay back on my bed, and I must have dozed off.

Groggy with sleep, I thought I heard or dreamed about a loud buzzing noise like a nest of angry wasps—no pun intended. The buzz grew louder in my head, and I woke up slowly. I sat up and shook my head. The noise came closer and closer to my house. I recognized the noise as yelling and cheering.

I jumped out of bed and ran to the bedroom window. I looked to my right up the street. I thought I saw a crowd of people rambling my way down the middle of the street. I ran out of my room and out the front door.

Standing on the porch, I stared down the street at a large crowd of kids and adults jumping up and down, yelling and cheering, and dancing in circles. In the middle of the crowd, someone was being carried on people's shoulders.

As the ecstatic group danced closer, I was shocked to see Rory being tossed up and down.

"Oh, no. It can't be…"

The jubilant crowd broke out into a chant: "Ro-ry! Ro-ry! Ro-ry!"

As they reached my house, Rory saw me on the porch. "Stop!" he cried and pointed at me.

"Yo, Hair-Less-Etta. We did it! We won! We won! And we didn't need you to do it!"

Jelly—Jorge—broke from the crowd and ran up to me. "He did it! He did it! Rory outran the Wasps' defenders with 10 seconds left, juked their goalie, and blasted a shot right past her. Magda blocked all 15 of their shots! We won, 1-nil! Ole´! Ole´!" he cried. He turned and ran back to the crowd.

I was too stunned to speak as they danced past and made their way toward Rory's house.

A red Mustang drove up slowly behind the crowd to the curb beside my yard, and Dad got out. Kim began to get out of the passenger side. Dad said, "Please stay here. This is between Sarah and me."

Kim protested, "Sam, find out what's going on. Be nice!"

All I could say was a weak "Oh no…"

"Honey, what happened? Why didn't you play? Are you all right?" Daddy said as he rushed up to me.

I cried, "Talk to mom. It's all her fault!" I turned and ran into the house to my room, slammed the door, and flung myself on the bed.

For the next two hours, my Mom and Dad yelled at each other as they had the worst argument I could remember, even worse than their fights when Dad was drinking so much. I stayed in my room, curled up on my bed and strained to listen to what they were saying.

I only heard bits and pieces of the fight—"She's my daughter and I decide what's best…" "What a stupid thing to do to a kid…" "You think you know everything now that you're 'recovered'…" "Maybe I'll sue you for full custody! You're not fit to take care of her…" "So now you think you can be a 'real' Father since you married that…that…" And on and on and on…It was terrible and all my fault…

I didn't hear Kim's voice again, and I don't know if she stayed in the car. She probably did because Dad never yelled like that when he was with her. I wished she had come in to try to calm things down. I was very worried that this terrible fight over me would push Dad over the edge and he would start drinking again. I couldn't stand the thought that I might be the cause if my Dad lost it and became a drunk again!

When Mom and Dad were married, that's what he had done after they had a fight. He just drank more and more after every fight. He stayed away longer and longer every day. I love both of them, and that day I felt so torn between them. I felt like each one was holding onto one of my arms and one of my legs and they were tearing me apart into large chunks. My life just exploded and I felt like there was nothing left of me.

Finally, I heard the front door slam and Dad's car drive away. Mom stomped down the hall, and I flinched as I feared she would barge into my room and blame me for their fight. I breathed a sigh of relief when Mom went into her own room and slammed the door instead.

I just lay there in a ball, thinking horrible things. They won the championship without me, and that idiot Rory kicked the winning goal! How did they do that? They didn't need me as much as I thought they did. That was my goal, my championship, and Mom kept it from me all because of her lousy life! Arrggghhh!

Chapter 12
Play Parent Ping-Pong,
And Only Pain Wins

As the sun set and the darkness deepened, I lay on my bed, listening to Mom crying in her bedroom for hours. I felt guilty because I had started this whole mess. I blamed Mom because she refused to do one simple thing: Call Dad's parents to find out where he was in the Bahamas so I could call him and explain why I wasn't playing.

Their fight was ridiculous and senseless to me. From what I could hear, Mom just wanted to take out her anger and misery on Dad. Dad lost his temper when Mom just dug in her heels.

I felt like they were playing ping-pong over who was the best parent and who "deserved" custody of me. "She's my daughter, too!" Dad whacks the ball over the net at Mom! "No, I'm her mother and I know what's best for her!" Mom returns the ball back over the net at Dad. And back and forth until they were too exhausted to go on.

Like they believed I was just a thing that they own and not their daughter, not a real person who has totally screwed up her life. All they could do was yell about which of them was the better person and the better parent. I didn't hear a lot of concern about me and my life at all.

For more than three years, I have felt like just a pawn in their nasty divorce game. I had hoped when Dad got sober and met Kim that Mom would move on and stop playing games with Dad over who controlled my life. It seemed like I was all she had left she could boss around.

Then, when Dad decided to marry Kim and was happier than I'd ever known him, Mom just fell to pieces and became even more desperate to keep me under her thumb. Like I was all she had left at all.

She was jealous that Dad had found someone to love and be loved by, and I felt she resented me and blamed me for a lot of her misery. She told me she couldn't go out on dates because she couldn't afford a babysitter. She couldn't invite men visitors for dinner because I was living there. There weren't any good men out there to date anyway; all the "good ones" were married or gay. Always some stupid excuse.

I knew a lot of ways she could have worked around me—I could spend a weekend with Dad's parents, I was at Dad's twice a month and for a month during summer break anyway. She had plenty of opportunity to go out with the women from her job and find a boyfriend. She is remarkably pretty when she does her hair, puts on a nice dress, and smiles.

But she has chosen to feel unhappy and blame Dad and me for all of her problems and not do anything about having her own life again. It seems like she doesn't know how to feel good about herself or anything anymore. She has been so unhappy for so long that misery is her only friend.

I felt squeezed like a giant hand had grabbed me and was tightening its grip. I felt like my ribs would crack and pierce my lungs. I felt like I would die because I would be suffocated from

Mom's never-ending demands on me. Demands to make straight As, be the perfect student, be the girl all the other girls wanted to be like, be the star athlete, and be the perfect daughter who would take care of the house, relieve her misery, and make her happy.

How was it even possible for me to make her happy? But I knew that's what I was supposed to do. It had become unbearable because I couldn't be all of that. It was impossible, as I'd done such an excellent job of proving the past few weeks. I just wanted to be who I am—Harry Chapman—and help that miserable dog.

I couldn't sleep as my brain kept tumbling too many angry feelings around in my head. "Everybody hates me…it's all my fault…why did Rory have to do something right for once…Mom and Dad will never get back together…Poor dog, somebody has to help it…He's all alone like me…Got to do something…Can't go back to school…"

On and on. I felt more and more desperate that I had to do something. I just couldn't take any more of Mom's misery, that blasted contract for dummies, the constant aggravation from everybody on the team, the shame and humiliation when I walked down the hallways and so many kids snickered at me behind my back. Cowards! I'd like to see them say something like that to my face!

As I felt more and more torn apart, I kept listening for Mom, hoping she would come to my room to talk about everything that happened. She didn't. Eventually, she did stop crying—at least I couldn't hear her anymore—and the house grew quieter and quieter as the hours passed.

I remained awake with my anxiety increasing. How was I going to go to school Monday and face everybody? Rory would be the hero and the "big dawg" on campus. He'd be insufferable and lord it over me for months. He'd never let me forget that he won the championship. What kind of slur would he think of to call me next? "Hardly-etta"?

Rory and the PBJs would show no mercy and make fun of me every chance they got. Magda, Keysha, and the rest would harass me in the girl's locker room, the girl's restroom, whenever I walked by them. I could never play on the Redhawks again, and it was the one good thing I had found in this lousy new school in this lousy new neighborhood. Now it was gone. Months of crap in school, grounded like a crashed airplane, and weeks of summer hanging around the house, bored to death. There had to be something I could do?

Chapter 13
The Worst Best Thing to Do

Then I got it, I knew what I had to do! I bolted upright in my bed. "But I have to be very quiet."

I crept out of bed, picked my backpack off the floor and slowly took everything out of it. I tiptoed to the dresser and slowly slid the drawers open one by one. I took out a bunch of clothes and stuffed them in my backpack. I took a long double Dutch jump rope out of my closet and put it in the pack. I dressed in jeans, a long sleeve shirt, a sweater, a jacket, and my best soccer shoes.

Moving carefully, I opened the door to the hall and crept to the door of Mom's bedroom. I listened and heard Mom's soft snore. "Good, Mom must have taken a sleeping pill like she used to after she had a fight with Daddy when he was drunk."

I eased slowly into the kitchen and opened the refrigerator. I took a package of cheese, several apples, and a bottle of water. Then, I took a small box of health bars from a cabinet and walked slowly back to my bedroom. I put the food in my backpack, put it on around my shoulders, and tiptoed toward the living room and the front door—away from Mom's room.

In the dim reflection of a streetlight outside the front window, I saw Mom's purse on the dining table where she'd thrown it. I knew I had to have some money. I only had a dollar in my pocket. I'd just borrow some from my mom and pay her back after I got a job.

I slowly opened the clasp on Mom's purse, took out her wallet, and looked at her cash. There wasn't much money there. I sighed and took a $20 bill anyway. I put the wallet back, closed the purse, and put it back like I had found it, hoping Mom wouldn't notice I had touched it, at least for a few days.

I tiptoed to the front door, grabbed the lock, and turned it very slowly. The lock clicked loudly. I jumped. I caught my breath and looked around and listened for Mom to wake up. I listened for about 2 minutes but heard nothing. I slowly turned the knob and opened the door. It creaked and groaned softly; I thought it sounded like the sigh Grandpa used to make.

I eased down the edge of the loose wooden steps to make sure they didn't creak too loudly. Then, I walked across the bare front yard into the night. Where my yard met the street, I paused and turned around. The streetlight cast ghostly shadows across our yard and our house. The windows seemed to stare at me like black, empty eyes. They didn't seem like they would miss me at all.

"This will be better, Mom. You won't have to worry about me anymore. I won't be in your way anymore and you can have your own life again," I mumbled. I took one last look, set my jaw, clenched my teeth, turned, and walked away.

I walked quickly and quietly to Horsham and turned onto the street. All the houses were completely dark, the only sounds were the rustling of dead leaves and garbage that scattered along the road. Then I was there. I stopped across the street from the dog's house and waited and watched for at least 10 minutes.

The house was dark, the dirty old pickup truck was parked in front, and the rusty, wheel-less jeep still rested in the high weeds. There were no lights on or sounds from inside the house. I hoped that terrible creep had gotten drunk again and passed out. That was my best hope for what I was about to do.

I stared at the jeep in the gloom. As my eyes adjusted to the deep black and gray shadows cast by the streetlights, I saw that the chain on the axle and the dark lump in the weeds were still there, so the dog was still alive—I hoped. Thank goodness!

Breathing hard and trembling, I inched across the street into the dog's yard. As I stepped, my foot made a loud "crunch!" I caught my breath and muttered about the gravel driveway. With weeds on one side of the drive and the house on the other, I felt trapped.

Then, the lump next to the jeep moved, rustling the weeds, and I saw two yellow-red eyes staring at me. The dog tried to growl, but only a soft whine came out.

"Shhhhhhh…" I whispered. "Shhhhhhhh…good dog…it's okay…" The eyes in the lump kept staring at me.

I waited, looking toward the house, poised to run away if I saw or heard anything. But no lights, no sounds. Slowly, I lifted one foot and put it down softly. No crunch this time.

One light, quiet step at a time, I moved toward the dog, cooing and whispering. The lump didn't move.

Four feet from the lump, I stopped, slid the backpack off my shoulder and rested it on the ground. I eased into a squat. "Shhhhh…it's all right. It's going to be okay. I'm here to help you," I whispered. It seemed like I was shouting in the dead of night, and I feared the evil man would come rushing out at any second.

The lump moved slightly, jostling the chain.

"Oh, the chain. I should have thought about that," I murmured. "How am I going to open that?" I stared at it; it was locked to the axle with a padlock. After studying it, I realized I couldn't see the end or how it was tied to the wretched dog.

'Well, in for a penny, in a for pound,' as Grandpa used to say, and I duck-walked toward the dog, keeping up my coos and whispers, doing my best not to rustle the weeds. A foot away from the dog, I stopped and slowly put out my hand, palm up. "It's okay…You know me…"

The eyes moved as the lump lifted its black nose toward my palm. It felt dry, cracked, and hard, another bad sign as I knew healthy dogs are supposed to have cold, moist noses. The dog sniffed my hand, sighed, and dropped its head back to the ground.

"Okay, good boy," I whispered and put my hand on the top of its head and gave it a soft stroke. Its hair felt wet and sticky, almost like glue. As I stroked down its head toward its neck, I felt its rough, hairless, scaly skin with wet ooze sticking to my fingers.

"Yuck! Poor dog…Jerk ought to be whipped, tied to this jeep and left here for days," I thought.

As I moved my hand down the dog's neck, I touched what felt like a dog collar with sharp edges. "Oh God, it's a choke collar!" I kept moving my hand along the contours of the collar and found that it was very large and just hanging loosely around the dog's scrawny neck. I slowly put both my hands on the sides of the collar and began to pull it toward the dog's head. It groaned as I raised its head very gently.

I stopped; I didn't know what the groan meant. I left my hands where they were for a moment. "It's going to be all right. I'm going to take you with me to a better place than you've ever been before. Trust me," I whispered, hoping the dog would accept my hands.

I pulled lightly on the collar and the dog remained quiet as I raised his head and slipped the collar off. His head drooped and I caught it before it could hit the ground and eased it down softly.

"Okay…okay…do you think you can walk? It'll be really tough to carry you without making a lot of noise," I whispered as I stroked the dog's head. I eased away from the dog a foot or two, held out my palm, and beckoned, "Come with me. Come on. Let's go."

The dog didn't move. I squatted and pondered for a moment. "Ah, right," I muttered. "I'd do the same thing. Why should you go with me when you feel so bad? Good question."

Slowly, I turned and slowly zipped open my backpack and took out the bottle of water. I twisted it open and poured a small amount into my cupped hand. I held it toward the dog. His ears twitched, he sniffed, and he tried to stand. His pink tongue darted out into my palm and lapped eagerly at the water.

"Good, now come with me, and I'll give you more," I murmured. I eased up out of the squat and bent over, holding out my hand with the droplets of water. I backed cautiously. At first the dog crawled along its belly, sniffing and lapping at my hand. Then, it staggered to its feet, trembling and shaking.

"Good boy, good boy. Now just take one step at a time."

It felt like we took an hour to back quietly down the gravel driveway to the sidewalk, making as little noise as possible. One small step at a time, one small splash of water for the dog at a time.

"One step at a time" popped in my head again from what my Dad always said, and I almost laughed out loud. I didn't think this is quite what he had in mind…or maybe he did.

I kept glancing nervously toward the house, expecting the drunk to burst out of his house at any second. No lights, no movement, no sounds. Good so far. This was the first—and only—time I had ever appreciated the power of alcohol to knock somebody out.

At the end of the driveway, I backed left onto the sidewalk and walked backward slowly, moving a few feet, watching the dog teeter along, and stopping when he faltered, about to collapse. I put another sip of water in my hand so the dog could drink more. We made our way gradually past several more houses on the street.

No lights came on, no sounds from the houses, no cars moving along the street. "Thank you, Whatever is up there or wherever You are!" I sighed.

I thought glaciers might move faster than the dog and I were, but we were making progress. The dog staggered every step toward the water, swaying and bumping against my legs to stay upright.

"Boy, you're a real 'booper,' you know. You're booping all over the place,' I chuckled.

After what seemed like far too long—we had to be long gone before sunrise or we'd be caught in a minute—we reached the corner of Horsham and Plum Point, Glenda's street. I stopped and sat down to give us both a rest. The 'booper' dog fell at my feet, panting. I felt exhausted, too, and we had barely gone a block.

I took the cheese out of her backpack and crumbled a few bits and held them on my palm. The dog gobbled them down. I got the apple, took bites out it, and fed them to the dog. The dog gobbled them, too. The dog seemed a little better already. "Let's see if we can speed things up a bit," I thought.

After the dog had eaten most of the apple and half the cheese and drunk most of the water, I took the jump rope out of my backpack, tied a loose loop, and eased it around the dog's neck. I stood up. I looked toward Glenda's house and the school.

Should I head there to get help? I shook my head. Glenda's mom would freak out. The school would definitely call my mom and report me to the cops for stealing the dog and creating a health hazard in the school since it had fleas and mange. I turned in the opposite direction and began coaxing the dog to walk with me.

"Come on 'booper' dog. I know where we can go, what we can do, and no one will ever find us. I'll take care of you and make you well. It's going to be just fine." The dog staggered to its haunches and looked up at me. His tongue lolled out of his mouth, his cheeks were pulled back, and his teeth were showing, so I thought this sad 'booper' of a dog actually might be smiling.

Suddenly, I realized, "That's his name! Booper, the wonder dog who boops along!" Sort of like a cross between a 'stagger' and a limp, but he kept moving.

As the 'Booper' and I began shuffling slowly west, I looked back. The false dawn of another cool, crisp, day began to show a glimmer of light on the horizon behind us. I felt a surge of hope that we were going to make it to safety, to a place where we would be happy.

Chapter 14
The Not-So-Lonesome Highway

As the 'Booper' slowly gained strength, we were able to move a little faster and reach the main highway a mile from my house. I stopped and looked both ways, startled at how big the highway looked from the street level with its four lanes and wide median.

"Wow, this is a lot bigger than it looks from the car. No sidewalk, either," I mumbled to Booper. "Now what?" I turned and stared back toward my house for a long moment. Should we go back and take our medicine or keep going? Mom would be furious, the evil drunk might go berserk and hurt us, I'd lose Booper for sure and never, ever see another dog, and I'd have to go back to school tomorrow to face the jeers and distain of my team. No way!

"Go west, young woman!" I said. It was an ironic riff on a saying from the late 1800s when some New York newspaper publisher name Horace Greeley had encouraged people who lived in the east to find opportunity beyond the Mississippi River. The real irony is that Greeley stayed at his desk and never left New York. Well, I wasn't going beyond the Mississippi, just far enough west to where I knew I would be happier than I felt now.

"Well, Booper, I'm sure I know how to get there, so if we're going, let's go. One foot in front of the other. The Chinese say a journey of a thousand miles begins with the first step, and we're only going about 50 miles or so."

So, I turned from the east and walked away from the sun as it began to rise slowly over the horizon.

We began walking very slowly along the side of the road and my scrawny, crippled dog limped beside me. Cars zoomed by us. I jumped the first time a driver blared his horn at us. I jumped again the first time a driver cussed at us. And we were almost knocked over the first time a huge tractor-trailer roared by, its backdraft slamming against us.

Almost worst of all were the catcalls from the young guys who drove by in their trucks or hot cars and whistled or yelled rude taunts.

The very worst were creeps who slowed down or stopped to offer us a ride. I had half a dozen "offers" in the first five miles. It didn't seem to matter how old or how young or how rich or how poor these men were. Rich men dressed in Polo shirts out for a Sunday morning drive in their Mercedes and dirty country boys in rusty pick-up trucks who were drinking from beer cans at dawn on a Sunday and playing country music way too loud.

They all had the same "offer." They smiled and asked me politely where I was going and if I needed a ride. But I could see in their eyes they had something else on their mind beside getting me where I was going safely.

I told every one of them a polite, but firm, "No thanks. I'm just taking my dog for a short walk. I live nearby, so I'm good."

One or two tried to coax me into their cars, offering to buy me a soda, breakfast, even give me a beer if you can imagine that! I discouraged them when I told them my dog didn't like to ride in cars and usually threw up after about two minutes. I told them I didn't want to mess up their cars. With that, they all took off, their precious cars a lot more important than getting this weird girl and her sick dog into their cars.

Mom and Grandpa had taught me what to say to creeps who tried to pick me up. They taught me to never, ever go anywhere with strangers. I had improvised about the dog puking in their cars; I thought that was fairly creative and laughed.

I figured we would get harassed all day, so I moved us as far over to the side as I could. We left the paved shoulder and walked in the grass and weeds, but that slowed our progress. We had to dodge all kinds of junk and garbage. People are such pigs and don't seem to care about the environment at all! I was sure I'd have lots of itchy flea and chigger bites by the end of the day from Booper and from the bugs in the grass.

I wanted to get off the highway, but long stretches were bordered on both sides by fences that separated business parks, virtually empty on a Sunday morning, from the highway. We couldn't climb the fences to walk through the parks away from the traffic.

As we moved slowly along, the sun rose and began to warm my back, so I stopped, drank a sip of water, and gave Booper some as well. I broke off pieces of a health bar, eating half and giving the dog half. We kept walking.

By mid-morning, I already felt hot—it was going to be a warm Indian summer day in late October. Both of us were a little tired and a lot hungry. We trudged for some distance more. Despite the dangers, I thought about hitchhiking a ride; maybe some old couple on their way to church would stop. Like anybody went to church anymore! None of the old people who had driven by so far had even stopped to ask us if we wanted a ride.

"What do you think, Booper?" I asked the dog, just to have

somebody to talk to. "It sure would be easier than walking all the way, but Mom and Grandpa told me never to ask for or take rides with strangers. So, I guess we better just keep walking. We'll be fine. It'll just take a little while longer to get there."

We trudged another mile or two past closed auto repair shops, used tire stores, one-story storage units, used car sales lots with grungy streamers flying around, and one-story warehouses. We hardly saw a soul at any of these places.

Finally, we got lucky when we saw a gas station with a convenience store. "Great! Booper, let's get some real food and go to the bathroom so I can clean you up a little," I said as I smiled and looked down at the dog. He looked back up at me with his huge, staring black eyes, panting rapidly and his tongue lolling out of his mouth in fatigue.

At the station, I left Booper outside; he wasn't going to run away with his limp and weakness. Worn out, his head drooped and he slumped to the ground. I didn't even have to tie his rope to anything.

I went into the station, asked the desk clerk for the restroom key, and came out with it.

We went around the corner, and I opened the door to a bathroom that was about the smelliest, dirtiest one I'd ever seen. Ancient yellow-brown stains of who knows what in the toilet bowl. The toilet seat was loose and cracked, ready to fall apart. Toilet paper—some of it looked like it had blood, or worse, on it—littered the floor. No soap dispenser. No toilet paper on the roller.

I held my breath and looked around the mess. Hallelujah, there were plenty of cheap, thin, brown paper towels on the toilet tank!

We really didn't have much choice, and I tried to nudge Booper into the bathroom. It was so awful even he whined pitifully and shied away, pulling me out the door back into the sort-of fresh air.

I dragged him back in to the room and began to wash him down with paper towels. Dirt, bloody ooze, and scraps of hair and skin fell off his back and belly and legs.

"Cripes! What a poor dog! That horrible creep!" I exclaimed as I threw wad after wad of paper towels toward the overflowing trash can.

As I gently wiped and wiped, Booper lurched and swayed and shivered, often whimpering when I touched a bad sore or open wound.

"I'm sorry, Booper. I know it hurts. Cleaning you up will make it better. That's what mom does to my cuts and scratches. Good clean water does the trick."

At least I hoped the water coming out the faucet was clean!

After about 15 minutes, I stepped back and looked at Booper. With most of the mud and filth removed, Booper looked like a black poodle with a close shave done by a crazy person. Hairless red welts and sores, patches of thin black hair, ribs that looked like they could pierce through the skin at any second, and big, black eyes that seemed to beg me for something I didn't understand. Food, water, affection, attention? Simple relief from pain might have been enough at the time.

"You aren't pretty now, but I'll find a way to heal those sores. With good food and water and tender loving care, you're going to be a beautiful dog, and you'll be all mine," I said to Booper. "Let's get something to eat."

As I walked back into the door of the station to return the key and buy food, the clerk yelled, "No dogs allowed!" Booper growled, so I left him outside again. This time, he sat facing the door, his eyes always searching for me as I walked around the store.

I tried to look like I did this every day so the store clerk and one or two other customers wouldn't notice I didn't know what I was doing. I picked up three bottles of water, a bag of potato chips, a package of cookies, and two small cans of cat food with lift-off lids for the dog.

"Like Booper knows the difference," I thought.

Heading toward the counter, I saw some medicines and got a tube of anti-bacterial cream to put on Booper's sores as soon I left the store.

At the counter, the clerk rang up the items and said, "That's $15.16."

"Huh!" I said, shocked by how expensive so few items were. If I bought these things, I'd have only $6.84 left to get us at least another 40 miles. At our slow pace, that could take 3 or 4 days.

Well, I was already in for a pretty large penny, so I better stay in for the whole pound. But I felt sure we would find something, or someone, to help us get there.

Unfortunately, someone found us instead.

Chapter 15
I Get What I Want—
I Should Have Been More Careful

After we left the station, Booper and I struggled along the highway for hours. I don't know how Booper kept going as I felt exhausted and he was in terrible shape. He whimpered with every limping step and sometimes staggered like he was going to collapse and never get up. We stopped often to let him nibble the cat food and drink some water.

Just before sundown, we ran out of food and water again. As the sun set, the Sunday afternoon traffic—and the harassment—slowed as well. I guess the bored old guys, drunk country boys and lonely truck drivers had had enough fun for one day.

The sun shone straight in my eyes as we kept plodding west toward Grandpa's. I didn't know what we were going to do when it got dark. We didn't have any money. We didn't have a place to stay or anything to eat or drink. I couldn't see any houses where it looked like anyone was home. Many of them were empty with broken and boarded up windows and some kind of legal-looking poster tacked to the doors. Of course, hitchhiking in the dark was unthinkable, but I began to seriously think about it, despite the dangers. I didn't know if Booper would be able to keep going the next day.

Just as it looked like Booper and I were going to have to either hitch a ride or find some shelter on the other side of the ditch, I heard a car or truck coming up behind us. It slowed as it came near. I turned to tell the driver we didn't need a ride. It was HIS rust-bucket truck.

The scraggly monster slowed beside us and stopped. He leaned over and looked out the open passenger window with a wide smile on his grizzled face. He had a knife in his left hand. A rifle sat on a gunrack.

"Get in the truck," he snarled. I could smell his boozy breath from 5 feet away. I instantly knew this crazy alcoholic wanted to hurt Booper and me. I'd seen my dad fly into rages after he drank too much and felt frustrated because he didn't get what he wanted when he wanted it.

But I knew the booze befuddled my Dad's brain and seriously slowed his reactions. I desperately hoped the same would be true of this drunken moron.

I turned to run away from the truck, back the way we came. We might have a few seconds head start if he turned the truck around. I yanked the rope around Booper's neck. He yelped, stumbled, and collapsed. I dragged Booper to his feet.

"Come on! Hurry! Don't you see who it is! We've got to get away!" I yelled at the crumpled dog.

He sniffed, snatched his head around, and saw his tormentor. His eyes grew as wide as terror could open them. With a deep groan and a growl, he staggered back to his feet and tried to run with me.

I looked back as the brute jumped out of his truck and began to chase us. As we turned to run faster, I stumbled over a large piece of tire that had been blown onto the shoulder. Off balance, I fell and rolled down the bank by the side of the road. I held onto the rope and Booper tumbled down with me. As we hit the bottom, the creep slid down the bank, caught up to us, and grabbed me by my jacket.

He yelled, "Now I've got yew!" He held the knife to my throat.

"Now, git back up thar and git in the truck, or I'm going to cut up this mangy piece of crap and let you watch it bleed."

"No! Don't do that!. I'll go! Just don't hurt Booper!"

I went limp, and he half-dragged and half-carried me back up the bank and along the side of the road to his truck.

I held onto the rope tied to Booper as tightly as I could. I never let it go as Booper stumbled and lurched with us.

Several cars raced by as he dragged me toward his truck. No one stopped. One or two seemed to slow down, but the drivers took one look at us and fled.

I'll never forget the face of one old lady passenger in a large, expensive Cadillac as her car slowed down. Her face had way too much makeup, as thick as a layer of pink adobe on the side of an old house. Her hair reflected a shiny blue rinse in the flash of passing headlights. Her mouth dropped open as she stared at us. She rolled down her window and said, nervously, "What are you doing to that girl?"

The maniac yelled, "She be my daughter, yer stupid cow! She run away from home and I found her. I'm taking her home to give her a good 'whupping.' Now get the hell away from us, or yew might get a whupping too!"

She jerked her head toward the elderly male driver and yelled as her window rose. My last hope disappeared in a tangle of blue rinse as the window shut tight. The Caddie took off like we were chasing it.

I thought bitterly that they didn't care about an idiot abusing his daughter. Maybe they thought I deserved a "whupping" for running away. That's one way they could have made excuses in their selfish minds for not helping. At least they stopped; I would have been scared if this filthy, stinking, drunken jerk had cussed at me, too.

As he dragged me and Booper to his truck, I prayed someone who had driven by us would call the cops. But the blue-haired woman obviously didn't and neither did anyone else. Thanks for your lack of simple kindness!

Chapter 16
Loose Lips Sink....

The monster threw me in the truck cab and grabbed the rope out of my hands. He slammed the door shut. I looked out the back window. He picked Booper up and threw him onto the truck bed. Booper yelped in pain.

I wanted to leap out of the cab and kill him with my bare hands. But he had Booper and a knife. I felt utterly hopeless. We had staggered for at least 10 miles in one day. Booper had shown the greatest will to live I'd ever seen, far more than I thought possible.

Crap and triple crap! If only one decent person had stopped and offered us a ride, we'd already be at Grandpa's farm! But now we were in more danger than I even thought possible. My mind couldn't imagine what this maniac would do to us, but all my fears burst into my brain—Booper sliced up into pieces while I was forced to watch would be the worst thing. I shivered and felt sick to my stomach.

I steadied myself because I was sure of one thing about my dilemma: Whatever the cackling, cursing crud tried to do to me, I would fight to the death with every ounce of strength I had to stop him!

"Lay down and shut up! Stupid dog! Yer already caused me more trouble than 20 worthless mutts!" He smacked Booper hard with his right hand. The dog cried out but slumped down quivering in the truck bed.

He climbed in the driver's side, waved the knife at me, then put it into a sheath attached to his belt on his left hip.

"Roll up the window and lock the door!" he snarled. I did what he told me to do.

The inside reeked of stale booze, stale cigarette smoke, stale sweat and stale fast food. I felt like I wanted to puke. The floorboard was caked in dirt and dried mud. The bench seat was made of partly shredded crimson vinyl so old and worn that it looked and felt like a parched Mojave Desert.

He picked up off the bench seat a pint bottle of what I knew was cheap liquor. I recognized the bottle; my father used to drink the same whiskey when he was at his worst. He gulped a long drink, started the truck, and roared down the highway.

He stared over at me and spat out, "So yew think yew was gonna git away wit' it? Now I'm going to show yew what happens to people who steal another's property! Where'd yew think yer going with my dog?"

I felt terrified, but furious. I yelled, "None of your business. Who do you think you are? Treating a dog like that, yelling at my mom, hitting me, threatening us when I'm just trying to help your dog? What's your name? I bet my Mom and Dad have already called the police to come look for me. Now you're in real trouble. You'll go to jail for kidnapping and assaulting a minor. You'll go to jail for years and years."

He laughed. "Now who's stupid? The cops will tell yer parents they won't do nuttin' for 24 hours. They'll tell them you'll probably come home when you get hungry or cool off like almost all yew runaways do. They'll say yer just mad at them and will come home soon enough. Do they know yew stole my dog? No! Do they suspect? Maybe. If they come by my house, they'll see that the jeep and chain has disappeared. That old hunk of junk jeep got hauled off today. They's going to find an empty house, a bunch of dirty weeds, and a patch of oil in the weeds.

"It's long past time I left that hole. If anybody else comes lookin', I won't be there and neither will yew. They won't know what to think."

He cackled, "Yew don't know how smart I am yet, but yew will.

"Where were yew going wit' my dog? I been looking for you all day. I knowed yew stole my dog. Yer just too damn stubborn or stupid to let things be—like my lousy wife. She just run off with all my money and all my good stuff and left me with junk. Like that damn dog that hates me and a stack of bills she didn't pay."

I pleaded, "Why do you treat him so badly? I bet that dog never did anything to you. What's your name?"

"Like I done told yew three times before, none of that is any of yer bidness. Now where was yew taking my dog? It's gotta be someplace special. Yew couldn't go home."

He took another drink.

"Yew got a friend? I seed your Ma ain't got no husband or boyfriend. To your Daddy's? Where does he live?"

I made a mistake. I said, "Daddy wouldn't buy me a dog either...but he'll kick your butt when he finds us. I know he is looking for me right now. Mom will have called him by now. They're out looking for me right now."

"Hmmm...so you ain't headed to yer Daddy's either. Where the hell are yer going? Tell me or I'm going to smack yew a good one."

He raised his right arm past his left shoulder like he was going to backhand me in the face.

I cringed against the truck door and threw my arms up to protect my face. "Don't you dare hit me. You're a coward, abusing defenseless dogs and hitting girls! You're going to jail!"

He laughed again and dropped his arm. "At least in jail, I'd get three squares a day, a hot shower, a color TV, a lot of exercise, and easy work. Missy, if yew think threatening me with jail is gonna scare me, yer barking up duh wrong tree. Me and jail is already old friends."

He put his right hand on the steering wheel, picked up the pint with his left hand and drained the rest of it. He held his left arm out the open truck window and threw the bottle over the truck cab. It landed on the shoulder of the road and smashed to bits.

"Now, see what a good guy I am. I cudda thrown it on the road so it wudda blowed out some folks' tires. But I throwed it off the road so it wouldn't hurt nothing. You might even say I am one of them en-vi-ro-mental ecofreaks," he cackled again.

"Hand me that bottle in the glove compartment. Don't even think about tossin' it out," he scowled. "Well, don't just sit there. Git me the bottle!"

I opened the glove compartment and grabbed a pint bottle of the same cheap whiskey. Underneath it I saw a piece of paper that looked like the registration slip Mom kept in her car. As I handed the bottle to the creep with my left hand, I quickly picked up the paper with my right. I saw the name "Thomas Michael Towns." So that's his name!

"Yew," he yelled. "Put that down!" He reached over and smacked my hand and the paper fell on the floorboard.

"Pick it up and put it back where it belongs and leave it alone, yer nosy brat!"

I did so and quickly read some more as I shoved it back in the glove compartment. The address was not on Horsham, but on Riggs Avenue across town.

"Michael…er…Mike, what are you going to do to me? We can't just drive around in this truck all night."

"Damn, so now yew knowed my name. That's not good for yew, missy. Yew shoulda just left well enough alone. But it don't seem like yew knowed how to do that. Yew done got yerself in big trouble. I was going to just drive out in the country and dump yew by the side of the road and take off with my dog. Wouldn't nobody come after me if yew showed up safe. Hell, half of 'em wouldn't even believe yer story. T'other half wouldn't care.

"Now tell me where yer was going to take my dog, or I might drop yer by the side of the road dead."

Crap! I'd stuck my big mouth into it again. The creep seemed to be getting desperate. I had to buy some time. I'd just been really scared and mad before. I'd thought he might just beat me up and let me go. Now, my heart pounded in my chest as I understood that he was on the run. Despite what he said, he had to be scared that he'd end up back in jail. He was trying to figure out the best place to kill me and dump my body. I shivered, terrified, and slid closer to the door.

Maybe I could open the door and jump out and roll on the road. It would hurt like the devil, but I'd have a chance to run. But if he came back and caught me, he might just knife me and leave me there, or worse…And he would still have Booper. I couldn't let that happen. Not after all this…

Chapter 17
The Painful Irony...The Truth

I needed time to think. I frantically thought of all the places I could tell him we are going. But it dawned on me. A huge irony—Tell him the truth. Tell him about Grandpa's farm! I know that farm like the back of my hand. Maybe I'd have a fighting chance there to get away and hide, but I didn't know how to take Booper with me.

I said, "Alright, alright. I'll tell you. I was taking Booper to my Grandpa's farm outside Otisville. Where are we now?"

Mike said, "Yer Grandpa's farm? Is he there? Your Grandma?"

"No, nobody's there. Grandma died a long time ago, and Grandpa died three years ago. It's been empty since then."

"Who's this Booper yer talking about? Is that what yer callin' my dog? That's a stupid name. His name is Ralph. Named him after my pa 'cause my pa had that same pointy nose and same sorrowful look in his eye. Worthless snake he was," Towns spit out.

He laughed. "So yew was just going to run away to some place yew knowed yer parents could find yew? What a stupid kid thing to do! If yew act'lly gonna run away, yew run away from everything yew knows and leaves it behind. But yew wanted mommy and daddy to save yer sorry butt."

"No, I didn't!" I started to complain, but I stopped. I realized he was right. My dream of getting to Grandpa's farm and living there with Booper now seemed like a dopey fantasy some kid would dream up. Mom and Daddy would know exactly where I was headed with or without the dog. It's a wonder they hadn't already caught me. Maybe I wanted them to find me to prove that they loved me. Maybe they would let me keep Booper—even being grounded for a year and giving up all my sports would be worth it.

Towns said angrily, "I ast you. Where is yer Grandpa's farm?"

"I said near Otisville. I know how to get us there. Where are we now? Where did you kid…er…pick us up. How long have we been driving on this road?"

"I caught up with yew about 10 miles from yer house," Mike said. "Yew wasn't exactly making a lot of time with my dog and yew limping along the side of the road. I drove around a couple of the main roads huntin' fer yew. Then I hit this highway heading out of town. I was just about to give up and take off when I saw yew. Lucky me!" he threw his head back and cackled again, with a manic look in his eyes.

Mike opened the pint I gave him and took another long swig.

He said, "We been driving on this road about 15 or 20 miles. Otisville oughta be about half an hour away."

I asked, "Have we gone by Route 37 yet?"

"Naw. It should be just up ahead. What of it?"

"You have to turn left there and drive about 10 miles to Route 1492. You turn right and drive about 5 miles 'til the road turns into a dirt road. Grandpa's farm is about a mile down the dirt road."

"What ar…are…are…you going to do me when we get to the farm?" My voice quavered.

I could tell Towns was getting drunker and drunker. I hoped he wouldn't pass out and wreck the truck. Well—maybe that wouldn't be so bad if I wasn't hurt and could get out and run. But Booper could get thrown out of the back of the truck. He could be killed. So very bad idea.

I needed to keep Towns talking so he'd stay awake like I did when I was a kid in a car seat and—I understood now—Daddy was driving drunk with only me in the car. Mom had always been frantic whenever we got home; she lived in a constant state of nerve-wracking fear when I was in the car with him.

"Mike, what are you going to do with me when we get to the farm?"

"Well, I guess that depends a lot on yew, now don't it?"

"What do you mean?"

"Yew tell me what I should do with yew. Yew trespass on my property a bunch of times. I warn yew to stay offa my yard and yew just kept coming. Now yew done stole my dog. Yew gonna sic the cops on me. Yew wanna send me to jail and throw away the key. Yew think I'm a scumbag and yew don't know nuttin' about me. Just what the hell should I do with yew? I think I been pretty nice to yew already. Yer still alive and I ain't touched yew," he glowered at me.

"I'mm…I'mm sorry. You're right. All I was thinking about was myself and your dog. It looked like it was so sick and needed help. I just wanted to help the dog," I pleaded.

"Like I done told yew a hunderd times, it ain't yer dog. Yew ain't got no right to come on my yard and mess with my property."

"But a dog isn't 'property.' It's a living being. It has rights, too!"

"Yew and yer lame lib'rl crap. A dog ain't nobody and it ain't got no rights. I OWN it. It's mine to do wit' as I want."

"Okay, okay," I said. "You're right. I was wrong."

I knew I had to agree with him to try to keep him calmed down. Just ahead, a sign for Route 37 popped up in the headlights.

"That's our turn. It's just ahead."

He slowed and turned left onto Route 37. Route 37 is a two-lane, oil-and gravel-paved country road with only a few small farmhouses near the road. The sun had set, the last reflections of the western sky shone pink, blue, purple, and gold. A gorgeous sunset, the last I might ever see...

As the light faded, all I could see was lights on inside a few of the houses. It was Sunday night, and a lot of the folks out here went to church then too. Unlike us heathens in the city! I couldn't think of any way to get help here.

He took several more swigs out of the bottle.

"Yew ain't answered my question? What should I do with yew?"

I panicked..."You could drop me off and take off. You'd have a really long head start before I could walk back to the main road."

"Bull…, nice try. Yew could run to one of them houses and call the cops in 15 minutes. Why don't I just shoot yew and dump yew at the farm so yer parents could find yer wortless body?

"I already been to jail, and they don't execute murderers in this state. I could live off the state for another 40-50 years if they caught me, and I doubt they could. I'd be long gone by the time they got around to finding yer body. Just another 'cold case,'" he guffawed with a manic grin. "Get it? Cold case – like a cold case of beer."

"I…I…I get it. But do you really want to die in prison? Don't you care about anything?"

"Yeah, I care about taking care of my own sorry butt. Ain't nobody else gonna do it. If I let yew live, yew 'member that. Don't nobody care about nuttin' except 'looking out for number one.'

"So what's it gonna be? Yew know my name. Yew know what I look like. I knowed yew'd just love to testify in court agin me and see me locked up for a long time. Why should I let yew live?"

Chapter 18
Stalling for Time, Desperate for Ideas

Oh my God, he was right, I realized in terror. He was getting serious about killing me! What an idiot I'd been! Freezing goosebumps rolled up and down my arms as I looked at him with new horror. I tried to shrink to nothing; I folded up my arms around my legs me as tightly as I could. I had to say something to distract him and try to focus his confused, drunken mind.

I blurted out, "You don't want to kill anybody! Have you ever killed anybody before?"

"Naw, but there always be a first time. But yew is an awful pretty girl. Maybe we'll just have some fun when we get to that farm...a little roll in the hay?" he leered at me.

"Uh...uh...I've never done that—rolled in the hay...maybe that'd be fun," I babbled just to distract him from killing me.

"Yeah, yer lying to me, girl! Ain't no girl like yew gonna want to do it with somebody like me. Do yew still think I'm stupid?"

"No, no...I can see you're smart. You found us really fast. You were smart to get rid of the jeep and take the chain away."

"Yep, I've got that chain right in the back of the truck. Maybe I should just beat yew to death with it and not waste a bullet."

He grinned at me with a mouthful of hideous yellow and green teeth. He drank some more from the pint. It was getting low and I didn't see any more in the seat or on the floorboard. I knew there wasn't any more in the glove compartment.

How much had he been drinking before he found me? Daddy had often passed out after only a pint or two. I didn't want this monster to pass out while he was driving. I wanted to get to the farm where I thought I might have a chance to survive.

"Do you want to stop to get more booze? There's a country store at the intersection with Route 1492 that sells beer and wine."

"Yew still thinking yer smarter than me. I knows that there ain't no beer or wine sold at no store on Sunday night in this county."

"Oh, I didn't know that. My Daddy drank a lot and he always was able to get more booze on Sunday when he ran out."

"Yer daddy is a drinker, huh? Him and me might have a lot to talk about, share a pint or two," he grinned again.

"Daddy WAS a drinker. He quit more than three years ago. He went to rehab, and he's been in AA and sober ever since. He just got married again last week, and he has a good life," I said more proudly than I should have.

"Oh gawd, not one of them," Mike complained. "'Holier than thou' bunch of do-gooders. I ran into some of them in jail. Wanted me to go to meetings with them. Bunch of crap. Surrendering my life to some God who never done nothing for me in my whole life. No way I'm goin' to listen to any of that bull. Not when I could always swap a pack of cigarettes for a pint of hooch with the prisoners who worked in the kitchen. I don't guess yer Daddy would be any fun at all.

"Yew still ain't givin' me a good answer. I won't take no pleasure in killing yew—too easy. Beating yew would leave a lot of scars on that pretty little body of yer'n. That 'roll in the hay' still might fun…It's been a while…" he leered at me again.

"Hey," I yelled. "There's the store. Rte 1492 is right there." As I feared, the store was closed. Nobody was around for miles.

Towns swerved the truck and made a sharp turn. He ran off the road onto the edge, but he whipped the steering wheel around, changed gears, and skidded back onto the road. "Yee haw," he yelled, as we roared down the road.

In a few minutes, we ran out of paved road and lurched onto the dirt road that led to Grandpa's.

"Where is yer farm?"

"Slow down. It's hard to see in the dark. It's just up ahead on the left. The house is wood painted dark red with white trim. There's a small red barn beside it. You see that wood fence with barbed wire on top over there," I said, pointing to my left. "The driveway is about 100 feet down."

He slowed down, drove by the fence, and turned into the driveway. The house and the barn were dark and empty. I could see by the headlights that weeds had overgrown all the flowers in front of the house. One of the white shutters that had hung beside the bay window had come loose and drooped like it was grieving being alone. A huge wasp nest hung down under the roof over the front porch. The red paint was faded and flaking.

The house looked weary and sad.

Towns stopped the truck and looked around where the headlight beams shone. "Well, well. Ain't this nice," he said sarcastically. He picked up the bottle, tilted it high, and drained the rest of the liquor. He dropped the empty on the floorboard.

He pulled the knife out of its sheath, pointed it at me, "Don't move." He got out and came around to my side and opened the door. "Get out of the car. Don't even think 'bout runnin' or I'll skin yew alive."

"Okay, okay…," I whimpered.

I climbed out slowly as he held the door and watched me.

"Yew still ain't answered my question. What is I gonna do wit' yew?" he said as he ran his left finger down the edge of the large knife and grinned at me.

All I could see were his hideous green and yellow teeth lurking just behind the deadly point of the shiny knife. It struck me how odd it was that the only clean thing about him was his knife. I knew what he meant to do.

Chapter 19
The Evil That Evil Men Try to Do

When I knew he planned to kill me, I felt stunned, shocked that this maniac was real, Booper was real, and I was about to die!

A crazy thought roared from deep in my mind: I had gotten what I wished for when I stole Booper and ran away—a quick trip to Grandpa's farm. Guess that'll teach me to wish for anything...

I stood with my back to the side of the truck so he couldn't get behind me. I looked past Towns to the house and the barn. The house was probably locked, but the side barn door might be open.

Maybe I could find a weapon in there; Grandpa always had shovels, tree trimmers, scythes, and tools like screwdrivers. If any hay bales had been left in the loft and other stuff stacked on the floor, I might have a chance to hide and get an advantage.

But how was I going to get past that knife and into the barn before this maniac caught me and stabbed me?

He stood a few feet away, looking at me with cold, dull eyes. I could tell he was thinking about how to attack me, but the last bottle of booze seemed to make him more confused. He swayed a little.

I begged—darn right I begged, "Why can't you just leave the

dog and me here and take off? You need a big head start, and now I can't get to any of those houses for at least an hour."

I thought about volunteering for him to tie me to a tree, but I immediately knew that was a stupid idea. He'd just stab me and leave me there to bleed to death. Dummy!

"Naw. Yew can identify me, so I gotta do something to keep yer mouth shut permanent-like. Yew never knowed. They might catch up with me," he snarled.

"I figure yew can make this quick and easy on yerself or try to fight me and make it hard and painful. I figure yew one for fighting and taking the hard way. Yew has been so far."

I snapped out of my fear. I hadn't been through all the failure I had endured with Dad and Mom to die now. I had been forced to move to my shabby neighborhood and my second-rate school; I had chosen to put my life on the line to save Booper.

He was right about that; he knew me better than I thought. I wasn't going to die without fighting with everything I had. Knife or no knife, stabs, cuts, blood. I would make him pay however I could and leave evidence on his filthy face that he had had his hands full before I died.

"Damn it," he mumbled and lunged at me with his knife aimed at my throat.

I don't how I did what I did. I ducked to my left and planted on my left foot; the knife whistled past my face. I pivoted in a half circle and kicked with my right foot as hard and fast as I could. My shoe hit him square in the groin. Towns screamed and dropped the knife. He sank to his knees, writhing in pain. "Oh, yew rotten little bitch," he gasped. "I'm really going to mess you up now."

I ran toward the barn, found the small side door, and slammed into it. It busted off its hinges, and I dived into the inky blackness of the barn. Although practically blind in the dark, I knew where the cow stall was and ran toward it at the far end of the barn. I wanted to hide there until I could see in the dark, but I tripped over a hay bale in the middle of the floor and fell on my face. It hurt like crazy, but I scrambled to my feet and kept moving. I hid in the stall and peered around the edge of the wall.

As my eyes adjusted to the gloom, I heard Towns cursing and screaming outside. "I'm gonna gut yew like a pig. I'm gonna hang yew up in a tree and watch you bleed out. Then I'm gonna leave yew so yer pitiful mommy and daddy find yer sorry carcass after the buzzards and crows eat yer eyes out and pull yer to pieces."

I scrambled from the stall toward the dirty, cracked window facing his truck. I peered over the ledge. He had his hands between his legs and he was hopping and staggering around. The knife was on the ground.

Maybe I had one minute to find something in the barn and escape before he picked up his knife and came after me. I knew the woods on Grandpa's 10 acres as well as I knew my bedroom. I could run, but I couldn't leave Booper behind.

I thought I could run toward him and grab the knife off the ground. But he was too close to it as he moaned and staggered in circles. I looked back inside the barn and saw shadows of boxes on the floor and tools hanging on the walls.

I scrabbled like a crab on all fours toward the boxes, hoping I could find something small but deadly, like a large screwdriver or a knife. Ole´! Some tools were left behind! I felt around and found gardening tools, nothing really good enough. I crab-walked to a table against a wall and pulled myself slowly up.

There was what I needed—a scythe. Thank the Whatever that Grandpa liked to exercise and trim the little bit of grass around the house the old-fashioned way. I didn't think an electric weed trimmer would help me much against the enraged Towns.

I grabbed the scythe. It was dull and rusty, but it would do. I began to run toward the stairs to the loft where I could ease out to the ground through the door to the hayloft.

Before I reached the stairs, Towns yelled again, laughing like a maniac. "But before I kill yer, I'm gonna do yew a special favor. I'm going to kill this piece of crap dog by slicing it up one limb at a time. And yer going to get to watch. So, yew got a choice—get yer butt out here now or I start cuttin' up the dog."

I heard Booper yelp and cry as Towns must have grabbed him out of the back of the truck. Booper howled and whined.

"Wait," I screamed. "Don't hurt him! I'm coming out! You can do anything you want to me but leave the dog alone!"

"Yew got 30 seconds to git out here," he yelled.

As I walked toward the busted door to meet Towns, I saw a small screwdriver on the table. I grabbed it and put in my back pocket. It didn't feel very big. I dropped the scythe on the edge of the table by the door, praying I would have a chance to get back to it.

I walked out of the barn into the dirt driveway. I could see the black, menacing figure of Towns silhouetted by the headlights. His shadow looked like a massive black monster—the Grim Reaper with a huge, sharp knife. He didn't need the long Reaper scythe.

I held up my hand to shield my eyes from the lights. Towns stood about 30 feet away. He was holding Booper off the ground by the scruff of his neck with the knife pointed at the dog's throat.

"Well, now missy. Ain't yew the he-ro-in—or her-o I should say to be po-li-ti-cally ko-reck," he laughed.

He dropped the dog. Booper hit the ground with a thud, whimpered, and lay still.

"Git over here. Now!"

I began to move slowly toward him.

"Faster. I ain't got no more time to waste wit' yew."

I began to step faster. With a swift movement, I pulled the screwdriver out of my back pocket and sprinted as fast I could toward him.

His bleary black eyes shot open wide as I leaped and lunged into his body, thrusting the screwdriver into his stomach. The screwdriver stuck in his gut as I pushed away from him.

He screamed and staggered backward. "Yew crazy bitch. What the hell?" He bent over, looked down at the screwdriver and grabbed the handle like he meant to pull it out.

"Oh no," he muttered. "Can't do that. Gotta leave that damn thing there, or I'll bleed out like a stuck pig."

I could see a smattering of blood on his shirt, but he wasn't bleeding as much as I thought he would be.

Wincing and cursing, he slowly stood upright and started limping toward me. I was freaked out that my stab had not knocked him off his feet. I didn't know how long he could keep moving and I had no intention of finding out. I looked frantically for a place to run. I started backing up quickly toward the barn to grab the scythe by the door. I made quick backward steps my soccer team had practiced every day for months; I wanted to keep him in sight so I could tell how fast he was moving.

I was widening the gap between him and me. I believed that if I could get into the barn and grab the scythe by the door, I could climb the stairs into the loft. Either he couldn't follow me up there, or he would be in terrible pain as he climbed.

I had the advantage as I could swing the scythe down at his head if he got near the top, or I could escape by leaping out of the loft door. I might even have time to run around the barn and get Booper before Towns figured out what I was doing. Carrying Booper would slow me down, but I couldn't leave him in this killer's hands. If we got to the woods, we had a fighting chance to survive because I could lead Towns to a steep ravine and try to trick him into falling into it.

As my mind raced forward and my legs moved backward, I stepped on a large, loose rock and twisted my left ankle, the one I had hurt earlier playing soccer this fall. I cried in pain and fell back onto the hard ground.

Towns roared a horrendous victory cry and limped toward me faster, holding his stomach with a bloody left hand and his knife in his right. I tried a backward crab walk on all fours, but my ankle gave way and I collapsed again. I stayed still and watched him come closer.

He stopped a few feet away from me. "Damn it, yew done hurt me bad, but not bad enough to kill me. Now it's my turn to cut yew a whole lot worse than yew cut me. But I ain't about to get close to those legs of yer'n again either."

He began slowly circling around me so he could reach my head. Despite the intense pain in my ankle, I clambered around to keep my legs between him and me. We did a slow, crazed dance around the clock as I turned as fast as I could.

He darted toward me and jumped back and forth. Every time I shifted, my ankle sent shooting pains up my leg. Every time he jumped forward, he swung his knife at me. He missed every time, but only by a few inches, and his swing came closer every time.

But every time he swung, he grunted in pain and gripped his stomach a little tighter. I didn't know how long it would take for him to collapse from loss of blood or for me to stop moving just once and give him room to leap on me for the kill.

Chapter 20
Saved by the Cavalry?
No—Much Better

Suddenly, I thought I heard over Towns' grunts a sound like a car rumbling in the distance. I strained to hear as I kept moving.

Yes! It was a car and it was moving fast down the dirt road toward the farm. I prayed that whoever was in the car would be a neighbor who would see the headlights at the abandoned house and stop to investigate. Towns seemed to be in too much pain to hear the sound.

He darted toward me again and swung his knife as I skittered to my right. My one-second lapse cost me as the knife sliced through my sleeve and cut my arm. He stepped back and yelled, "I got yew! That's just the first one of a lot more to come!"

I screamed as blood began to ooze from the cut. I skittered around, but driven by the smell of blood, he jumped at me again faster than before and landed on top of me. His weight knocked the breath out of me, and I struggled to breathe.

As he swung the knife down toward my face, I blocked it with my left arm, but I heard a crack in my forearm from the force of the blow. I swung my right fist at his stomach, I hit the screwdriver and pushed it hard. He fell backward off of me to the ground, groaning loudly. The screwdriver was still stuck in his belly.

He got up slowly, panting and staggering. He stared at me with intense hatred. I scrambled backward to put more distance between me and him. Where was that damn car?

Just then, a small pickup truck swung wildly into the dirt driveway and skidded to a stop beside Towns' truck. I stared at the truck as Rory jumped out of the driver's seat, and Peter, Bu, Jorge, Magda, and Keysha leaped out of the truck bed. They ran toward us. Then Glenda stood up slowly in the truck bed and gawked at the incredible scene silhouetted by the headlights.

They screamed my name, "Harry! Harry! Where are you? Are you all right?!"

Bewildered, I only thought, "Rory's only 13. He's not old enough to drive a truck!" Stupid me, I guess he could.

Towns jumped up and swung around at their shouts and roared, "Who the hell are yew? Get out of here. Ain't none of this any of yer bidness." He swung the knife around at them. They screeched to a stop.

I yelled, "Rory, I'm here behind that maniac. He's got a rifle in the truck. Get it and shoot him!" I really wanted Towns dead.

As the others looked on, Rory ran to the truck, pulled the rifle off the rack, turned around, and pointed it at Towns. He said, "Drop the knife, or I'll pull the trigger."

Towns looked at him with a wicked grin and said, "Do yew think I'm stupid enough to leave a loaded rifle in my truck? And yew ain't even knowed how to load a round in the chamber, even if it was." He laughed wildly, but bent double as pain from the screwdriver wound shot through him.

"Rory, I stabbed him in the stomach. He's hurt bad and bleeding," I screamed as I lay on the ground about 10 feet behind Towns. "Do something to put him on the ground!"

Rory yelled back at me, "He's got that knife. Did he hurt you?"

"I twisted my ankle and fell, and he just nicked my arm, but I'm okay. Don't worry about me. Figure out a way to stop him!" I cried.

"I've got an idea," squeaked a voice from the back of the truck. Glenda was standing, holding a bag of soccer balls. She opened the bag, dumped all the balls in the truck bed, and started throwing them one by one at the—well—MY—Redhawks.

She squealed, "Kick the balls at his head. Knock him down!"

"Yes!" I shrieked. "Spread out all around him. Kick the balls at his head. Kick the balls at his stomach. Keep kicking 'til he falls!"

Rory, Peter, Bu, Jorge, Magda, and Keysha each leaped to a ball and spread out in a semi-circle, facing Towns. He looked at them like they were crazy. He laughed loud and then doubled over, grimacing in pain. He had no idea what was about to hit him. He learned quickly.

They rolled the balls around with their kicking feet to set the best angle. Rory cried, "Now!" All six kicked the balls straight at Towns. Rory's hit him right in the nose, Peter's the left side of his face, Bu's his left ear, and Jorge's his right side. Keysha's hit the screwdriver in his stomach, and Magda's slammed into his sternum. They chased the bouncing balls, Glenda helped run down a couple, and they formed their semi-circle again.

As they got into position again, Towns, in a daze of pain, booze, and something new—fear, gibbered, "What the..." He wobbled and toppled to the ground. He writhed in pain, curled up in a ball, and puked two pints of rotten whiskey all over himself. If I hadn't hated him so much right then, I might have thought how pathetic he was.

Instead, I whooped for joy! "There's a chain in the back of his truck. Get it and chain him tight like he did poor Booper. Bu, there's a strong rope in the barn in one of the bins under the counter on the left. We'll tie him up just to make sure he's not getting up off the ground."

Rory laughed and yelled at me, "Still the one giving orders, are you, Bossy-etta!" At least I had enough shame to keep my mouth shut and blush at his joke. Thank goodness it was dark so he couldn't see me!

Rory and Keysha got the chain and tied it around Towns' legs. They dragged him to the front of his truck as he groaned pitifully. They found the lock in the truck bed where Towns had thrown it, so they used it to lock the chain to the front axle. He wasn't going anywhere. His arms were still free, so Bu and Jorge grabbed his arms and tied them behind his back.

Towns screamed when they pulled his arms and shoulders tight behind him. "My stomach! Yer killing me! Get me to a doctor before I bleed to death," he whined.

I was still lying on the ground. I called to Magda to ask her to help me stand up. She quickly walked over, reached down with her long right arm and virtually lifted me off the ground with one hand. She was strong!

Leaning on her arm, I hopped over to look down at the rotten scumbag. I said bitterly, "Five minutes ago, you were about to cut my throat and now you want us to get you to a doctor. You miserable coward!" I spluttered.

"You can wait and suffer. You're not going to die. I just want you to know what it feels like to be chained to a truck for a little while. It's too bad it can't be for days and days in the rain and mud and heat without enough food and water like what you've done to poor Booper for so long."

I really wanted to kick him again and again and again, and I even moved my right leg, but Rory grabbed my left arm and my ankle hurt badly when I stepped down on it. "Oww," I wailed, hopping away from Towns. I guess revenge is best left to others.

I was furious at Towns but amazed at what had just happened. The guys and even Glenda had searched for me and found me and taken down a crazy criminal with brilliant footwork! I was yanked out of my reverie when I heard another moan.

"Oh no, Booper! Booper! Where are you?" I screamed. "Peter, Bu, did you find a dog anywhere?"

"Yes, I saw what might be a dog on the other side of the truck. Holey moley, it looked like a pile of rotten carpet and a bag of bones," Bu said. "It didn't make a sound when we went by to get the chain."

"Oh, thank God!" I cried. "Magda, please help me get to my dog." She half-carried, half-dragged me toward Towns' truck. I let go and slid down next to Booper.

"Oh, Booper," I sighed, as I wrapped my arms around him. "I am so sorry he hurt you again. He'll never do that again. I promise…"

Rory, Glenda, and the rest of my team gathered around us to look at the dog.

"So that's the dog Glenda told us about. That's what started this whole mess," Rory exclaimed.

"No, you're wrong," I snapped. "That maniac chained to the truck started it when he began to abuse this poor, beautiful creature. I just wanted to have a dog, and I found one I knew needed help. I didn't count on that drunken monster losing his mind.

"Wait a minute," I said, coming to my senses—what little I had left. "How did you know where I was and how to get here?"

Rory grinned at Glenda. "Oh, Glenda is your real hero. Your Mom called her at 8 o'clock this morning, absolutely terrified because you were not in your bed when she woke up. Your Mom ran all the way to this bum's house, didn't find you or him, and didn't see the dog or the truck. Glenda, you tell the story from here. It's really your story.

Glenda looked down at her shoes and said, "Well, Rory's right. Your Mom called and said you were gone and the guy with the dog was gone too. Everything—his truck, the old jeep, the dog. The house was empty when she looked through a window.

"She was terrified that you had woken up early and snuck over to check on the dog. She was sure the creep had caught you and kidnapped you. Just to make sure, she called me to see if you were staying over with me or had told me where you were going.

"I told her all I knew is that you were threatening to run away with the dog, but I didn't take you seriously. But how did you get here if he kidnapped you?"

Towns continued to groan and rattle the chain and whine for help. We ignored him. We had checked and the bleeding from his stomach had slowed. I was hoping that if Booper and I were lucky, he would get blood poisoning from the rusty screwdriver the longer it stayed there.

I said. "Actually, Mom was mostly right. I felt so ashamed and devastated yesterday when you won the game without me. I thought the only thing I could do was run away to a safe place. Towns—oh, that's his name, Thomas Michael Towns—drunken bum for short—didn't grab me until Booper and I had walked—if you can call limping slowly—about 10 miles outside of town.

"He just lucked out. He drove all over our neighborhood looking for us after I took Booper. When he couldn't find us, he just fled the city, I suspect to avoid getting caught for some other crime we don't know about yet. He happened to leave on the main highway. He saw us by the side of the road, stopped, and grabbed us."

"Boy, what rotten luck or bad karma!" Bu said, shaking his head.

I agreed, "It's bad something, that's for sure! But Rory, Glenda, how did you find me?"

Rory grinned, "That was the easy part," looking at Glenda.

"Jeez, Harry," Glenda said. "All you ever talked about was your Grandpa's farm and how much you missed it and wanted to go back there. You told me where it was and how to get here like 100 times.

"After your Mom called me—and woke my mom up and made her very, very mad, by the way—I knew you had stolen the dog…"

"I didn't steal it," I protested. "I saved it from Towns' abuse."

"C'mon, Harry. 'Fess up. It wasn't your dog, and you didn't report it to animal control. You stole the dog because like you also told me 100 times, you really wanted a dog."

I said sheepishly, "Well,…I did take the dog because it was suffering so badly, and nobody cared about it but me. Mom, Mrs. Jackson, Mrs. Reynolds, all of you ignored its suffering."

Glenda sighed and said, "Let's not start all that again. OK…?"

Rory interrupted, "To pick up what we did, Glenda called me and told me everything. Last week, she had told us some of the stuff about why you couldn't play in the game.

Glenda spoke up, something amazing for her to do, "I knew you had made your Mom really mad at you by disobeying her over the dog. But I didn't realize how dangerous this jerk was and how likely he was to hurt you until this morning. Your Mom and I both felt terrified something awful was going to happen to you, if it hadn't already."

"Harry," Keysha sighed, looking me straight in the eye. "We were mad at you because you were being really selfish. You wanted everything your own way. You thought you were better than the rest of the team and you didn't need our help to win.

"But we're a team, Harry, and none of us wins alone and none of us loses alone. "That's why we're here. You are one of our team, even when you act like a snob and know-it-all."

Rory laughed, "Since we knew you'd be in trouble—as usual, I called the rest of the guys—and girls—and sort of 'borrowed' my brother's truck. He took me out to the country a lot last summer and taught me how to drive it. I'm almost as tall as he is, so it's easy to work the pedals, shift gears, and steer.

"But geez, my parents are going to ground me! My brother is going to kill me when we get back, but it was worth it. I've never helped catch a criminal before, especially by playing kick practice with his face!"

We all cracked up at that. When we stopped laughing, the rest of my team looked at me solemnly, shaking their heads. Keysha said, "Rory's right. We didn't know about all the stuff you were going through. We just thought you were the conceited new kid who had to show us up. We didn't see how unhappy you were. You shoulda trusted us and talked to us. We woulda helped you."

"Guys, I am so sorry." I broke into tears in front my teammates for the first time. I sobbed, as I hugged Booper, who whimpered when I grazed his open sores.

"I felt so angry at my Mom for not letting me have a dog. For working all the time. I felt so alone in school when no one seemed to want to make friends with me. My Dad's problems…I've just felt so confused. When Mom grounded me and I couldn't play and you won without me, I thought I was going to die of shame.

"I hated being the new kid. I've been obnoxious and tried to make you to treat me like the boss. I believed you hated me but hung out with me because you needed me to help you win.

"Yes, Keysha, you're right. I didn't trust you except when we played, and I knew you would pass me the ball so we could win. It was all about winning so I didn't believe I was so worthless.

"Thank you for saving me! I owe all of you my life, and I'll do anything you want me to do to make up for my terrible mistakes."

Rory grinned and said, "Oh, we'll think of something…"

"Oh, yeah, we have big plans for you in the winter and spring," Magda said, with a twinkle in her black eyes.

"Okay, okay, whatever it is, I'm willing to do it. But I still don't know how you got here," I said.

"Oh, that was easy," Rory said. "Glenda told us the farm was just off Route 1492 near Otisville on a dirt road. I used my smart phone to search for it. The location popped up in about 30 seconds, so we drove out here as fast as we could. We would have been here sooner, but I had to round up everybody I could find. This sorry group were the only ones I could find late Sunday afternoon."

"What 'sorry group' are you talking about, Mr. Ro-ry Supa-Star?" Keysha said, with her hands on her hips but a smile on her face.

"Harry, just to let you know," she said, looking at Rory with a wicked grin. "Rory told us after the game that the only way he made the winning goal was to copy your juke move on the goalie. He even said he missed you."

"I did not!" Rory protested lamely.

I laughed, "That's alright, Rory. You can steal any of my moves any time you want to. And guys, you have no idea how much I missed you and the chance to play with you in that game.

"It really wasn't about my scoring the winning goal like I said; I felt so angry at my Mom since she wouldn't let me finish what we started together four months ago when I walked out to my first practice…Alright, enough of this touchy-feely stuff! I still don't understand how you got here."

Rory added, "Like I said, I had the location on my GPS. But my stupid brother had let the gas tank run down to almost empty, so we had to stop and buy some gas.

"By the way, you owe us 20 bucks," he kidded me.

"More than happy to pay—with interest!" I said.

"Boy, you should have seen the face on that store clerk when he saw me give him the 20 bucks for gas," Rory joked. "He asked me how old I was, and I said I was 17, but looked real young for my age. I'm sure glad he didn't ask for a driver's license," he chuckled.

The rest of us almost choked we laughed so hard at the vision of Rory buying gas and driving away while the clerk stared at him and wondered if he was even close to 16, much less 17.

"Okay," Glenda interrupted. "What in the world are we going to do now? As much as it sounds like a great idea, we can't leave Towns—is that his name?—tied to his truck bleeding."

"Maybe we could just chain him to the back of his truck and drag him to the hospital," I said, with an innocent, angelic look on my face. "Maybe the fresh air would do him some good."

"Harry, you're so full of it," Jorge laughed. "*Hermana loca*!"

Rory said, "As much fun as this is, we've gotta call 9-1-1 and get the cops and an ambulance out here. Harry, you better have your story straight. You've got a lot to explain to a lot of people."

He pulled his smart phone out of his hip pocket and opened it. Just as he began to dial, we heard sirens blaring and saw flashing lights cutting through the limbs of the bare trees. We heard the rumble of several cars as they hit the dirt road at high speed.

"Well," Rory said with a deadpan look. "I guess the cavalry is here just in the nick of time to save us."

Chapter 21
The Cavalry Isn't So Helpful After All

All of us were laughing hysterically as Dad's red Mustang flew into the driveway, followed by a county sheriff's cruiser and a state patrol SUV.

Mom leaped out of the back seat of Dad's car, ran over and fell to the ground with me. She hugged me so tightly and it felt so great.

"Oh, Harry, are you alright? Your arm's bleeding. What happened...I've been so scared to death...Did that terrible man kidnap you...Did he hurt you? Did he...uh...touch you...? Where is he? What happened to him?"

On and on, until Dad ran up to us and asked Mom to calm down and listen to me. For a change, I thought, but I kept that idea to myself.

We all started jabbering at once, about my dog rescue, the kidnapping, my fight with Towns, the team's search for us, their soccer practice on Towns' head. All our words made one big mess no one could understand.

From behind Mom and Dad, a deep voice roared, "Enough! Be quiet! I am State Trooper Knowles. I'll question each of you one at a time, and you'll give me a straight answer." The directions came from a burly black state trooper who looked like he meant business, so we shut up.

A county deputy sheriff, a tall, lanky white guy, had gotten out of his car and seen Towns chained to the truck. He walked toward the truck to examine Towns.

"Arrest that little bitch," Towns roared, pointing at me as the deputy reached him. "She tried to kill me! I got a knife in my gut and I'm bleeding out. Call an ambulance! I'm dying!"

The deputy looked down at him and said, "Ah, if it ain't my old buddy Towns! Surprise seeing you here! We hoped you had already gotten away so we wouldn't have to waste any more time on a scumbag like you.

"So you really want me to believe that little girl," he chuckled, pointing at me, "she tricked you, attacked you, and knifed you in the stomach? You're always shooting your mouth off in every bar in town how tough you are. I think I'll make the rounds later tonight and tell all your drinking buddies how a little girl was a better man that you were!"

Towns roared, "Billy, yew m@%#%f!&!!&, yew say a word about this to anybody and I'll come after you!"

Billy laughed and kicked Towns' right foot. He cried out, "That be police brutality! My lawya is going to sue yer butt for evahthing you got!"

"Well, Towns, I sure am sorry. I wasn't looking what I was doing and I must have tripped over your foot!" Billy mocked Towns. Then he said, "You sue me, you piece of sewer trash. Be my guest. It will be kind of hard to do that since you're broke and you're going right back to state prison for about half a dozen probation violations I can think of off the top of my head."

Towns mumbled under his breath. "Well, get me some help! It's your duty as a police officer!"

"Yeh, you know all about my duties and what I have to do for you and all the other vermin of the earth," Billy said disgustedly.

He turned and walked a few feet away from Towns. He wailed, "Don't leave me, get me outta here!"

"Neither you nor I are going anywhere, fool. I'm calling an ambulance and the detectives. This whole thing looks like a real mess."

All of us had remained stock still, astonished at what deputy Billy said to Towns. I grinned and knew I liked that deputy a lot!

We watched him use his shoulder radio to call for ambulances, crime scene investigators, and detectives. The farm was going to get very busy very soon on what must by then have been the middle of the night.

Knowles, standing behind us, harrumped, "I need to talk to all of you right now."

Before Knowles could start asking questions, my Dad spoke up, "Trooper, these kids are only 12 or 13 years old. Shouldn't you notify their parents and have them come here if you're going to question their kids?"

Trooper Knowles looked at my Dad like he wanted to rip his tongue out, but he clinched his teeth. He said, "Yes, sir, you're correct. Is that girl yours? Seems to me like she's the one I'm most interested in, so do I have your permission to start with her?"

Dad looked at me, but before I could speak, my Mom said, "She's my daughter, and I have full custody. Her Dad only has visiting rights, so Trooper, you might want to ask me that question."

Dad rolled his eyes, and Kim grabbed his arm and moved him away toward their car before he could say anything and start an argument with Mom.

Mom looked at me and said, "Harry, you have a right to have a lawyer present. You've watched enough TV shows with me to know whatever you say can be used against you. These officers are just trying to do their job, but they are not your friends. So, what do you want to do?"

"Mom, at the moment, I think I'd like to get my arm bandaged and my ankle and my forearm checked out. I don't know if they're broken. And I'm beginning to feel woozy."

All the adrenaline that had flooded through my system all night and all day had suddenly drained away, and I felt light-headed and exhausted. I hadn't eaten anything or had any water to drink in hours, and I was dehydrated and starving.

All that was true, but it certainly was a good way to stop Knowles from asking me any questions when my head was as foggy as a morning in San Francisco, as Grandpa used to say. The fog was rolling into my brain, my ankle hurt as badly as it ever had, my left forearm ached, and the cut on my right arm had started a slow trickle of blood again.

"Oh God, when will the ambulance be here?" my Mom, always ready to get hysterical, cried.

While we waited, Knowles asked for and wrote down the guys' names, their parents and phone numbers. We had to give him that much. Still fuming, he went to his car, radioed in the information and barked at the dispatcher to call their parents and get them out here as fast as possible.

Knowles had to satisfy himself with asking questions of Dad, Mom, and Kim. None of them really knew very much about the truth. My Mom, of course, told him how rotten Towns was and how he had threatened us. But she didn't help me out when she said I had gone onto the creep's property to help the dog. She didn't realize she had just gotten me charged with trespassing and theft.

Finally, a car with two detectives and two ambulances arrived at the same time. Wearing thick gloves, two EMTs asked us for the key to the lock on the chain. Rory gave it to them. They unlocked and untied Towns and gave the chain and the rope to the detectives. The detectives put them in a plastic bag, I guess for evidence. The EMTs examined the creep, and stuck a blood transfusion in his arm, not very gently either.

As they loaded him on a gurney, he looked over at us and cackled, "Yew idgits, the rifle was loaded. All yew had to was cock it and pull the trigger! Yew missed yer chance. Now I is going to do everthin' I can to make yer puny lives a living hell!"

One of the EMTs told him to shut up. He fell back laughing like the maniac he was. They basically threw him into the ambulance, making him groan. They raced away, siren blaring. I hoped the ambulance hit every pothole in the dirt road so he would suffer some more. I hoped Towns' stomach would have a new belly button to remember me by.

Deputy Billy followed Towns' ambulance to make sure he was placed under guard at the hospital. I had a feeling he wasn't going anywhere anytime soon, despite his threats. Little did I know then how far Towns would go to keep his word.

The other EMTs examined me in the back of the second ambulance so I would have a little privacy. They thought my ankle was just badly sprained, and they found the slash on my arm wasn't very deep and wouldn't require stitches. They cleaned it and bandaged it. They squeezed my left forearm and although I said it hurt, they were sure it wasn't broken, but a bad bruise was turning blue and purple.

The woman EMT asked the male EMT to leave so my Mom, she and I could be alone in the back of the ambulance. The EMT shut the door and asked Mom and me for permission to examine the rest of me. I turned bright red but remembered from TV how many abused girls refused to be examined from shame. I didn't feel ashamed, I felt angry!

Mom and I agreed to the exam, and the EMT asked me embarrassing questions about whether Towns' had abused me. I told them the truth that in fact, I had kicked him between the legs and stabbed him.

She looked at me weirdly—like I was either a superhero or a fool. I couldn't tell which they thought I was. They chuckled and asked me if I wanted them to take me to the hospital to have my ankle and forearm X-rayed. I asked if I could have my parents drive me to the hospital later. They said it was fine with them as long as my ankle and forearm didn't swell more than they already had.

After the techs helped me out of the ambulance, I realized I didn't know either—whether I was a hero or a fool, probably a little of both, but more naïve fool. I just wanted to help the dog, yet all this terrible trouble happened because I stuck my nose in where only I thought it belonged. Speaking of which, in all the excitement, I had forgotten to check on Booper. Some dog mom I was going to be!

"Where's Booper?" I exclaimed as I got out of the ambulance and limped toward the group. "Booper, my dog. Magda, where's the dog, Booper's his name! What happened to Booper?"

"He is fine. Peter, Rory and Bu picked him up off the ground and put him in the back of Rory's truck. That creep's truck is disgusting!" Magda said. "The dog is lying on a blanket on the bed of Rory's truck. We gave him some water and some snack bars we had in our backpacks. He really loved those!"

"Oh, thanks so much! You can be his Godmother," I said, only half-jokingly.

Magda looked me in the eye and said seriously, "I don't think I am ready for such a high honor. I think Glenda is most deserving of that pleasure."

Glenda looked a bit startled at that idea. I said, smiling at her, "Well, you ready to be the Godmother of a 'bouncing baby Booper?"

She grinned shyly, "I guess so, but you have to promise me you'll never go nuts like this again. Cross your heart and hope to die!"

I dutifully crossed my heart and promised to keep Glenda away from my problems. But I knew in my heart that Glenda and I were going to experience together a lot more than we could even begin to imagine. Like who could have imagined this craziness just a few days ago? Anyway, I didn't believe in that heart-crossing, dying superstition, so I wasn't too worried.

As the sun began to rise, the crime scene team, like the CSIs on TV, arrived next and start doing their thing—stringing the obligatory yellow crime scene tape around the entire driveway and the barn, putting little, numbered tents by every little mark in the dirt, dusting the creep's truck for fingerprints, photographing everything, scraping blood samples off the dirt, taking blood samples from my skin, even taking my bloody shirt when they found out Mom had brought some of my clothes with her.

However, last I saw, the screwdriver was still lodged through scumbag's belly button, so they'd have to go to the hospital for that critical piece of evidence. I hoped the screwdriver that saved my life wouldn't turn around and become the jerk's primary defense.

The CSIs worked methodically, mostly looking down at the ground in the driveway and searching carefully through the minutest particles of dirt and dust in the barn. They were doing whatever it is they do. It didn't look nearly as exciting as it does on TV. No wretched, half-dismembered body with maggots eating its guts, no organs to slice up like on TV. Just some crazy kids, an abused dog, and a maniac. Probably all in a day's work.

Two by two, the guys' parents began to arrive. Rory's brother was with his parents; he was furious that Rory took his truck, but he calmed down and gave him a hug when he learned Rory had not wrecked it and had been a hero by capturing Towns. He burst out laughing when Rory complained he had left the tank almost empty and he'd had to pump gas with 20 dollars of his own money to get here.

After all of the parents had arrived, except Glenda's, Trooper Knowles asked for permission to speak to the guys. A few said yes, and the questioning began. The interrogations went on for what felt like hours until mid-morning. The cool fall morning was a cloudless, bright blue, and the sun felt warm on my face. It was going to be another Indian summer kind of day. My ankle and forearm ached even worse so I found a place to sit on the front porch in the shade to watch the show. I asked Dad and Kim to keep an eye on Booper to make sure he was alright.

As the crime scene techs worked and Knowles and the detectives interrogated Bu, Keysha, and Rory, I realized they were wasting their time. Only Towns and I knew the truth behind everything that led to my 'dognapping' and his kidnapping me. Jeez, I assumed Towns would go on trial for kidnapping me, but I realized that we could end up testifying in court as "He said, She said." That could swing a judge or a jury either way. I needed to help gather more evidence.

I yelled in the direction of the trooper and the detectives. "Please be sure to examine my dog in the back of the pickup and take lots of pictures. There's probably a lot of blood and puss all over the bed of the other truck. That's where Towns threw him. That jerk abused him for months, and you'll need the evidence to prove it in court. Can you call a vet to examine him like the EMTs examined me in the ambulance?"

Trooper Knowles stopped talking with Bu and his parents and stared at me. "What did you say? You think the dog is an important piece of evidence?"

"Yes, sir," I said respectfully. Our not-so-great experiences with Dad and the cops had taught me to always speak nicely to them. "Booper, er...the dog, was badly abused. I think it would be important to add animal abuse charges to whatever else Towns is going to be charged with."

The trooper looked at me, "You think so, do you?"

"Yes, sir. I've seen the pattern of abuse for months, and..."

Dad interrupted me and came over. "Yes, Trooper Knowles, please call a veterinarian and an animal control officer to examine the dog. I suspect my daughter is correct. She's usually right about these things."

"She is, is she?" Knowles said with suspicion in his voice.

"Yes, sir," my Dad said extra politely. He had learned his lesson the hard way, too. "I'd hate to see the man who almost killed my daughter get away with it because of a technicality like not showing evidence of severe animal abuse."

Trooper Knowles sighed, "I see your point." He called to one of the detectives and murmured to him. We heard the detective say quietly, but sharply to Knowles, "Of course the damn dog is important so we have to make sure it gets examined, the evidence properly collected, and a full profile of its injuries and abuse cataloged."

Great! I thought, but then, my Dad leaned over and whispered in my ear, "I know you want to do the right thing and help the dog, but you almost said too much. Talk with me about what and how much you tell the investigators. Unfortunately, you know I know too much about that."

"Yes, Dad. I'll be more careful. Thanks!"

During the whole mess at the farm, the only parents who didn't show up at all were Glenda's. I felt really sorry for her as she waited and waited for them to arrive. I mentioned it to Dad, and he spoke with Knowles. Dad said the trooper promised to send a town patrol car to Glenda's home to find out if her parents were home and in any condition to drive to the farm and pick her up. I saw the trooper speak into his shoulder radio.

A few minutes later, a patrol car radioed back, and we heard Glenda's parents weren't in any shape to come get her. We learned later they were so drunk that they couldn't understand what the officer was trying to tell them. They even denied Glenda could be anywhere but in her bedroom because she was so sickly. They were lucky they didn't get arrested for being drunk and disorderly and the cops didn't send Social Services to their house. I already knew you can get as drunk and wasted as you want in your own house. I never intended for that to happen in my house, ever!

Despite her pitiful parents, Glenda was the real hero that day. I felt so proud, grateful, and happy for her since she had stood up for me, called Rory, and started their fantastic rescue.

In just a few minutes, an animal control officer roared up in a town animal shelter truck. She jumped out and yelled, "Where's the injured dog?"

"He's in the back of the truck. He's really in pain. Be careful and don't hurt him," I shouted as she began to trot toward the truck.

The woman, medium-height, brown-haired and dressed in a khaki uniform, stopped and looked at me with a "What?" kind of look. She said with a tight grimace, "I would never deliberately hurt an animal. I'll take care of him."

Wow! I hoped I hadn't insulted her. I began to reply, "I…," but she turned and ran the few steps to the back of the truck.

She quickly began to examine Booper, looking all over him first and taking pictures with a small camera.

Wanting to make up to her and help her, I limped over to the truck and introduced myself to her. Leaving out the part where I "technically" dognapped Booper, I explained what kind of horrible shape the dog was in when I first saw him several months ago. I explained how I had kept an eye on the dog for weeks and how he had gotten worse and worse. I told her where Towns had lived and suggested that she check out the driveway and inside the house. I told her Towns probably tried to clean up the evidence, but they might find some anyway.

I described how I had cleaned Booper up quite a bit when we stopped on the way to the farm. I even remembered to tell her where the gas station was and how they might still find the dirty paper towels soaking with blood, ooze, hair and lots more in the restroom.

I told her how Towns had thrown Booper in the back of the truck and hit him. I even told her how he threatened to kill the dog if I didn't come out from hiding.

The animal control officer interrupted my babbling stream of advice: "Slow down, Harry. Is that your name? I'm Anne. I can see poor—what's the dog's name? Booper?" I nodded yes.

"Okay. I can see he's in terrible shape. I'm going to give him a quick examination here to collect the obvious evidence. Then I'm going to take him to the emergency veterinary hospital for a thorough examination, X-rays, blood tests, everything we can do to collect all the evidence we need to find out what happened to your dog.

"You really seem to care about this dog. Between you and me, I am appalled at what this man Towns has apparently done to such a good dog. He hasn't growled at me or tried to bite me. He just looks like he wants to be loved and love you back. I'm going to do everything I can to help bring this man to justice, and I will need your help to do it."

I promised, "You've got it! I will do everything I can to help you. That creep needs to go jail for what he did to Booper. It was horrible watching Booper get worse and worse and not be able to do anything about it…"

"Why didn't you call us?" Anne asked earnestly.

Oops, I didn't want to get my Mom in trouble so I stammered, "I didn't know what to do or how to contact you…"

I fidgeted, and Anne gave me a look that said she knew I wasn't telling the truth, but she let it slide. "Well, for now, let's help this dog, and we'll talk more later."

I sighed and said, "Thank you so much. You have no idea how much this dog means to me."

"Oh, I suspect I'll find out soon enough," Anne said with a grin.

Anne examined Booper gently, tssking when she saw the awful mange and even made a noise that sounded like growling when she saw the swollen, bloody ankle naked of hair where Booper had been chained as well as the bruises, mangy skin, and injuries all over his body. She took dozens of photos and asked me to help move Booper around so she could photograph every inch.

Booper whimpered when we moved him, but like Anne said, he didn't try to bite us or show any fear. He just stared at us for a moment, and then he sighed and his eyes closed and his body relaxed. It seemed like he understood we were helping him.

After about an hour, Anne gave Booper a shot of painkiller, picked him up, and laid him gently into a cage lined with blankets.

"I'm going right to the vet emergency hospital. Here's my card. Call me later this afternoon, and I'll let you know what kind of shape he's in and how long they plan to keep him."

Anne got in her truck and raced away with its emergency lights flashing. She didn't tell me, but I knew from her sudden sense of urgency when she stopped her exam that Booper might be lucky to be alive tomorrow. I prayed to Whatever Wherever to continue to protect Booper, keep him alive, and heal him!

As Anne sped away, I turned and saw that the crime scene techs were wrapping up, and Trooper Knowles and the detectives had ending their questioning of the guys. I limped back to the porch where Rory, Keysha, Magda, Glenda, Bu and Jorge were sitting.

I stopped when I saw all of our parents a few yards away talking among themselves. From the way she was hugging herself tightly with both arms—what she does when she feels worried or scared— Mom seemed to be telling them what she thought happened and defending what she had done.

She hadn't met any of the parents because she had to work most Saturdays and hadn't been able to go to any of my games. Although she had not met Keysha's and Jorge's dads, they had been two of the parents who had called and yelled at her when she wouldn't let me play. I imagined the conversation was tense. I learned later that some of the parents tried to blame me for their children running off in a truck driven by a 13-year-old to save me and a stolen dog.

Like the guys even knew what was going on! They didn't, except Glenda knew some of it. She didn't know I was actually going to run away with Booper. And I didn't "steal" the dog! I saved it from awful cruelty, unspeakable suffering, and a miserable death! I wanted to shout the truth at them, but I stayed away from the parents. I knew they could turn on me if I limped over there, and I knew better than to tell angry adults I was right and they were wrong.

However, I was very happy to see Dad and Kim standing with Mom. Kim, as usual, appeared to be trying to make peace among the parents since she was the only neutral person there.

It was going to take some time for the parents to calm down, and who knew what kind of punishment they were going to wreak on the guys. When they arrived and found the guys safe, they had been all relieved and hugging and crying. But they became upset when they heard the bits and pieces of what happened, and they seemed to be blowing everything out of proportion.

I felt shocked by the turn of events since the cops, the detectives, and the parents had arrived. I thought the guys would be treated like heroes for catching a dangerous criminal who was about to kill a friend of theirs. I thought we'd be praised for our courage in standing up to evil and doing the right thing.

When I got to the porch, all the guys told me that they thought the detectives were treating them like criminals and their parents were mad at them. That was when I knew for sure this whole mess was going to end very differently than I had imagined. I always have been a dreamer.

Chapter 22
FINALLY!
Someone with Power Who Cares!

Within 24 hours after Towns was arrested and we returned home from the farm, I learned to my horror—and my joy—that Booper was lucky to still be alive.

The horror crawled in like a fog that begins as a gray mist that skulks at the edges of a sunny day. The edges began to turn gray in the late afternoon of the day we captured Towns. Anne, the kind animal control officer, took Booper to the emergency vet. Trooper Knowles and the detectives finally allowed all of us and our parents to go home to recover from the most incredible and most dangerous thing we'd ever done.

Mom, Dad and Kim took me to the hospital. They all blathered at me at once, trying to get me to tell them everything that happened. I was exhausted and woozy with thirst, hunger and pain all over.

After about 10 minutes of their babbling, I interrupted, "Wait a minute, please! Didn't Dad tell me to say as little as possible so I didn't say the wrong thing to anyone? Mom, didn't you tell me not to talk to the cops? Well, I don't know, but maybe whatever I said to you could be told to the police by mistake. Maybe they could try to trick you into telling them something they could misunderstand. That's what happens in every episode of *Law and Order* I've ever seen. Maybe I'd just better be quiet. Anyway, I am worn out and I'd like to get some rest." I closed my eyes, leaned to my right, and rested my head on the corner of the backseat.

Dad whispered, "She's probably right. She's going to need a lawyer. I have a good friend who handles criminal cases. I guess she shouldn't say anything more right now. We can talk with her when she's feeling better and knows her status with the police."

Mom whispered back, fiercely, "You may not care about what happened, but she's my daughter, and I have a right to know what happened to her!"

I heard Dad sigh a very deep sigh. "Yes, Sarah, you do. It's not about your right to know, it's just a matter of when it is best for Harry to explain to us."

Mom seemed to choke on her words as I heard her gasp and cough and growl. But she didn't start a fight with Dad. Probably because Kim was in the car. A fight would have been the worst!

I did doze off for a few minutes after they stopped talking. I popped awake when we arrived at the emergency room entrance and stopped. We got out and I limped in the door.

In the ER, it was "Lucky me!" My ankle was severely sprained and my forearm was severely bruised, but they weren't broken. My right arm would heal on its own if I kept it clean and bandaged. The ER doctor put an air cast on my ankle and told me to rest for several days—Yea! No school! Mom, Dad, and Kim took me home and wanted to make a big fuss about everything.

But it was already 6 p.m. Monday. During the past 39 hours, I'd walked for miles with an extremely sick dog. We'd been kidnapped, terrified, attacked and almost killed by a maniac. We'd been saved by my amazing friends in a crazy battle. We'd been interrogated for hours by the police and our parents. I'd been poked and prodded by EMTs and asked horrible questions. Towns had threatened all of us—again. Worst of all, we "heroes" had been treated like criminals for doing the right thing.

When we got home, I couldn't take anymore! I told Mom, Dad and Kim I was exhausted and just wanted to go to bed and sleep for days!

I went to my room, collapsed on my bed and fell asleep in seconds. It was about 8 p.m. Monday night.

I didn't wake up until Mom came in at 7 a.m. Tuesday morning and told me she had to go to work. She looked haggard, her hair mussed, dark bags under her eyes, and drooping shoulder, like she was utterly defeated. I doubted she had slept at all. I limped out to the living room with her. I felt like every muscle had been beaten with baseball bats. But I was more alarmed by how my Mom looked.

"Mom, are you alright? You look terrible!" I asked with real concern.

"I didn't get much sleep," she said like she was drained of all energy. "I'm so worried about what's going to happen! The way those terrible detectives talked to us…was it only last night? No, it was two nights and a day ago! I can't even remember…You might get arrested and charged with serious crimes! That would be unbelievable!

"I am mad at you for stealing that dog, but I'm also proud of you for doing what you thought was the right thing. And that awful man! I hope they send him to prison for the rest of his miserable life!

"What a mess! Who knows what's going to happen! But I've got to go to work. We need the money now more than ever!" Mom fretted, always ready to feed her anxiety and fear.

"Mom, I'm so sorry I've made another mess," I said. I limped on my ankle cast to her and hugged her. Tears began to roll down my cheeks as she stroked my hair and hugged me back. "Mom, I'm so sorry about all this. I'll make it up to you somehow! I promise!"

"Well, we'll figure all that out later. I've already called your school. The principal said he agreed with the doctor you should stay home for a few days.

"But that's only part of what he cares about. I think the main reason is what I saw on the TV news. Dozens of reporters and TV crews and gawkers are piled up around the entrance to the school looking for you and your teammates. It's insane!

"The principal doesn't want you or your friends to show up and cause a riot. He said the police have put up barriers in front of the school, keeping the crowd away so the buses and parents can drop kids off. They're even diverting the walkers to the back of the school. The reporters are chasing the kids and teachers, and the police have to cut them off and send them back behind barriers!" Mom exclaimed.

"Those vultures, those idiots!" I seethed. "I'm not some dead cat in the road they can tear the flesh from!" I pulled away from Mom and tried to limp to the couch to get the remote to turn the TV on. Mom grabbed my arm and stopped me.

"No! Stay away from that television! They're reporting all kinds of stupid rumors and you don't need to worry about them."

Mom said the principal agreed to tell the media that I was already in school and would not be allowed to speak to anyone. We all hoped that ruse kept the creeps camped outside the school and away from our house.

"Harry, if anyone, anyone at all, shows up at the door, DO NOT open the door, do not talk to them, and act like you are not here.

We'll close all the shades. You keep them closed! Don't answer the phone! If anyone refuses to leave our doorstep, call 9-1-1. And remember, you're still grounded!"

"I will! I don't have anything to say to those ghouls! But, Mom, can't I call the guys and see how they're doing!?"

"Okay, but that's all!"

"Yes, ma'am," I said, happy with that little bit of freedom. And I meant to keep my promise—as I always think I do…

Mom hugged me again, ran out the door, climbed into her car, and drove quickly away. I watched as she even took a different way than she did every morning. I knew she was really rattled. Me, too! In a way, I wish she'd stayed home from work. It would have been nice to sit on the couch with her, snuggle under our blanket and watch sappy soap operas and eat popcorn.

I limped back to bed and fell back to sleep, hoping Towns did not taunt me in my dreams. I was so tired I didn't dream at all. It was just a lovely, peaceful blackness.

After what felt like one second of peace, the phone rang. I looked at the clock. About 9 a.m. Oh goody! Two more hours of sleep. I staggered out of bed and stumbled on my air cast to the living room to check who was calling. Caller ID flashed a number I didn't know, so I decided not to answer it. I thought it was going to be some jerk reporter.

The message machine kicked on and I heard a familiar voice leaving a message. It was Anne, the animal rescuer!

I quickly picked up the phone, "Anne! It's Harry. Are you there!?"

"Harry? Yes, it's Anne. How are you?"

"Oh, I'm going to be fine. Just a sprained ankle and a lot of bruises. Coulda been a lot worse…But how's Booper?! Is he alright?

"Glad to hear you're going to be okay. You taking care of yourself?"

"Yes, I'll be okay," I said impatiently. "But how's Booper?"

"I've got good news. The emergency vet examined him, took photos of his wounds, gathered evidence samples, recorded the facts about his condition, and tended to the worst of his wounds. I didn't think you had pet insurance to leave him at the vet hospital. It's hundreds of dollars a day. So I took him to the animal control shelter and gave him to the director. I explained to her what had happened. I'm sure he's going to be okay."

"Can I call the shelter and check on Booper? Can I go see him?"

"Sure, you can call, and I don't see why you can't visit him," Anne said.

"Anne, thank you so much for helping Booper! I'm sure you saved his life!

"All in a day's work," she demurred. "I can tell that when Booper gets well, he is going to be a magnificent dog! And I know you're going to love him and take care of him better than anyone else.

"He's going to need a lot of patience and loving care. He's been through some of the worst abuse I've ever seen, yet he's not snapping or fighting to get away. Most abused dogs are freaked out. They can be terrified of people for weeks or months. They can try to bite people, even people who love them and are trying to help them. But even through all his obvious pain, Booper seems to be just happy someone is taking care of him.

"So that's what you're going to have do. Be very patient, be very gentle, and give him time to trust you. I'll be happy to work with you and him a few times after you take him home."

I sighed with a huge sense of relief. "Oh, I'm so happy he's going to be okay! I was so worried about him! He looked so bad

Sunday night! I was scared that he might not make it through the examination.

"I am going to give him the best care I can! And I'd really appreciate your help when I bring him home! Do you know when I can pick him up?"

Anne said, "It might be a few weeks or more. The shelter will have to make sure his wounds don't get infected and heal properly. We're always worried about his mange spreading to the other cats and dogs, so he has to be isolated for a few days until we're sure the mange is not infectious anymore.

"Don't worry, though. The vet at the emergency hospital is a great doctor and a good friend of mine. She paid extra special attention to Booper after she heard what happened. She is as mad as I am at that, that b#$&!!$ Towns," Anne spluttered. "Both of us hope we get a chance to testify at his trial! We want to confront that jerk with the terrible harm he did to that wonderful animal and make sure he pays for it!"

"Wow, Anne, that's amazing!" I said. "Tell the vet I'm so grateful she took such great care of Booper. It's such a relief that finally, after all this, people like you and her really care about Booper!" I cried.

"You bet we do, and we're with you and Booper all the way. So call me anytime you need help with Booper. I've got to run now. I just got a call that another dozen kittens have been found left in a box by the side of Highway 54. Harry, you know, it never stops, the evil some people do, but we have to keep fighting!"

"You take care of those kittens, and I hope you find whoever abandoned them and give them hell!" I cried!

"Don't worry. I'm going to do my best," Anne said as she hung up.

Chapter 23
Saving Booper Again!

Despite what Mom told me to do, I immediately called the animal shelter to check on Booper's condition and was forwarded to the Director, a Ms. Marion Kerry. She turned out to be very different from Anne. She was very brusque, "So you are the famous young lady who rescued this dog," stressing the 'famous' and 'rescue' sarcastically.

I hate being called 'young lady'; I ground my teeth but didn't say anything.

"You understand the dog is in very poor condition," she stated haughtily. "He's got the worst case of mange we (she said it like the "royal we"!) have ever seen. He is so weak that he may not recover. He could spread the disease to the dozens of dogs and cats we already have here, and we could have a mini-epidemic on our hands. He's also badly infested with fleas. The vet gave him a flea bath, but I think there were so many the infestation could reoccur.

"It might be a blessing to the dog if we put him to sleep now rather than let him suffer more pain and die in a few days. Otherwise, we would have to devote substantial time and resources to care for the dog to the detriment of all the other animals we have here. We can stretch our limited budget only so far to accommodate one very sick animal."

"No!" I cried into the phone. I was livid! "Booper is such a special dog. I didn't save him from a drunken madman just so you could kill him now! I'll come get him and take care of him. My Mom has agreed to let me keep him. My Dad is going to help pay for medical bills and his care! I promise I'll take great care of Booper."

I didn't know if Dad was going to help or not, but I had to say something to get Kerry to back off and buy some time.

"I can't let you do that," Kerry said flatly. "Right now, the dog is under quarantine for the mange and the fleas. We have to keep it isolated for at least a week or put it to sleep if its condition doesn't improve."

She didn't seem to care about Booper at all. She was more worried about her budget than a horribly abused animal. She even seemed to really dislike me before she even spoke to me. I was going to have to be very careful or something terrible might happen to Booper.

"Can I at least come see him this afternoon and bring him some treats?" I asked.

"No, I'm sorry, you can't. Quarantine means just that. No contact with anyone from the outside."

I kept trying. "Is Anne going to take care of Booper? She seemed really nice, and I'm sure she can help Booper recover fast."

"Anne is our external officer. She enforces the law, captures unleashed or abused animals, and brings them to the shelter where the internal staff takes care of them."

I realized I wasn't going to get anywhere, so I retreated. "Thank you for discussing Booper's situation with me, Ms. Kerry. I'm sure he is in fine hands and you will do your best to help him. Can I call back in a couple of days to see how Booper is improving?"

"Yes, if you'd like, but remember if the dog's condition

deteriorates, we may have to make an unfortunate decision." She hung up before I could object. She didn't even offer to call me if Booper got worse!

I felt furious and frantic. I screamed and stormed as I limped around my empty house, ankle cast and all! "Lose Booper now after all this? How could this happen? Doesn't that nasty witch know Booper is special? She doesn't care at all. I bet she doesn't plan to take care of him at all. Heck, if he were human, they would take great care of him. He might have to be called as a witness to testify in court…

"Wait! That's it! Booper's a witness! And living evidence! I bet Kerry can't do anything to Booper until the trial is over and that will be weeks or months from now!" I yelled joyfully and limp-danced around the living room.

I thought I was right, but I didn't know who to call. I remembered we had copies of some papers the detectives had given us at the end of the terrible 18 hours at Grandpa's farm. They had to have somebody's name on it I could call. I rifled through the pages. At the end, I saw a name, Eric Scarano.

Oh yeh, I remembered him! How could I forget! He was the hunky detective who had chewed out that miserable state trooper about getting someone to examine Booper to gather evidence against Towns. He was tall with dark black, wavy hair, strong muscles rippling under his jacket and shirt, olive skin. But who noticed!??

I called the number on the report and asked to speak with the detective. I was lucky. He was at his desk.

"Hello, Detective Scarano, this is Harry…"

"Oh, yeh! The super girl hero and dog savior! How are you feeling?" he said.

"Uh," I stammered. "I'm doing okay, a bit achy, but I'll be

alright."

"I bet you will. You're quite something else, you know, to take on a criminal like Towns."

"Uh…thank you," I blushed, glad he couldn't see my red face. "I don't feel very super or special today. I ache all over, and I just got some bad news I need you to help me with."

"Ok, anything for super girl. What's up?"

I wished he would stop calling me that. Geez, I didn't need a crush on a cop!

I explained to him how Kerry had threatened Booper and how I thought Booper had to be kept alive because he was living evidence of Towns' crimes.

Eric said, with disgust, "That was a really lousy thing for her to tell you after all you've been through! You may be right, but I don't know for sure. I know who does. Lynne Tarantollo is the assistant district attorney who's prosecuting Towns. She would know what you can do."

He gave me her office number and told me to call him back any time I needed any help with my next "super girl crime fighting adventure"! He teased, "You don't have a super girl cave or anything like that, do you?"

I laughed, "No, but I have a super girl soccer field and a team of superheroes who are pretty good at taking out criminals with their soccer moves!"

He laughed, so I thanked him, and hung up. I called Ms. Tarantollo's number, but of course, her voice mail said she was tied up in court all morning. I left a message, begging her to call me back. "A matter of life and death," I sobbed at the end.

For the next hour, I limped around the house almost out of my mind with worry. My fear for Booper's safety began to crawl under my skin and clinch my stomach. I needed to calm down. Lynne

Tarantollo was the weapon to convicting Towns. In this new crisis, if she was enthusiastic about the case, she might go out of her way to protect Booper. If she wasn't, she might not return my call because she had so much else to do.

Another hour of agony. I limped around the house until I was exhausted. I flopped on the sofa and wrapped myself up in a warm wool blanket my Dad had brought back from an Indian tribe he had visited in New Mexico. I dozed as my blood sugar crashed— I hadn't eaten all day—and my adrenaline rush ebbed.

The phone rang and jolted me from a pleasant dream about Booper and me running in the woods near Grandpa's. I leaped over the couch to reach it and pain shot up my ankle when I landed, but I didn't care.

It was Lynne! I told her I was calling because I wanted to find out what happened to Towns since he had been arrested and how long it would be before the trial.

She asked me, "Why are you so curious about this now? I am very busy, and I don't know if I can help, but I'll try. What do you need?"

I quickly explained what the animal shelter director had said and the danger Booper faced. Then I asked, "Is it possible that Booper could be a witness in court? That way, the shelter would have to keep him alive and take good care of him."

She said with sharp skepticism in her voice, "Marion Kerry said what to you about the dog, what's his name, Booper?" She sounded angry.

I repeated what Kerry had said.

"How insensitive can she be!" Lynne exclaimed. "Not 24 hours after you've been through probably the worst day and night of your life, and she tells you she might put your dog to sleep! That's outrageous!"

Two words thrilled me, "your dog"! She already believed that Booper should belong to me. I felt a surge of hope!

"I have a dog of my own, a beautiful female Labrador, and she's part of our family. I've been reading the police and vet reports about how Towns treated his dog and what he apparently tried to do to you.

"Trust me. Towns is not going to get away with it. I'm going to do my best to put him in jail for a very long time. As for Booper, we'll see about Ms. Marion's ridiculous stance. I think I can work with your idea. I'll see if I can get a judge's order to protect Booper, is that his name? I'll call you back tomorrow morning to let you know what I can do."

As soon as she hung up, a wave of relief swept through me, and I fell on the sofa and began to cry. No one else was around, so it was okay. Finally, Anne and Lynne–people who understood what loving and caring for a dog could mean! Finally, people who listened to me about how much Booper meant to me! Finally, people who cared enough to do the right thing!

Two hours later, my Mom didn't share my enthusiasm when she got home from work. I babbled about my phone calls, the threat to Booper, and Lynne's promise to help us. I didn't notice she looked very tired and irritated.

"Harry, slow down! I've had a terrible day. There were reporters at the factory this morning. They yelled stupid questions at me and pushed all around me until the security guard had to grab me and pull me through the crush.

"Everybody I work with had heard about the whole mess on the news. A few were nice and told me they were glad you were okay, but most of them avoided me and just stared at me all day long. Even the people I normally eat lunch with ignored me.

"My supervisor called me into his office and pretended to be sympathetic, asking if you were okay. But he made a point about how everyone felt upset because the building was surrounded by reporters and news cameras. It wasn't that bad, but he said they tried to get people to talk about what kind of person I was. How obnoxious can you get!?

"He also hinted that if the disruption continued, he might put me on leave so the press would go away. He even wanted to know how much time I might miss dealing with all the legal issues and going to court.

"Harry, I've only been there less than a year, I'm still on probation, and I don't have much leave saved up. I have to work, and I have to have this job!" my Mom cried. She paced around the room, pressing her fingers to her temples like she did when she felt a migraine headache coming on.

"I hardly slept last night, and I'm exhausted. And I told you not to use the phone! Even now, after all you've been through you can't mind me for one day! You're infuriating! I'm going to bed. Make yourself a sandwich or something for supper. I don't care. Just cut it out!"

"Mom, I'm sorry it's been so bad today. But can you listen to me for just a minute? They're threatening to kill Booper!"

"What? Who's threatening to kill the dog?" she stopped her pacing and stared at me.

I told her the whole story about the shelter director and her nasty comments and how Lynne the prosecutor promised to help.

Rather than take my side, Mom looked at me wearily and said, "You know, Harry, the shelter may be right. Do you want the dog to suffer needlessly?"

I was furious! "Mom! How can you think that?! Booper just needs somebody to take good care of him, someone who loves him. And you promised last night that I could keep him! Now, you're breaking your promise. Arrgghhhhhh!"

I ran down the hall toward my bedroom as Mom yelled behind me, "Harry, you can't have everything you want when you want it. You have to think of what's best for the dog and not just yourself!"

I stopped, turned around, and said cruelly, "I am only thinking about Booper. I am not thinking about myself. That crazy bum abused Booper for months. He threatened you and me. He tried to kill me Saturday night, and if it hadn't been for my team, I'd probably be dead right now. All because you wouldn't stand up to him in the first place. You refused to report him to the police, and you couldn't convince anybody to listen to you when I left."

Mom retorted, "Don't blame me! If you had stayed away from the dog like I told you to, none of this would have ever happened. No dog in the universe is worth the danger you put yourself in!"

"Yes, he is! So is every other animal that is being abused by vicious people!"

"You can't, and I can't, save every animal in the world. Nobody can! Terrible things happen to millions of people and thousands of animals every day. You need to grow up and realize that there is darned little you can do about it!"

"So, I should just do nothing," I retorted. "I should have let that rotten criminal keep hurting that dog for as long as he wanted to. That's terrible!"

"That's enough, Harry! Stop it! My head is killing me. I'm going to bed. Fix something to eat or not. See if you can take care of yourself for a little while without worrying about saving the world," she shouted at me. She turned around and walked quickly to her room and shut the door.

I stood there, fuming. I really want to scream at her through her door, but I had already made a bad situation much worse. I had given Mom an excuse to take back her promise, so I might never be with Booper. I couldn't believe she got so angry so fast; all I wanted to do was share the good news that the prosecutor was dedicated to helping us and Booper. My big mouth again, I thought. When will I learn?

I did make myself a sandwich. It was NOT a PBJ, but bologna and cheese. I ate it, drank a glass of milk, and went to bed. My arms ached, my ankle ached, my head ached, and my heart ached.

The next morning, Mom got up early and left for work, probably to avoid any lurking reporters and suck up to her boss. She didn't even leave a note.

So far, the "mad media" hadn't found out where we lived since we rented and paid the landlord cash every month.

Our landline phone was listed in Mom's family name, we have only a pay-as-you-go cellphone, and we don't use social media. Luckily, the reporters appeared too lazy to dig deep for information about how to find us.

It also seemed like everybody at school had kept their mouths shut. I don't know if Rory and the guys had gone back, but I suspect they put the word out through their brothers and sisters to keep quiet.

Feeling wretched about my fight with Mom and worried about Booper, I pushed cornflakes and milk around in a bowl for breakfast. I couldn't eat. I was tempted to turn on the TV, but I was still grounded, so I thought better of it. I moped around the house, leafing through magazines for a little while.

Then, a fantastic idea popped into my head—a "jailbreak" out of the shelter! Heck, if I could rescue Booper once, I could do it again. I certainly wouldn't head toward Grandpa's; I did learn a little something about being too obvious.

I started thinking about how I could break into the shelter and take Booper. I needed to find out how late people stayed in the evening, how many people worked on weekends and for how long, what kind of tools I would need to break into the shelter and open Booper's cage. My mind worked furiously…and I became more and more determined to do it.

No one, certainly not some horrible hag, was going to kill Booper. Booper was going to live a long, happy life with me, and I didn't care what it took, how it happened, or where it was.

Chapter 24
Dog People Are the Best People

I was saved from another colossal mistake by the bell—well, by the phone. I limped-ran to pick it up. It was Lynne!

"Hello! Harry? Great news! I did some research, and I decided the law states I can ask a judge to put Booper in the custody of the court until Towns' trial ends. He is living evidence of the crime, and his potential presence in the courtroom could be considered 'testimony.'

"There are a number of cases, especially in contested divorces, where a judge has brought a pet into court and allowed the pet to choose which person it wanted to live with. A pet may not speak English, but its actions can speak louder than words!"

"Oh, that's awesome!" I cried. "How long do you think it will take you to see a judge and get the order?"

"Harry, one of the tricks of my trade is knowing which judge to ask for an order like this. I've got my assistant checking to see which judges own dogs. As soon as he gets back to me, I'll go see that judge."

"But that awful woman could put Harry to sleep any time!" I bawled.

"Don't worry about that. I will call Ms. Marion and tell her she can expect to receive a judge's order later today and she needs to keep Booper safe and sound."

"That's wonderful! Thank you, Lynne! You're incredible!"

For the rest of the morning, I couldn't sit still. I limped around the house from room to room I was so nervous waiting for Lynne's call. Finally, about 1 o'clock, she called.

"It's done. A judge with three dogs and a farm had heard about you on the news and was happy to sign the order protecting Booper. He is as appalled as I am about what Kerry had been considering. The sheriff's deputy is carrying the order to the shelter now.

"The shelter doesn't have its own lawyer since it is a public agency, so our 'good friend' Marion won't try to appeal the order. As a bureaucrat, she'll go with the flow. You can relax now and focus on getting better. We're going to have to get together in a couple of days to talk about the case. I'll call you by the end of the week. Oh, you'll have to bring your Mom or Dad since you're a minor."

I thanked her over and over, and she said, "Don't worry. We're going to make sure Towns never hurts another living thing and Booper lives a long and happy life."

After she hung up, I felt so happy I jumped around on my good leg, singing and yelling. I just knew everything was going to be alright! I wish it would have been that easy. One of these days I'm going to learn that achieving the right outcome by doing the right thing is much, much harder than it looks.

Chapter 25
A Ray of Hope

I waited two days for Kerry to calm down after receiving the protection order. Mom calmed down when she heard the judge had intervened, and we had two relatively pleasant evenings.

I still stayed home from school, but Glenda had gone back. She brought my books and assignments to me on Wednesday afternoon, the third day I was out.

Mom made sure I stayed up on my homework; she took it to school early every morning, sneaking through the back door to avoid any remaining media vultures and picked up my new assignments. No rest for the weary of school like I was.

She gave me plenty of extra chores to do so I stayed busy, constantly thinking about how I was going to make a special place in my bedroom for Booper, how we would go running every day to help both of us stay in great shape. I'd even teach him to knock the soccer ball around with his nose and his head!

I called the shelter on Friday morning.

When she picked up her line, she said, "Oh, it's you, our celebrity victim. How can I help you?" Not good at all. I struggled to be extra polite, but I imagined venom dripping from her mouth.

"Hello, Ms. Kerry. It's nice to speak with you again. I was calling to ask if I can visit Booper tomorrow for a little while."

"Miss Chapman, per the judge's order, we're taking very good care of the dog. He is showing significant improvement, but he is still in quarantine. It would be inappropriate for me to grant anyone special visitation rights at this time. The quarantine period will end on Monday," she said stiffly.

"I understand, but I'm sure he wouldn't be infectious to me," I told her. "I've already handled him several times, and I've never gotten infected. I wouldn't stay more than a few minutes. I just want to see him and bring him a few treats. I'm sure Ms. Tarantollo would think it would be OK."

I played my ADA card when it wasn't a great idea, but I had to see if Kerry was telling the truth. I had to protect Booper.

"So, you have interacted with the dog before," she said.

"Yes, ma'am. When Booper was suffering the worst, I was very close to him a few times." My ploy worked.

"In that case, you may visit tomorrow at 8 a.m. for 5 minutes. And do NOT bring any reporters with you. I hope this is not some underhanded scheme to get publicity for you."

Aghast, I insisted, "No! I have been avoiding the reporters all week. We don't want anything to do with them. I just want to see Booper."

"As I said, 8 a.m. tomorrow for 5 minutes. I'll be expecting you."

"Thank you very much, Ms. Kerry. "You are very kind." We hung up, and I thought, "Snooty…" Little did I know!

I told Mom that evening about the arrangement, and she told me I would have to walk because she had to go to work early. I said I didn't mind since my ankle was feeling better. Of course, she reminded me I still had to do the weekly chores and the extra ones she had written down. She was taking this grounding thing very seriously!

Chapter 26
Blue Eyes Are Not Blue Skies

On Saturday morning, I limp-walked the two miles to the shelter. The pain was worth every step. I arrived promptly at 8 with a small bag of the dog biscuits Mom had bought. Maybe, just maybe, she was beginning to come around.

I knocked and Kerry immediately opened the door like she had been waiting for me. I was shocked at seeing the real person!

Kerry didn't look anything like what I thought she would. Since she was so rude and arrogant, I imagined a vulture-like hag, scrawny with wisps of white hair, dressed in black. In fact, she looked like a middle school principal—medium height, well-groomed gray hair, a bit plump, pink cheeks, blue eyes, and a formal, no-nonsense manner. The only way you knew she worked in an animal shelter was that she wore brown work pants, a stained white smock, and comfortable brown walking shoes. As I soon learned, working in a shelter is filthy work.

I introduced myself. She barely replied, let me in, and led me back through the rows of cages of howling dogs and screeching cats to Booper's cage. I was thrilled to see him and limped to his cage.

My 5 minutes with Booper were five of the best minutes of my life!

She huffed, "As you can see, we have given it an extra-large cage. It is examined and treated for its injuries daily. It is fed high-quality dog food twice a day—soft food for now because its teeth are in poor condition. It is walked three times a day so it can relieve itself, but it is still limping so we are taking extra precautions."

She was speaking formally but couldn't resist sneaking in a dig. "We are highly cognizant of the dog's special status and your celebrity."

I said as humbly as I could because I felt like wringing her neck, "Thank you so much, Ms. Kerry. He looks great. I am so glad you are taking such good care of him. I'll be sure to let Ms. Tarantollo know what a fine job you're doing with her witness."

"That will be unnecessary, Miss Chapman. I send the ADA an email every two days to update her on the dog's condition."

She just can't bring herself to call him Booper. She kept calling Booper, a male dog, an "it." Very weird. She either hates me or him or both or can't stand to get close to the animals she is responsible for. After all, either they are adopted out quickly or they are put to sleep. To give her the benefit of the doubt, it must be difficult to make decisions every day to put animals to sleep.

She let Booper out of his cage. He limped over to me, and I sat down on the dirty floor, hugged him around his beautiful neck, put my face into his so-thin black fur, and crooned, "Oh, Booper, I'm so glad you're alive...I miss you so much...I love you so much..."

He sighed and leaned against me. When I leaned away, he raised his face to me and licked my face. His eyes shone in recognition.

"Booper, you remember me!" I sobbed. I took the dog biscuits out of my pocket and fed one to him. He gobbled it down and gave me the first real smile I had ever seen on his face! Asking for more.

But Kerry, who was standing a few feet away, said, "Not too many biscuits. His stomach is still getting used to solid food. We don't want him to fall ill and create a mess, now do we?" she said like sugar dripped from her tongue.

Jeez, she was more worried about Booper creating a mess she would have to clean up than whether it made him sick.

"Yes. I understand. I want Booper to get better and wouldn't do anything to hurt him."

I hugged him and whispered to him for the next few minutes. I told him what a hero he was, how the team had saved us, how Towns was never going to hurt him again, how he was going to live a long and happy life with me, how I was going to take such good care of him.

Kerry, who apparently had the super-acute hearing of a bat, interrupted my whispers, "Ms. Chapman, I need to advise you not to get ahead of yourself. After the trial ends and the judge's order is rescinded, assuming the dog is in adoptable condition at that time, he will be put up for adoption according to our formal procedure. If you wish to apply to adopt the dog at that time, you will have to follow the same procedure as everyone else. You and your family will have to prove you have the resources to give the dog a good home. He does not appear to have been neutered, so you will have to pay for that.

"Other people may file applications, especially after the dog becomes as notorious during the trial as it is likely to become. We will consider all applications and decide which family is most likely to be able to provide the best home for the dog."

I jumped up, staggering on my bad leg. "What? I saved this dog from horrible abuse and almost got killed by a madman doing it.

Booper means more to me than anything in the world, and you're saying I go to the bottom of a pile of applications because I might not be good enough to take care of him!"

She looked at me with her blue eyes as cold and uncaring as ice in Antarctica. "I understand your sincere concern for the dog. But rules are rules, and if we break them for everyone who claims a special case, the shelter could be accused of personal or political favoritism. That would be both illegal and unethical. You must understand that in my position as Director, I must be completely fair and above board."

I couldn't believe what she said. I knew she was lying because I had learned in Civics class and by watching TV news that people in public offices did legal favors for other people all the time. It was the way the system worked, rules or no rules. You just had to know how to work the system so you could do the right thing.

I knew I had already made an enemy by going over her head, so I stopped complaining, took a deep breath, and replied, "I see, Ms. Kerry. You're correct. I'll be happy to follow the rules, and I'll trust that the shelter will do what is best for Booper. That is all I want, too."

"Thank you for seeing my point of view, young lady. Now, your 5 minutes are up."

I hugged Booper again and told him I would come see him again soon. I promised him everything would work out fine. I forgot how hard promises are to keep, but as I said, I was naïve. I ignored the queasy feeling I got as Kerry put Booper back in his cage.

I hesitated a step and quickly tossed another biscuit through the opening in the fence into Booper's cage. He gobbled it down and smiled again. Goal! Ole´!

After that first visit, I arranged to visit Booper once a week and snuck him treats as often as Kerry turned her back. He grew healthier, stronger, and more beautiful every time. The shelter worker, Abeo, a Nigerian immigrant, was doing a wonderful job, helping him heal and grow stronger.

Best of all, Kerry couldn't interfere; she knew I would complain to Lynne if I saw any sign that Booper was not getting the best possible treatment. This happy pattern continued for several weeks. I grew more and more hopeful Kerry would change her mind so I could bring Booper home with me. Naïve, like I said.

Chapter 27
One Simple Law of the Universe

So a month later, life felt as good as it had since before Grandpa died. The Redhawks had caught the evil guy and he was going to stay in jail for a long, long time. We had saved a wonderful abused dog. Booper was safe in the shelter and getting healthier by the day. The team had won the league championship for the first time in our history. All of us—Rory, Keysha, Magna, Peter, Bu, Jorge, Glenda, and even I—had shown an amazing amount of courage, ingenuity, creativity, and even love for one another in the face of deadly danger.

You'd think that we'd all be heroes. Right? Well, as nasty as the cops were at the farm, that was not even close to what happened to us.

Well, we were heroes to the kids at Carver. It was like a circle whisper game run amok! In the game, you sit in a circle and the first person whispers a simple sentence to the person next to them. The second whispers to the third and so forth around the circle. Of course, by the time the circle is completed, the final sentence is light years from the first one.

Like in the game, the stories about us grew more fantastic every time they were retold and spread across everybody's Mebook page, EgoGram account, ChatPix, and Birdy feed.

The stories became so exaggerated that we laughed hysterically. Just a couple of examples—Towns had an AK-47 rifle and shot up the barn, wounding me. I knocked him out with one punch—or Rory or somebody did. All six soccer kicks hit him in the groin and now he is, ummm…, incapacitated for life. Towns sliced half my arm off, Rory picked it out of the dirt, and reattached it with string.

Like I said, hysterical. We tried and tried to tell everyone the truth, but eventually, we just let the kids have their fun and we basked in the glory at school.

However, our parents, the police, and the courts reacted in a very different and very difficult way. All of us got into some kind of trouble, me more serious than the others. We learned the hard way the one simple but most important "Law of the Universe": Actions *Always* Have Unintended Consequences.

In our situation, they were painful for us and our parents for many months.

First, Towns did his best to keep his promise and make my life a living hell. The court gave him a legal aid lawyer since he was "indigent," that is, a drunken good-for-nothing bum. From his prison hospital bed, his lawyer and he cooked up against me charges of grand larceny—claiming Booper was worth more than $500—trespassing, harassment, and assault with intent to kill. They hounded the police to charge me as an adult.

Between you and me, they were right; I did all those things. To save Booper, I would have done even more.

They also filed assault charges against the guys but didn't argue when the guys' cases were assigned to juvie court since they were only 12 or 13 and none of them—nor I—had ever been arrested before.

Well…we had done some things I won't explain here because we never got caught. We weren't angels, just lucky! It's strange how your life can go in a completely different direction just because you were lucky enough to get away with doing something stupid. Often those unlucky enough to get caught for the same not-so-serious "crime" end up so much worse. Life is not fair at all…Consequences—good and bad—are not evenly shared.

Our parents were stuck with unfair consequences as well. They had to hire a lawyer to defend us. Unlike the "indigent" idiot Towns, our working-class parents made too much money for us to qualify for legal aid attorneys. Our parents barely get by on what they earn! My Mom works double shifts and weekends half the time or more just to pay our bills! It's ridiculous that they had to pay thousands of dollars out of their own pockets or go into debt, like I know some of the parents did, to protect their kids when the scum of the earth like Towns get free lawyers.

Yeh, I know everyone has a right to a defense, but the system is totally screwed up: it gives the criminals free lawyers and the rich can afford the best lawyers and use their power to get away with their crimes. Both have a huge unfair advantage over the struggling middle class! Like I said, life isn't fair at all.

Fortunately, with my Dad's help, our discouraging position turned into a great one. My Dad knew an experienced criminal lawyer—who also happened to be a friend of his in AA, so I won't use his whole name. I'll just call him Jerry. He generously agreed to defend all seven of us in juvie court for the price of one, so our parents were able to split the cost.

Dad and Kim even stepped up and paid 80 percent of my share, but I am going to have cut their grass, rake their leaves, and do odd jobs around their house until I'm a senior citizen to pay them back at minimum wage. Maybe I'll join the movement to increase the minimum wage to $15 an hour so I can pay them back faster! Not likely they'd agree!

Seriously, I know how much I owe them, and I am happy to keep their yard and do whatever chores they want me to do. They did more than I could have ever hoped to keep me out of the godawful juvie detention hall. I would have been plunked in with teenage drug addicts, thieves, murderers, prostitutes, just really disturbed and violent girls. I might not have survived. I would have never become who I am now and the better person I hope to become.

Mom was pleased that Dad helped out so much, but to pay her share back, I had to wash the dishes, take care of what little yard we have, take out the garbage and recycling twice a week, clean the house and my room every week, AND oh yeah, be completely responsible for Booper.

Yep, I got to keep Booper after the trials, and it seemed my life was golden, but again the consequences of doing the right thing that threatened Booper and me were—well, that's actually a different story.

Today, Booper has become the incredibly wonderful dog I had dreamed of for so long and love so much. Now, I'm better than the post office. Whether rain, snow, sleet, sun or dark of night, seven days a week, etc., etc.—like the motto carved in granite above the door to the headquarters for the Post Office in New York City.

The motto, *"Neither snow nor rain nor heat nor gloom of night stays these couriers from the swift completion of their appointed rounds,"* was adopted from a Greek historian, Herodotus. He actually wrote the sentence to describe how well the Greeks' mortal enemy, the Persians, communicated across their huge empire.

I'm not a Greek, Persian, or New Yorker, but I'm as dedicated to Booper as any caregiver can be! No matter how cold or how hot, how wet or how dry, how dark or how light—I walk Booper, pick up his poop and throw away the bag twice a day. I feed and water him twice a day, bathe and groom him once a month, "try" to keep him off the furniture (not likely!), check for fleas and ticks, and just love him more than anything! He is my best friend and playmate, running and "playing" soccer with me just about every day!

Of course, being Booper's "Dog Mom" has been the "tough" part of my punishment!

Unfortunately, Mom also kept her promise for what would happen if I went back to Towns' house. I remained grounded for three months during the winter, but she relented and did let me go to basketball practice and play in the games. I just had to come home immediately after school, practice or a game and do all of my homework and turn it all in on time. I couldn't watch any TV unless she invited me, and I couldn't talk on the phone except about school assignments. I sorta, kinda followed her orders… most of the time.

Oddly enough, I found out I liked to read books from the school library. Mrs. Reynolds recommended that I read books about famous women who did amazing things. I loved them! I read about Amelia Earhart the famous female pilot, Marie Curie who invented the X-ray, Harriett Tubman who freed slaves through the "underground railroad," Susan B. Anthony who fought for women's right to vote, and many more.

I was deeply impressed by how courageous, smart, and talented they were. Despite very strong opposition from a male-dominated society, they broke the "rules" and made huge changes in the world. Reading about them showed me that an individual, passionate about an idea or a cause, can change the world for the better. I hope I can become one-tenth as courageous as those women were.

Thankfully, I had such a powerful woman, who made our county a better place every day, on my side. Lynne T., the prosecutor who had saved Booper, worked behind the scenes with my attorney to fight off Towns' scheme to have me tried as an adult with a jury, and helped me through the whole scary courtroom thing.

Lynne turned out to be incredibly sharp both in and out of the courtroom. She wasn't fooled at all by Towns' legal attacks against us. She saw through all of Towns' bull, and she helped me understand that I was very important to her case.

During our first meeting, she told me, "Well, Harry, since it looks like you and I are going to be working together for some time, why don't you just call me Lynne. And I've got to hear your story about why your name is 'Harry.' I bet it's something else."

"Its…uummm…interesting," I stammered. "I'd enjoy that." Wow, she asked me to call her Lynne instead of Ms. Tarantollo or ADA Tarantollo. How cool was that!

However, she appeared to be caught in an ironic legal dilemma: She or someone from her office was supposed to prosecute all of us in juvie first and then she would prosecute Towns for multiple felonies. It appeared to be a conflict of interest. But she convinced both the juvenile court judge and the district court judge to let Towns' lawyer "assist" her in juvie court and she'd prosecute Towns in regular court.

I don't know how she pulled it off. I heard she argued that all the cases were "inextricably entwined." I guess that means everything that happened related to each other, and the courts could save time and money by letting her do both. Thank goodness for a tight budget, a shortage of county attorneys, and lazy judges! I was going to be tried in juvie court with the guys!

Towns, in turn, was charged with kidnapping, first degree assault with intent to kill, multiple counts of animal abuse, malicious wounding for cutting my arm, reckless endangerment for driving while drunk, drunk and disorderly conduct, and other minor charges. Oh—and since he was already on parole for assault in which he almost killed a guy in a bar fight, he was charged with multiple parole violations and kept in jail without bond—that is, he wasn't getting out.

I'd like to know what the heck he was still doing on the street when I first saw Booper! He had been driving around town for months drunk as a skunk, hanging around low-life bars with other felons, and carrying a rifle in his truck and a knife on his hip. Something is very wrong when the county doesn't have enough money to hire enough parole officers to keep criminals like Towns in line, yet the county has millions of dollars to build a fancy new building for the county executive!

In any case, even before Towns went to court for all the terrible things he did to me, he was going back to jail for at least five years for the parole violations. That felt good, but I was still worried; he might get out of jail in two or three years for "good behavior." I doubted he could act that way for very long!

Before this tough situation got better, however, the guys and I had to face the music in "juvie" court.

Chapter 28
The Juvie Jive

With Jerry and Lynne on our side, the "magnificent seven" Redhawks did really well in juvie court. Perhaps worse, Rory, the PBJs, Keysha, Magda, and Glenda had to face their parents. Except for Glenda's parents, their parents grounded them for three months, except for going to school, practice and games. They also have to do extraordinary chores to pay their parents back for their share of the lawyer's fee.

Our parents acted like they were very angry with us, but we all heard stories that our parents were telling their friends how proud they were and how courageous and selfless the guys had been to save me. Darn right!

That is, everybody's parents except Glenda's. They never showed up for any parents' meetings with Jerry so he agreed to represent her for free, but we never told her that. Actually, all the parents kicked in a few extra dollars for her. She wouldn't have wanted to accept charity.

Her parents also didn't show up for her juvie hearing; the judge, surprised and upset, consulted with the attorneys. Lynne told me she explained about Glenda's parents, so the judge let Jerry also serve as her temporary guardian for the hearing.

Glenda wouldn't talk, even to me, about what happened at her house, but I could swear I saw some bruises on her arms when she rolled up her sleeves once. But as soon as she saw me glance at her arms, she quickly unrolled the sleeves to hide her arms. She always wore jeans so I couldn't see her legs.

I was very suspicious about Glenda's parents and how they neglected her. If they physically abused her, I didn't know what I'd do, but no child should endure anything like that. If I ever get any solid evidence, I'll find a way to stop it. Nobody hurts Glenda without my protecting her!

As for the rest of the guys, for "borrowing" his brother's truck, Rory had to face additional charges for auto theft and driving without a license. Of course, his brother didn't want to pursue the auto theft charge; his Dad and his brother had already had a— um—vigorous discussion with Rory so the judge dropped that. But he did have to face the juvie judge for driving without a license.

In court, all of us testified why he was driving without a license and how his actions had helped capture a dangerous criminal and save me. With Jerry's guidance, Rory agreed to plead what is called "nolo contendere," or no contest. It means that although he was not pleading guilty, he understood the prosecutor probably had enough evidence to convict him.

Since this situation was his first offense and his actions so heroic, the judge sentenced him to "probation before judgment," or believe it or not, PBJ. Rory can't escape being surrounded by PBJs, and I will never let him forget it either!

A legal PBJ means an offender like Rory can avoid having a conviction entered against him and keep the offense off his permanent record. Instead, Rory was placed on PBJ for six months—no, he didn't have to eat peanut, butter, and jelly sandwiches for six months. For Rory, that would have been a treat!

Instead, the judge delayed any further action as long as Rory stayed out of trouble for six months. Then, the court would dismiss the charges, and Rory's record would stay clean. His brother never lets Rory within 100 feet of his truck anyway, and Rory's Dad keeps him too busy working around the house for him to even think about getting into trouble. The court also ordered him to do 200 hours of community service working at a homeless shelter, helping to clean the place and serve meals.

Right after he started working at the shelter, Rory surprised the heck out of me one day at lunch.

He said, "I've never seen so many people in such awful trouble. It's mostly men, but I see women and kids, too. Most of the men are mentally ill, alcoholics, or drug addicts, probably both, but some of them just lost their jobs and can't find another one. Instead of helping them, their landlords kicked them out of their homes when they couldn't pay the rent.

"Most of the mentally ill have been dumped out of hospitals or treatment centers with prescriptions for their medications but absolutely no help at all. They're just lost and confused. The alkies and addicts don't seem to want any real help, just more money to buy booze or drugs. A lot of times, they don't even want to eat.

"Many of the women with kids have run away from abusive husbands. Some of them have terrible scars on their faces and arms and probably other places. They just ran without anyone to turn to. They don't even have enough money to rent a tiny room, or they're too afraid their husbands will find them and drag them away.

'It's awful! They tell me there's not enough beds at the shelter for everyone at night, so many of them end up on the street."

"It's about time you see how the 'other half' really live!" Keysha interrupted bitterly as she leaned across the table toward Rory. "I see this crap every day in my neighborhood. And no one in city hall gives a damn about us until it's time to vote. Then the jerks in their black Caddies drive down our street giving out $50 bills and a sheet of paper that tells them who to vote for.

"I don't know why my people keep taking their bait. Nothing ever gets any better. The slumlords own all the apartments. Not even one black family owns a store. Heck, we can't get the inspectors to make the landlords fix the heat or call a plumber to fix a busted water pipe! You don't know how lucky you are!"

Rory looked shocked. He stammered, "Geez, Keysha, I didn't know you had it that bad. I'm so sorry!"

"Well, sorry ain't good enough. You can't do anything much about it now, but you better do whatever you can do to help those folks in that shelter. You better remember them and me when you grow up and do something about it!" Keysha warned.

"Okay, I promise! I hate to see those people suffering. I thought my family was having a tough time because Dad got laid off and can't find a job. At least Mom is working at the hospital and we have our own place. I'm getting it, Keysha, I really am," Rory said.

"You better. I'm going to hold you to it, and you know I don't forget a promise—either one I make or one somebody makes to me!" Keysha stressed.

Rory and Keysha leaned back and looked at each other in the eye for a few seconds. Rory suddenly stuck out his hand toward Keysha and said, "I promise to help make this town a better place and help poor people, period. Deal?"

Keysha grabbed his hand, gripped it hard, and shook it up and down, and said, "Deal! You'll be a better man!"

The rest of us were astounded. We just sat there staring at them and at each other. We didn't know what to say or what to think.

Peter spoke up first, "Rory, I'm proud of you for saying that, but you have taken on a very great obligation. Do you understand what your promise means?"

"Not entirely, but I know I'm going to keep working at the homeless shelter after my PBJ is done," Rory said.

Then, we all started laughing. Sitting on Rory's plate was a half-eaten PBJ sandwich!

Keysha hooted, "Boy, you better not think our deal ends when you finish that sandwich!"

Rory looked down at the sandwich and his face turned red. "Oh crap! Don't worry, I won't…maybe after I eat the second one in my bag…"

Keysha reached across the table and tried to swat him lightly on the head as he put up his hands and ducked. She grazed his hair and laughed as she sat back down. We laughed some more and settled down to finish our lunches.

I sat there, feeling very surprised to see this "new" Rory. Something changed in how I felt about him. He's always going to be a wisecracking jerk who teases me whenever he gets a chance. Yet, since that day, he has kept his promise and become more mature and more caring about other people.

For the rest of them, their juvie court hearings went just as well. Even the PBJs received PBJs—every time I think about the three PBJs, I start laughing! The PBJs, Keysha, Magda, and Glenda also pleaded "nolo contendere" and had to do 100 hours of community service. Lynne T. pulled a few strings and arranged a cool PBJ for all of them.

The team had to go to the Police Athletic League gym for 8 hours each weekend for three months and teach the younger kids how to play soccer. Glenda wasn't any good at soccer, so she got to read to the youngest kids and teach them their ABCs. Nobody had to pick up trash by the side of the road, and everybody got to do something they loved to do and help disadvantaged kids. A really good deal! If only mine had turned out as well as theirs…

Chapter 29
An Evil Frog Trapped in a Hot Pot

My 'juvie jive' was more difficult because I had to face the much more serious charges Towns and his jerk lawyer had pressed against me.

A week after the guys' hearing, I had my juvie hearing for stealing Booper, trespassing, and assault. Towns showed up in court dressed in a cheap suit, Goodwill dress shoes shined, his hair cut and combed, his face clean-shaven.

His lawyer, who was supposed to "assist" Lynne, had claimed Towns being brought to the hearing in an orange prison jump suit and shackles would prejudice the court against him as a witness. Jerry argued against his dressing up, and Lynne didn't say anything, but the judge let Towns come dressed like he was a decent human being. He even limped into the hearing room on a cane—the faker! He almost looked like an upstanding citizen, except for the scars on his face, his sunken cheeks, his menacing grin when he looked at me, and his cold eyes.

Lynne had a strategy. She had met with Towns' lawyer and easily convinced him how he, not her, should question me. Towns clearly didn't trust her to really want to help him—smart man for a creep. After all, she was going to prosecute him in a few weeks.

It seemed to me she had set them up. She could represent his interests like she was supposed to in case his lawyer needed help. But she could avoid harming my case if Towns' lawyer overlooked things that might help him. She didn't have to volunteer any ideas. Like I said, a very sharp woman!

Towns testified—unfortunately for me truthfully—that I had trespassed on his property several times and took his dog without his permission. On the surface, his "reasonable" explanation looked bad for me. He portrayed me as a loony kid who didn't respect property rights, refused to abide by his legal right to privacy, disobeyed my mother, was a sneak thief, and tried to kill him when he took his lawful property back from me.

His lawyer said the charges against me called for at least three years of detention and three years of probation until I was 18 years old! That scared the bejesus out of me!

Then, Jerry went to work on Towns' during his cross-examination, setting him up like a frog dropped into a pot filled with cool water. The frog "thinks" life is good—until the chef turns on the gas burner and the water slowly heats up. By the time the frog figures out he is not basking in the pool at an amphibian beach resort, it is too late for him to jump out. His froggie self is slowly cooked.

Jerry started with the low heat. He showed the judge police photos of Booper's terrible condition that I had insisted be taken at the farm. Towns claimed I had done those injuries after I stole Booper. Jerry entered statements from Anne, the animal control officer, and the emergency veterinarian that the injuries had taken place over many months. Towns stammered and tried to deny it.

Next, Jerry asked him about how Towns kept the dog from running away, and Towns admitted he kept him tied to the old jeep. The jeep had been found in a junk yard before it was crushed, so photos of it were used as evidence. Jerry pressed him on the kind of restraint he used, and grudgingly, he admitted it was a chain.

Jerry continued his attack on how often Towns fed, watered, and groomed Booper. He asked Towns if he took Booper to the vet regularly and asked for vet records. Towns mumbled answers and slowly his face began to get redder and redder. The water was getting warmer and warmer.

Jerry switched gears on him and asked him about his criminal record, whether he had served prison time, how many years he had served for first degree assault, how many arrests and convictions he had for drunk driving and disorderly conduct, whether he was now in jail for probation violations, and if he was about to go to trial for a series of felony charges related to this situation.

Towns' weasel of an attorney objected that Towns' previous record and current legal situation had nothing to do with my stealing his dog and trespassing.

Jerry countered that it was critical to the defense because he needed to show Towns' background and character so he could challenge his credibility as a witness and show a pattern of neglectful behavior. Lynne sat silently and didn't help Towns. The judge let Jerry's questions stand and Towns had to answer. Lynne smirked just a little.

Of course, Towns minimized his atrocious record and tried to blame everybody else for his troubles—his ex-wife took all they had and left him with an overdue mortgage he couldn't pay and a sick dog. He blamed the other guy in the bar for picking a fight with him, so he had to defend himself.

To his credit, Jerry had done his research. JERRY introduced testimony from Towns' divorce hearing that his wife claimed physical abuse when Towns was drunk, which she said was most of the time.

Turning up the heat a notch, JERRY tossed in testimony from

Towns' criminal trial for assault. While it was unclear who had provoked the fight—both men were drunk and arguing with each other—Towns had flown into a rage and kept bashing the guy's face and head with a beer bottle until four men dragged him away. Then, he ran out of the bar and tried to escape capture.

Jerry asked him if he had had a job; since obviously he didn't, Jerry pressed him on how he managed to pay for the house and buy the booze he drank to excess.

Towns' replied with a growl, "None of yer bidness."

Jerry proclaimed, "It is indeed the court's business to know how you have the resources to stay in your house, pay for your truck, feed yourself, and buy so much alcohol that you can drink every day if you so choose!"

With a shifty look in his eyes, Towns mumbled that he got odd jobs around town that paid cash or he traded work for booze or food. He knew how to fix his truck himself.

Jerry pressed him again: Wasn't his house, which his wife had given him to get out of their marriage, in foreclosure and he had not made a payment on it in almost a year? Towns grudgingly admitted that was true. The heat kept rising.

Jerry asked him if he had filed tax returns for the past several years to declare his cash income. Towns snarled, "None of yer bidness."

Jerry poked him again, "You are correct. It is not my business, but it is that of the Internal Revenue Service. I suspect that they will be very interested in reviewing your tax status. But it is this court's business whether you had the resources to care properly for your dog rather than buy booze and stay drunk much of the time."

Towns snapped, "How I spend my money ain't none of yer bidness neither!"

As Jerry kept pressing Towns' and revealing his lies one after the other, Towns got madder and madder. Towns' water began to simmer and he was about ready to boil over.

When Jerry asked him why he wanted to seek revenge on me—"this child," Jerry called me—ugh—Towns stood up and screamed at Jerry, pointing at me, "That little bitch stole my property after I dun told her to stay away three times. That mangy mutt was mine to do with as I pleased, and she ain't got no right to take it from me. She's lucky she's still alive after what she done to me."

The judge silenced him and threatened to throw him out of court. He sat down, fuming and glaring at me.

Then, Jerry stuck the proverbial knife in to make sure Towns the frog was cooked: "After what she—this 12-year-old, this 7th grader—did to you, a big, strong man like you? Are you sure you were not taking out your rage toward your ex-wife on this girl and that poor dog you abused?"

Towns' lawyer leaped up to object, and Towns tried to jump out of the witness stand to attack Jerry. "I shoulda killed 'em both when I had the chance," he roared. "I gave that little slut a chance to choose how she should be punished, but she kept shooting her mouth off at me. I was being nice to her 'cause she was a girl!"

The judge slammed the gavel repeatedly and ordered the bailiffs, the sheriff's officers who kept order in the court, to haul Towns out of the hearing room.

As they dragged him away, he yelled at me and sent a chill up my spine, "We ain't done yet, yew and me!" So much for 'good behavior'!

Jerry just turned and grinned at me. He had destroyed Towns' credibility and goaded him to anger the judge. Especially important, since Towns' outburst was now part of the court record, the prosecutor could use it against him in court. Smart guy, Mr. Jerry! Lynne just sat there, looking properly perturbed, but she did glance at me and wink! Smart girl!

Next it was my turn. Two can play the dress-up game, so I was dressed in a nice new knee-length tartan skirt, a plain white blouse, and a dark blue school jacket that Kim and Mom had gone with me to buy. They made a big fuss about it, but they seemed to be "bonding," as the pop psychology articles call it, so I didn't complain—too much. I also wore polished new shoes and stockings. My hair had been cut by a professional stylist. I looked like the proper preppy—an act I knew how to play well since I had gone to St. Brendan's for six years.

Jerry cut through the legal truth quickly to get to the larger, moral truth. He asked and I admitted I had trespassed on Towns' property several times and ultimately taken Booper. I admitted I had ignored Towns' warnings, but I added the part where Towns had come to our house very drunk and threatened my Mom and me, not once but twice.

His lawyer objected and said how did I know he was drunk, but I handled that easily. A softball question for the child of a recovering alcoholic, so I hit it out of the park. I said that I smelled the strong stink of alcohol on his breath every time he came near me, and he wobbled on his feet both times he was standing at our door. I added I have the unfortunate experience of having an alcoholic father, so I knew the signs of drunkenness very well. I made sure to add that my Dad was now sober, in recovery, happily remarried, and doing well.

Mom, Dad and Kim were in the courtroom, and I saw him smile at me and nod his head. It felt good to know he was okay with my "outing" him in court.

Showing the pictures of Booper's injuries again, Jerry asked me and I described in graphic detail the condition Booper was in when I first saw him and how his condition became worse and worse every time I checked on him.

Towns' lawyer thought about objecting and stood up, but Jerry interrupted and reminded the court that the vet's report had proven the dog's very poor condition and how long the abuse had gone on. Mr. Legal Aid sat down.

Jerry then asked me the million-dollar question: Why did I take the dog and run away? I told the truth—well, most of it.

I said fiercely, "It is immoral for anyone to abuse another living creature. I'd begged my Mom and my teachers to do something, but they ignored me. I believed I could take Booper (I used his name and the judge gave a slight smile) to a better place, Grandpa's farm, so I could heal him and take care of him so he could live the good life he deserves."

Jerry ended his questions.

Unluckily, since this case was limited to the trespassing and theft charges against me, we couldn't discuss what happened afterward—the kidnapping, the fight, and the rescue at the farm. All that would have to wait for Towns' criminal trial.

The claws of Towns' legal eagle were not as sharp as Jerry's, so he apparently never found out about the mess of motivations that led me to take Booper: my anger over being grounded, my shame at missing the championship, my reaction to my Mom's misery, the nasty divorce, my Grandpa's death, and all the other things I felt angry and depressed about at the time. The entire mess confused me, enraged me, and drove me to feel so closely attached to Booper that I convinced myself my only choice was to steal him and run away.

Towns' lawyer asked only technical, legal ones: "Do you know stealing someone else's property is wrong and against the law?"

"Yes, if it was a bicycle or a lawnmower, but not a living creature that was being abused!" I exclaimed. "There are laws against abusing children and abusing animals. I was doing my duty as a citizen, under the law, to protect the dog and "*HIS*" legal rights as a living creature! There is a higher, moral law that every living thing is God's creature and we should treat all of them with respect!!"

Towns' lawyer stammered about the law being the law, and Jerry, Mom, Dad, and Kim just grinned at me. He had no more questions, and I left the witness stand and sat down, satisfied I had done my best.

Jerry and Towns' lawyer summarized their arguments. Towns' focused on the narrow legal definitions of stolen property, trespassing, and the right to recover one's property. Jerry focused on how upstanding a citizen I was at such a young age to have recognized Booper's suffering and done something about it when the so-called responsible adults had ignored the abuse. He went on in that vein, and I felt embarrassed. At heart, I just wanted a dog, and poor Booper's suffering gave me a chance to have a dog and do something good for a change.

In the end, the judge's decision was fair. Based on my age, my clean record, my school and athletic record, and my future "potential to be a good citizen,"–ummm, maybe—she gave me two years' PBJ. During that time, I was going to have to do 500 hours of community service at the county animal shelter, cleaning cages and taking care of the animals.

I couldn't have asked for a better "punishment"! Helping dozens of dogs and cats and snakes and other cool animals for two years! It couldn't get any better than that, could it??

Chapter 30
The Harsh Mistress of the Shelter

A week later, Marion Kerry got the shock of her life! At 8 o'clock on Saturday morning, I walked into the animal shelter carrying a copy of the judge's order. I hadn't called to make an appointment to see Booper like I usually did.

"Good morning, Ms. Kerry," I said as sweetly as I could. "I've been ordered by the juvenile court judge to perform 500 hours of community service at the shelter. Here is the judge's order. How I can help you?"

Her face turned as red as a volcano and I thought she was going to start spewing lava at me. "What are you talking about? No one has informed me. Give me that paper," she growled as she snatched it out of my hand. She was furious!

Then her stare turned from red hot lava to glacial ice.

She read the order intently, glancing up at me a few times. She was clinching and grinding her teeth so hard I could hear them crunch.

I just stood there, doing my best to maintain my 'innocent'" wide-eyed look. I hadn't used that since I was about eight years old when I broke Mom's favorite porcelain vase, back when we had such things. I didn't think it would help. Maybe I just wanted to irritate Kerry some more. I thought she would get madder—and she did—but I didn't think about the consequences—again.

Instead of yelling at me, she took a deep breath. "Well, it will be good to have another set of eager hands to help us," she said pleasantly, with what passed for a smile on her puffy face that pinched her eyes to tiny slits. "There is so much to do and never enough volunteers, time or money to take the best care of these poor animals. It seems with 500 hours of service, we'll have your assistance for the next couple of years. Do you think you can handle that?

"Yes, ma'am," I said quietly. "I'm here to help the animals as much as I can. I know it's at least 2 years, maybe more. I love animals, so it's the best place I can think to be."

She said, "Remember that you are here to work, not to play with the animals, especially with our special guest. By the way, when is the criminal trial going to start?"

"Oh, my trial is over…Oh, you mean Towns' trial! In a few months I think. I'm not sure," I fibbed. I knew the trial was going to start in a few weeks, and I could tell she wanted to get Booper out of the shelter as soon as possible.

I had taken seriously her threat to adopt Booper out to someone else. I wanted him to stay there long enough so I could help Mom save enough money so we could adopt Booper before anyone else. I planned to save the few dollars Mom gave me each week to buy milk at school or other stuff. I figured it would take about 3-4 months to save about half of what I needed and then I'd hit Dad up for the rest.

Marion's voice roused me from thinking about adopting Booper. "Well then, you'd better plan to be busy before then," she said nicely. "When can you go to work?"

I felt startled at her abrupt change of heart. She had never spoken to me nicely before. Maybe she was grateful to have more help, or maybe she thought she had me where she wanted me.

"I can start right now," I said. "I can work every Saturday or Sunday for up to 8 hours. If I have a game on Saturday that runs late, I'll work on Sunday. Or I can come in after a morning game on Saturday and work Saturday afternoon and Sunday. Does that work for you?"

She thought about it for a few minutes, turning to look from me to the ceiling now and then with her familiar haughtiness. She was figuring something out. I didn't think she was trying to figure out how to make my life easier.

That was okay with me. I didn't expect anything but grief from her. I was there to do my PBJ, help the dogs, and spend as much time with Booper as possible.

"Yes, that schedule will be satisfactory for now. Be aware that if we receive a late emergency call to handle a lot of dogs or cats at night during the week, you could be called in to help. Will your Mom let you do that?"

"Yes, ma'am. I'll work it out with her. It will be fine," I said. I really didn't know what Mom would say, but I wasn't going to give Kerry a chance to send me back to the judge.

That seemed to be that. I was dressed in a Redhawks sweatshirt, jeans, and sneakers. She gave me a blue smock with the shelter logo on it. I was now an official "volunteer," just another juvenile delinquent working off her sentence.

For the next two Saturdays, Kerry tried her best to make me quit. Each day, she gave me every nasty chore to do—cleaning out cages where animals had had diarrhea, scrubbing filthy cages and floors on my hands and knees when the animals in them had been adopted, hauling out and dumping the heavy buckets of animal waste, and much more.

The very worst was when she made me help hold the animals

when they had to be put to sleep. I had to watch Abeo, the shelter worker, or Kerry insert the needle into a dog's leg vein and see the blue poison flow through the tube. At least, the animals seemed to just fall asleep and their hearts stop beating. I felt so sad and grieved every one. My only consolation was that they died peacefully and Booper wasn't one of them.

It was very hard on me. Sometimes at night in my bed, I cried bitter tears for them. I felt utterly helpless to prevent their deaths. I felt so powerless to do anything that helped them at all.

Giving them food and water and keeping their pen clean for a few days or weeks before they were put to sleep seemed cruel. I felt like I was the prison warden who knew when the prisoner was going to be executed, but the prisoner didn't. Beyond words awful!

Or maybe it was better. I don't know if it would be better to know when I was going to die or be oblivious until it happened. Maybe the animals are the lucky ones.

I knew from my disastrous report to Mrs. Jackson's class— geez, that seemed like a lifetime ago, not just a few months—that there are millions of stray, abused, and abandoned pets in this country, and not enough people or money devoted to caring for them. I knew that some private shelters either raised enough money or were owned by rich animal lovers so that they never had to put an animal to sleep. There was a private shelter like that near my old neighborhood, but I couldn't volunteer there because my PBJ specified community service at a public facility.

The private shelters could help only a very few. Most abused animals died in great pain or were put to sleep at shelters. I had to do this terrible job the hard way so—I hoped—I would learn that every life is precious and that we have to convince the public to do much more to help solve this serious problem.

The best news was that I got to see Booper as often as I could sneak away from my chores. Since I usually worked alone, I brought him extra healthy treats every time I worked. He was so happy to see me he'd jump up and down in his cage and start barking. I had to calm him down so Kerry wouldn't hear him bark with joy when I showed up.

A few times, it was a close call when he barked and she came rushing into the cage area. I always managed to skitter behind a larger cage down the aisle. She never bothered to look for me. If she had caught me, she would have given me even worse chores to do, like putting the euthanized animals in the incinerator. I don't know if I could have taken that.

Luckily, she really hated to come into the animal area. The stink was horrible until you got used to it. You'd think she would have, but I think she just didn't like the animals. The dogs always began to howl and the cats scream when she opened the door. I had no idea why she was working there, but I was determined to find out.

Despite everything Kerry tried to do, I never complained. I did everything she told me to do, and I did it to the best of my ability. I expressed my sadness after the first few times I had to help put a dog to sleep. She wasn't impressed, but I made a friend of the shelter worker.

Abeo, pronounced like Ah-bay-o, is a true African immigrant. He is from western Nigeria and loves animals because he was born on a tiny farm. He had a dog and raised goats and cows. By the way, I checked a Nigerian name dictionary and his name means "happiness bringer," and his name fit his personality.

I never asked him how he came to the United States and our town, and he never volunteered anything about it. I did wonder what his story was. Whether he was legal or not wasn't my problem. I am all in favor of immigration. We're all immigrants or their descendants, no matter how long ago. After all, that's what the Declaration of Independence means and that's what the Statue of Liberty proclaims!

"Give me your tired, your poor—Your huddled masses yearning to breathe free—The wretched refuse of your teeming shore. Send these, the homeless, tempest-tost to me, I lift my lamp beside the golden door!"

Abeo appeared to be one of those "tempest-tost' who only wanted a fair chance to live a better life. I'm all in favor of allowing many more good people like Abeo to come to America to pursue their dreams.

I felt that way because of how Abeo treated the wretched animals in the shelter. The first time I was forced to hold a dog while he was given a "blue shot," Abeo also seemed distressed. After my second time, I walked away shaken, and he walked up to me and talked to me to shift my attention. He told me how he had grown up on a small farm where they raised animals for food. He explained how some animals had to die so we could eat, but we could also thank the animal for sacrificing its life so we could live.

I replied, "But, we're not eating these poor dogs and cats. They're just sick and abandoned and no one cares. It's an awful world…"

He gently explained, "I too feel very sad as you do when we have to waste these lives. As you do, I want them to have nice families and live happy lives. But some things are beyond our understanding for now. I do not understand how in this very rich country, you spend so much money on silly things like fast cars and huge palaces and acres of green grass. You waste so much food in a day just in this town that I could feed my village for years. All I know is that we can do the best we can each day to treat every living thing with kindness and compassion."

He was wise and kind, but I believed then and believe now that we can do much more than we are doing, that we have to change our priorities to focus on what is loving and meaningful.

Chapter 31
Justice Is Served Hot,
Not Cold Like Revenge

Abeo's keen sense of morality, compassion for animals, and clear sense of justice stood in stark contrast to the torturous, often unjust, workings of our judicial system. Towns' criminal trial for me was an embarrassing and enlightening experience; I learned exactly why it is so hard to overcome the devious manipulations of defense attorneys so justice can be served and the criminals held responsible for their evil deeds.

Before Towns' trial, he got a new lawyer, a sharply dressed guy named Barry Pelotzi. His new lawyer seemed smarter and more experienced than the one he had at the juvie hearing because Pelotzi negotiated tough plea bargains with Lynne.

I wondered how Towns could afford such a good lawyer who dressed in expensive clothes and was obviously not a court-appointed one from Legal Aid. Lynne said he belonged to a fancy criminal law firm in town and was doing this trial as part of his yearly *pro bono* work. That is, attorneys in large firms are expected to take a few cases a year for free to make the firm look like its doing its share of public service. They turn around and charge the rich criminals $1,000 an hour to keep them out of jail!

The real reason, though, was that Pelotzi held a grudge against Lynne for beating him the previous year in another high-profile *pro bono* case. She warned me, "I've known Barry since law school where we competed in everything. He hates to lose, especially to me, so he's going to come after you and will be as mean as he can get away with. I'm going to fight back just as hard but be prepared. This is not juvie court; this is the real thing."

By the end of their negotiations on Towns, Lynne and Pelotzi "split the baby" on the lesser charges. Lynne dropped the charges for drunk driving since the deputy had failed to do a sobriety test at the farm. It also had taken the hospital lab so long to test his alcohol levels that the results showed Towns' level had been only a little over the legal limit. Since he had thrown up at the farm, most of the alcohol was out of his system. Worse, the crime scene techs failed to test his puke for alcohol. This confusion turned out to be a minor problem during his trial, but we worked around it.

Lynne also skipped the moving violations for his truck's expired license plate, expired inspection sticker, a burnt-out headlight, and other petty stuff since he wasn't going to be driving on the roads for a long time.

In turn, Towns agreed to plead guilty to Class C felony animal abuse—I felt very angry about that. I wanted a Class A felony conviction that would put him away for at least 15 more years. In my mind, what he did to Booper was far worse than what he tried to do to me. Booper, like a child, was totally defenseless; as the guys and I showed, we could defend ourselves.

But Lynne calmed me down when she reminded me we would use his testimony and outburst at the juvie hearing against him. She convinced me that convicting Towns on the very serious charges was more important and would mean he would spend most, probably all, of the rest of his life in jail.

They also limited the charges against him to those crimes he committed against me. The guys weren't involved in them, only the rescue. Pelotzi did not want six more fresh-faced, well-groomed, well-dressed, intelligent 12- or 13-year-olds from diverse ethnic groups to get on the stand and testify what a creep his client was and how they had taken him down so easily. Lynne knew we had plenty of other evidence to convict him for what he did to me without the guys' testimony.

Towns refused to plead guilty to kidnapping, 2nd degree attempted murder, and aggravated assault. He knew those would mean the very stiff sentences Lynne had promised to pursue.

As the trial began, the courtroom was packed with reporters, news trucks were outside the courthouse, and a lot of kids had skipped school to be there with their parents. Mom, Dad, and Kim sat right behind the railing separating them from where I sat with Lynne at the table to the judge's right.

This time, Towns had to sit with his lawyer in his "best" orange jail jumpsuit. He wasn't shackled or handcuffed. The bailiffs—officers of the court—stood close by because they knew what he had tried to do at my juvie hearing. The guys and their parents had to wait outside if the situation changed and they had to come in one by one and testify.

Towns also chose a jury trial; Pelotzi hoped he could find one juror who would side with Towns and cause a hung jury. In a jury trial, all 12 jurors must agree to convict the accused on the charges; if only one refuses, the judge rules a mistrial based on a deadlocked or "hung" jury. Then, the prosecution has to start all over again, change or drop the charges, or negotiate a plea bargain with the defendant.

The jury Lynne and Pelotzi chose seemed fairly neutral to me. Pelotzi struck from the jury, that is, prevented them from taking part, a couple of died-in-the-wool dog lovers who obviously knew about the abuse charges and looked at Towns with obvious loathing. Lynne struck a couple of DINKs—dual-income, no-kids—types who didn't own pets and who didn't seem to like me much. We ended up with eight whites, two African-American women, and two Latino men. Four of the whites—two men and two women—were retired senior citizens. The other four were women office workers. The two African-American women worked as nurses at different clinics in town. Of the two Latino-American men, one owned a *bodega,* something like a neighborhood convenience store, and the second worked as a construction worker.

To begin the trial, Lynne quickly questioned Trooper Knowles, Eric the detective, the CSIs, and the doctor who eventually examined me at the hospital. I did have the sprained ankle, the cut on my right arm, the severely bruised left forearm, and lots of cuts and scratches. Unfortunately, by the time of the trial, I had healed and looked and walked normally. I hoped the pictures Lynne showed the jury would be convincing. I couldn't tell from their faces when Lynne passed them around.

She walked the officers and investigators step by step through what they found at the farm and what their investigation disclosed. With one exception, all of them supported the facts as they happened. Eric, bless him, even added that he thought we were the most courageous kids he had ever known, but Towns' lawyer objected and the judge instructed the jury to disregard the comment. Of course they wouldn't. Score a goal for us! Ole´!

However, Trooper Knowles, the pain in the neck he is, caused some difficulty that Lynne had to work around. During the cross-examination, Pelotzi got him to say that he thought we had gone too far when the guys kicked Towns with soccer balls since he was bleeding from the stab wound I had inflicted. Knowles testified he was not pleased Rory had pointed Towns' rifle at him and was about to shoot him. Worse, he said he was surprised we had not called for help as soon as we captured him and tied him up. Not good for us. Score a goal for Towns.

But Lynne asked, on what is called "redirect," how six children were supposed to defend themselves from an enraged drunk with a sharp knife who was about to kill their good friend? She got Knowles to grudgingly admit that Rory didn't know how to fire the weapon and that a soccer ball in the face is a "gentler" way to be disarmed than being shot.

She also got him to admit the police were almost too late in figuring out where I was heading so they could find us at the farm. She embarrassed him and the other officers when she forced him to admit they had disregarded my Mom's frantic pleas for help.

She blamed them and stressed that the entire situation could—and would—have been avoided if the police had done their jobs by arresting Towns for parole violations months earlier and by heeding my Mom's pleas for help. She asserted that they should have sent out both State Police and county patrol cars to look for me and issued an Amber alert to the surrounding towns as soon as my Mom called them. Goal! Ole´!

After Knowles was excused—he was still really mad at my Dad and me as he scowled at us as he walked by and sat down behind us—the real "fun" began. It was my turn to testify.

I didn't feel frightened to get up in front of the judge, jury, and people in the courtroom. I felt more relieved that I was finally getting my chance to tell my truth. I felt incredibly determined to show everyone what an evil creep Towns truly was.

As I walked toward the witness stand, I stopped for just a moment and looked Towns straight in the eye. He scowled at me with pure hate, but he shrunk away from me in his chair almost like a caged animal does when you peer into its cage.

"Good," I thought. "He's scared of me, the weasel. He better be because I am going to put every nail in his proverbial coffin I can."

The fierce resolve I felt inside was belied by my appearance. Lynne had told me to dress up in my prep school girl outfit again so I would look what she called "demure," that is, modest and reserved. When I told the guys that, we all laughed so hard tears rolled down our cheeks. No one is less "demure" than I am!

But I learned from Lynne that just as both Towns and we had tried to shape the judge's perceptions at the juvie hearing, I had to shape this jury's perceptions as well. I guess it is a ridiculous and hypocritical truth that today, we have to manage people's perceptions of us so we can tell the truth.

Maybe it has always been true. I remembered how we had learned in Civics class that George Washington refused to have a portrait done showing his teeth because they were false and made of many materials. From ivory and gold to horse, donkey, and even some human teeth.

There's a bit of a debate whether good ole George took or bought those human teeth from his slaves. The records at Mount Vernon are vague; they only say he did buy some slave teeth for one-third as much as he would have paid a free person for their teeth. The records don't show whether or not the teeth came from his own slaves or someone else's.

Believe it or not, selling your teeth was a common way for poor people to raise money in Colonial days. Yuck!

In Washington's portraits, his formal look and fancy uniform shaped a perception of him as a serious, intelligent leader. In my case, I was about to learn how important perception would be to the jury during cross-examination.

After I took the oath to tell the truth, Lynne led me through the questions and answers we had practiced many times before. As Jerry had done during the juvie hearing, she asked me to discuss how and why I had taken Booper, and I told my truth—I thought about writing "story" here, but like the word "perception," the word "story" could imply my testimony was something fictional, something I made up. What I said was not that. I lived it so I know what happened, and I had to make sure the jury understood that and believed me.

Lynne made sure she asked me if I had taken responsibility for taking "Booper" so Pelotzi couldn't use my juvie hearing against me later.

Believe it or not, before I could begin to answer, Pelotzi objected to Lynne calling the dog "Booper." He actually said, "Your Honor, the dog's name is Ralph and should be referred to as such. My client named the dog Ralph and that was the name the dog was known by at the time these alleged events occurred. The witness' name for the dog is irrelevant, and her use of it could imply she owned the dog at the time. That implication could influence the jury."

Lynne responded, "Your Honor, the defendant has already pled guilty to animal abuse charges. Since the defendant's attack on Miss Chapman, the dog has been housed at the county animal shelter. He continues to be treated for multiple external and internal injuries, malnutrition, mange, and a flea infestation. Miss Chapman saved this poor animal from incredible abuse and neglect by the defendant, so I would ask the court to rule that witnesses can refer to the dog by whatever name they prefer."

The woman judge, the Hon. Mary Francis O'Shields, pondered a moment and ruled, "Anyone who treats an animal the way this dog has been treated and caused it to suffer forfeits his legal right to ownership of the dog's name. Therefore, I agree with the prosecutor's recommendation. Each witness can name the dog as he or she sees fit." Goal! Ole´!

Lynne repeated the question about my taking responsibility. I repeated what I said at the juvie hearing about how my pleas to my parents and my teachers to help the dog had been ignored and how I had both a legal and moral duty to protect the dog.

But I did say I understood I had been wrong—legally—to trespass on Towns' property and had followed the wrong procedure to help the dog. I simply stated the truth that for "rescuing"—I used the word deliberately!—Booper and trespassing on Towns' property, I was under a PBJ order from the judge. I said I was performing 500 hours of community service at the public animal shelter and would continue to volunteer at the shelter after my PBJ ended.

Although we hadn't practiced it, I threw in a comment: "My parents also punished me. My Mom grounded me for three months—straight to school and straight home after basketball practice. No TV and no video games. And I will be doing extra chores for Mom as well as Dad and his new wife for the rest of my life!"

The jury liked that as some of them chuckled and the rest smiled. Lynne gave me a stern look for "freelancing," but also gave me a slight smile when she saw the jury liked it.

Next, she asked me about the kidnapping. I explained how I was walking along the highway with Booper toward my Grandpa's farm so we'd be safe and I could take care of him. I told them in detail how Towns had told me he had been looking for us but was about to give up and leave the town. I explained how it was just pure bad luck that he chose that highway to flee and just happened upon us. I told how he threatened me with the knife, forced me into the car after I fell down the embankment and he grabbed me, abused Booper, and forced me at knifepoint to tell him where I was going.

Lynne made sure I added the specifics about how he was drinking heavily and I learned his name for the first time when I was getting another bottle of whiskey out of the glove compartment. She also asked me if this was the first time I had smelled alcohol on his breath.

Pelotzi objected, but the judge let the question stand when Lynne argued that she intended to show a pattern of behavior. Goal! Ole´!

I repeated my testimony from my juvie hearing and described how I had smelled the heavy odor of alcohol on his breath every time he found me talking to his dog. I described how he had come to our home twice, reeked of alcohol, and threatened my Mom and me. I also said that I had seen him stagger across our yard and down the street.

Pelotzi objected to that, too, arguing I could not know how much Towns had been drinking, if the police had given him a sobriety test, or whether Towns had a medical condition that might make him wobble on his feet. The judge rolled her eyes but sustained the objection.

Unfortunately, since Lynne had decided not to prosecute for DWI, driving while under the influence, she could not bring up his long arrest record for DWI and disorderly conduct. Score one for Towns. Drat!

Lynne then asked me about what Towns said to me while we were in the truck. I described his veiled sexual suggestions. Lynne interrupted me and asked, "So, he said he was going to rape you?"

Pelotzi leaped up and objected that I had never mentioned the word "rape" and that the question was extremely prejudicial. The judge upheld his objection, struck the question from the record, and told the jury to disregard Lynne's question.

As she turned away from the judge, she smiled a little smile: We had practiced that question and knew that his lawyer would object, but the jury heard the word. In truth, I couldn't say that he threatened to rape me because he never said the word, but his intentions were very clear through what he said and how he leered at me. We just had to find a way to show the jury the truth of his intentions. Goal! Ole´!

We reviewed how Towns asked me repeatedly what he should do with me. She asked, "The defense may argue that Towns' repeating that question shows he did not intend to kill you. This is a critical point," looking straight at the jury as she asked, "At what point were you convinced that he intended to kill you?"

"When I was held captive in his truck and I saw his name and address on the truck registration," I explained. "He told me then he would have to make sure I could never tell anyone who he was. That is when I knew he intended to kill me because I had figured out he was running from the police."

Pelotzi objected and called my comment speculation, that I could not know Towns' 'state of mind.' The judge upheld the objection and struck it from the record, but I had said what I needed to say and the jury heard me. Only a little "ole´!" this time.

Lynne rephrased the question: "What did Mr. Towns say he planned to do with you before you learned his name?"

"He told me he didn't know what he was going to do with me. That is why he kept insisting on learning where I was taking Booper. He seemed to be considering his alternatives," I replied.

Lynne then asked, "But he changed his mind after he understood that you knew his name?"

"Yes, as soon as he knew I knew his name, he threatened my

life."

The defense couldn't object to that logic. I glanced at Towns, I could tell he was infuriated. He knew we were slowly heating up his frog again. Every question and every answer was like the hand of justice slowly turning up the knob on a gas burner so the truth would slowly boil Towns to a life of misery in prison.

Finally, Lynne asked me to describe what happened after we reached the farm. I told the truth about how I was terrified for my life, how and where I kicked him, why I ran into the barn, why I came out after he threatened to kill Booper, how I had stabbed him with the screwdriver, how I had tripped and fallen, how he had cut my arm, how he jumped on me, how I had blocked his stab at me and hurt my arm, and how he was trying to stab me again when my teammates arrived.

I described how all six of them had hit him with their kicks the first time they tried and how he had fallen to his knees and puked all over himself. I freelanced again, "That shows you why my team won the league championship." That got a laugh from everyone in the courtroom.

The guys later told me that they heard about my comment and loved it!

I finished my direct testimony with Lynne by describing how we captured and restrained him and how the police and my parents had arrived just as we were calling for help.

Lynne thanked me and said that was all she had at that point but reserved the right to redirect.

Pelotzi took over for cross-examination; he was vicious and mocked me.

"Miss, you have admitted you trespassed on my client's property. Yes or no?"

"Yes, but…" I tried to continue, but he interrupted me. "Just answer the question 'yes' or 'no.'

He was trying to irritate me and push me to lose my temper. It came to me that since he was a smarter attorney, he must have done some research about me and my temper so I had to stay calm and remain "demure." As that thought flashed through my mind, I almost laughed out loud, but I remained "demure."

Next, he asked, "And you stole my client's dog despite repeated warnings to leave it alone. Is that correct?"

"No, I did not 'steal' the dog. I had a legal and moral obligation to save the dog from abuse."

"But you trespassed on his property and took his property without his permission. Isn't that correct?"

"I don't consider a dog 'property'…" I began, but he interrupted me again.

"Objection, your Honor, the witness is being argumentative."

Judge O'Shields looked at me and said, "Under the current laws of this state, the situation is ambiguous. A pet is considered a person's property, but as a living being, that type of property also has certain rights that are protected by the law. If you want to change the law, then you must lobby the legislature. Technically, you must answer the question as counsel has stated it."

I boiled inside because I wanted to tell them how stupid and cruel the laws were, but I held my temper.

"If you put it that way, then yes, I took his 'property,'" putting my best sarcastic tone in my voice.

Next, Pelotzi asked, "So, technically, my client was searching for his stolen property and had a legal right to retrieve it. Is that correct?"

"I don't know. As the judge just showed me, I clearly don't understand these laws and what the defendant's rights would be under the laws that cover badly abused animals." Goal! Ole´!

He countered, "So, you took the law into your own hands and did what you wanted to do. You stole my client's dog because you wanted a dog and Ralph was the closest one you could find. Isn't that correct?"

I was shocked! How did he know I wanted a dog so badly? I thought frantically.

Lynne saw my distressed look, stood up, and said, "Objection! Your Honor, the defense is badgering the state's witness."

Pelotzi replied, "It seems like a reasonable question, your Honor. I have no intention of badgering this young girl. Did she want a dog or not? Did she consider Ralph the most convenient one for her to take?"

The judge overruled Lynne, but she had given me a few seconds to calm down. I said, "Yes, I wanted a dog. But I went onto the property to find out if Booper (I stressed the name!) was doing better or worse because he was being so badly abused.

"Mr. Towns (how I hated calling him 'Mr.'!) refused to help Booper when I pleaded with him. He just said the dog belonged to him and he could do with it what he wanted. And no one else would listen to me and stand up for what was right."

Pelotzi knew he was losing this battle about me as a thief, so he changed to an even nastier direction.

"Let's move forward to the morning that Mr. Towns found you with Ralph. After you got in the truck, did you not make sexual advances toward him so you could keep the dog, so you could 'buy him off,' so to speak?"

I was horrified. "No! Never!"

"But didn't you say that you thought it might be fun to have 'a roll in the hay' with my client in your late grandfather's barn?"

"I was terrified for my life….," and he interrupted again.

"Please just answer the question 'yes' or 'no.'"

Lynne stood up and objected, "Your Honor, if the defense is trying to get to the state of mind of the state's witness, she should be allowed to explain what is clearly a gray situation that cannot be answered with a simple 'yes' or 'no' answer."

The defense argued, "Your Honor, it is a simple question. I am not trying to discern the witness' state of mind, just whether she made the comment or not."

Fortunately, the judge recognized the real intent behind the defense's question and response to Lynne's objection. She ruled that I could explain my state of mind.

I added, "While he was talking about what to do with me, he leered at me and said that rather than kill me quickly, he might want to have a 'roll in the hay' first. I said I had never done 'it' before, but it might be interesting. I ONLY said that to keep him talking, to distract him from thinking about killing me."

He tried to trap me: "Did Mr. Towns ever directly say he was going to kill you?"

I deliberately looked stricken at the memory. "I remember very clearly that he had held a knife on me for more than an hour. He forced me…"

"Your Honor!" Pelotzi interrupted. "The young lady has testified to her point of view on direct. I asked a simple question, so she is the one who apparently does not want to answer the question."

This time, Judge O'Shields upheld his objection. Drat! One for Towns!

"No, Mr. Towns did not explicitly say he was going to kill me, but…"

"Thank you," Pelotzi turned and walked away, stopping me from continuing.

Pelotzi changed directions again to the fight at the farm.

"Let's move forward to the incident at the farm. Your family owned the farm at one time. Does your family still own the farm?

"No."

"Why not?"

"We had to give it back to the bank after my grandfather died. He was my mother's father, and she was his only child, so it was left to her in his will. After my mother and father got divorced, my Mom could not afford to pay for the mortgage, taxes and maintenance on the farm, so we had to give the farm back to the bank."

"So, you not only trespassed on my client's property, you also trespassed on the bank's property? Isn't that correct?"

Knowing he was technically correct, I simply said, "I knew we did not own the property anymore."

"So, in the law, we call that trespassing," he said.

Devious creep, twisting the truth. "At that time, did my client say he was going to harm you with his knife, or did he just tell you to get out of his truck?"

I said, "He told me to get out of the truck, and I believed I had no choice because he had been holding the knife on me for more than 50 miles."

"Once again your answer does not respond to my question. Did he threaten you with the knife at that time?"

"No." I let well enough alone.

"Moving on, at the farm, you assaulted my client, injuring him severely. Isn't that correct?" Pelotzi changed directions again.

"I kicked him between the legs, if that's what you mean by 'assault,' after he forced me to get out of the truck by pointing his knife at me. He looked at me for a few seconds and then he lunged at me with his knife."

Pelotzi asked, "How far away from you was he standing?"

"I don't know. Maybe 4 or 5 feet."

"Was it dark where you were standing?

"Mostly. The headlights of the truck were on."

"But they were shining away from you, weren't they?"

"I suppose so," I said, wondering what he was getting at. Lynne looked worried, too.

Then, Pelotzi sprung his trap. "Is it possible you imagined that he lunged at you and he was merely waving the knife at you?"

If that was the best he had, Towns was as good as boiled to a nice dark green, dead frog.

"No, it's not possible. If he had been standing still, how could I have kicked him between the legs? I'm only 5-7, so my legs aren't long enough to have reached him since he'd been standing 4 or 5 feet away."

Pelotzi tried one more time, "Is it possible in your concern about your situation that you stepped forward so you were close enough to kick my client before he moved?"

"Oooooohhhh. That jerk!" I thought frantically. I shot a look at Lynne.

She leaped up, "Your Honor, objection! Counsel is splitting hairs to turn the impossible into the possible. If he wants to establish his client's movements, let him put Mr. Towns on the stand and testify in his own defense—which I understand that for very good reasons, he has no intention of doing!"

Pelotzi glared at Lynne. "Your Honor, it's just another simple question. Did she or did she not take a step forward so she could assault my client?"

"That's not what Counsel asked, your Honor," Lynne said. "He asked if it was possible that the victim in this heinous crime took a step forward. Anything is possible, so it's a specious question the state's witness should not have to answer."

"But your Honor, the entire case against my client might hinge on that one step," Pelotzi fired back. Oh, he was sly!

"A hypothetical bit of fevered imagination," Lynne said caustically.

Judge O'Shields banged her gavel, "All right, counsels! Enough. I see a simple solution. The witness can testify to what she did. If the defendant doesn't like it, he can take the stand in his own defense."

"Wow, what a Solomon-like way to split this baby," I thought as I sighed and took a deep breath. I could tell my truth and Towns could either put up or shut up.

The judge said, "The witness will answer Mr. Pelotzi's question."

I was relieved I had the extra minute to think. "No, ma'am, I am quite sure I did not step toward the defendant. I wasn't about to get closer to the knife, and I remember that I was holding the door handle so I could brace myself." Goal! Ole´!

Pelotzi tacked again. Seemed to me he was trying to find anything to stir a niggle of doubt in one unsuspecting juror's mind. I hoped Lynne thought he wasn't getting anywhere. I wasn't looking much at the jury so I couldn't tell what effect my testimony was having.

He took a "jive step" and asked, "After you ran into the barn, you came back out and attacked my client and stabbed him with a deadly weapon. Yes or no."

"I only came out of the barn because he threatened to kill Booper. I wasn't going to let him do that."

"Your honor, the witness once again refuses to answer the simple question. I'm not questioning her thinking process. I asked her if she came out of the barn and stabbed my client with a deadly weapon?"

The malicious devil was making a speech he hoped would make my action look like an unprovoked attack!

Lynne didn't object, and I didn't understand why at the time. This question made me look bad.

Judge O'Shields sighed and frowned, trying to think of a reason to refuse his objection. I could tell she didn't want to make me, but she did, "The witness will answer the question."

I minimized my answer, hoping Lynne would know how to straighten it out later, "When I came out of the barn, I ran at Mr. Towns and stabbed him with a small screwdriver."

"Did you ask, even demand, that my client put his property down before you attacked him?"

"No, but when I was in the barn, he yelled…"

"Thank you," he turned away again and strolled back to the defense table with his back to me.

"Grrrrr…," I clenched my jaw and wanted to scream at him for turning the truth into lies of omission when his client committed the most horrible crimes against Booper!

He turned again and sat on the edge of his table and asked quietly, "When you first came out of the barn, were you walking or running?"

"Walking."

"Did you show my client your weapon?"

"No, I put it behind my back."

He stood up quickly and walked toward me. "So, when you ran at my client with a hidden weapon in your hand and you did not give one word of warning, didn't you intend a surprise attack to catch my client off guard?"

"Uhhh," I stammered. "No, I just wanted him to let Booper go!" Uh oh!

"Was my client holding his dog in one hand and his defensive weapon in his other?"

"Yes," I said in a low voice, hoping the jury wouldn't hear me.

He spat out questions:

"Did you start running faster and faster so you could leap at my client and inflict the worst possible damage on my client?

"Didn't you lunge at Mr. Towns and stab him with a deadly weapon while he was holding his dog and basically defenseless."

"Didn't you intend to kill him because he had what you wanted most in the world—his dog!?

"What right did you have to attack my client like that? It was his dog, and as the judge has aptly stated, he had the right to do as he would with his dog, even if it meant he could be arrested and charged for mistreating it?"

I heard a few members of the jury suck in their breath. Were they offended by how Pelotzi had attacked me so viciously, or had they just realized he was right? I really didn't want to know at that point.

He was doing his best to convince just one person on that jury that my taking Booper was a serious crime and that I had no right to interfere in the first place. That Towns was the victim, not Booper, and I was the perpetrator. Again, that "horse's petute," as my Grandpa would have called him, was twisting everything into legal Gordian knots that the jury might never unravel.

Of course, in strict legal terms, he was right. The "legal" thing to do would have been to report Towns to the county animal control officer and let her handle it. However, the morally, ethically and spiritually "right" thing to do was to save Booper and get him away from Towns as fast as I could before that wonderful dog died from neglect, disease and abuse. I would find out soon enough if the "law" had any room left for morality, ethics and spirituality.

After he stopped his machine-gun questions, I paused for a few seconds. His harsh criticism, veiled as rhetorical questions, had shoved me way off balance.

I could feel my suppressed fury swirl around my mind. I felt heat soar into my face and knew I had flushed a bright red. Truthfully, I wanted to leap off the witness stand and strangle Pelotzi. Yet, he was right; he had me nailed. I wanted to save Booper and take care of him more than anything. I wanted Towns to suffer for what he had done to Booper and me. If he had died, I wouldn't have felt sorry. That doesn't make for very good testimony!

Lynne looked at me sternly and shook her head slightly from side to side. She meant me to see that she was screaming "No! Don't take the bait! Hold your temper! Be demure!"

He interrupted my moment of panic, "Well, do you have any adequate answers to these serious questions, young lady, or is the truth now obvious even to you?

Lynne reared up like a mother lion protecting her cubs: "Objection! Your Honor, Mr. Towns is obviously a very large man. It is hard to understand how he could be 'defenseless' against a 12-year-old girl."

I cringed when she called me that. Yuck! But if I had to act like a St. B's preppy little girl to save Booper and get Towns, I could do it for a few minutes.

Lynne, just as sly as Pelotzi, gave her own legal "knife" a big twist in Towns' gut. "Even if he was holding a dog up in one hand," she said as her voice rose in indignation. "he still held a large knife in the other. Unless the defense wants to stipulate that the defendant was too drunk to defend himself."

Pelotzi shouted, "Your Honor, there is no charge against my client for drunkenness or any action related to drinking on trial in this case!"

"Alright, Ms. Tarantollo, that's enough," Judge O'Shields said. "No more references to the defendant's drinking and alcohol abuse. You made your choice about which charges to bring." What an awesome way for the judge to slip in the Towns' alcohol abuse into my testimony without me saying a word! Goal on a deflection from the judge! Ole´!

"Thank you, Your Honor. I strenuously object to the people's devious attempt to defame my client. Please strike the record and instruct the jury to disregard her comments," Pelotzi almost bowed when he said that.

Lynne didn't fight it because Pelotzi had just reinforced her point for her.

The judge sighed heavily again—she must be an Irish grandmother. Only grandmothers can sigh like that! "The jury shall disregard the people's reference to the defendant's relationship with alcohol—if any."

Pelotzi sputtered and looked like he was about to object to her wording, but he stopped, turned and walked back to his table. He realized if he pursued his objection, he would make it very clear to the jury that Towns was hiding something about his history with alcohol abuse.

He turned back toward me with a nasty look. "Let's put it this way. You lunged at Mr. Towns and stabbed him after he simply told you to come out of the barn and walk over to him. Didn't he say that he would let the dog go if you came out of the barn, so your fear for the dog's safety was unfounded at that moment. Isn't that correct?"

"No, I had been afraid for the dog's health and safety for months. I did not trust the defendant to keep his word."

"But you did lunge at him and stab him before he ever actually did anything to you. Isn't that correct?"

Lynne objected, "Your Honor, asked and answered!"

Pelotzi replied, "I'm just reviewing a few key points, your Honor."

She snapped, "Then, cover it quickly and move on! The witness will answer the question," she said looking down at me.

"I was afraid for my…"

"Again, it is a simple 'yes' or 'no' question."

"At that moment," I said in a loud, slow tone, "he was not doing anything actively to hurt me. But by holding Booper off the ground by one leg, he was hurting the dog as he had…"

"Thank you," he cut me off. "So, it seems to me that you assaulted him and stabbed him before he ever tried to do anything to you. You had reached the farm. You had a chance to escape, but instead you came back to kill my client because you were enraged that he took back his rightful property that you wanted. Aren't you the one who should be on trial for attempted murder?"

Lynne jumped to her feet, "Objection! Your Honor, the defense is trying the old game of diverting attention from the real criminal to blaming the real victim with inflammatory remarks. The state has no evidence that would support such a ridiculous accusation; to the contrary, the evidence clearly shows the defendant is the real instigator and the state's young witness was only defending herself from his malicious intent."

The judge said, "Objection sustained. The jury will disregard counsel's question. And enough, both of you! Save it for your summations. You're both being argumentative instead of eliciting useful testimony. Move on!"

Whew, close one for me! But I worried because the defense used the same tactic we had—asking a bombshell question knowing it would be thrown out, but also knowing it had been planted in the jury's minds.

Pelotzi had one more nasty thrust. "Let's review the time after your friends attacked my client, knocked him to the ground, and tied him to his truck. At that time, was he not begging for help and didn't you all ignore his pleas?"

"We were very scared and confused about what to do next," I fibbed just a little.

"Did you walk over to my client while he was bound in chains and bleeding and tell him you wanted him to suffer? Yes or no?"

Uh-oh! I felt trapped because that was the truth. Ok, "demure" I was supposed to be, so "demure" I acted.

I sniffled—yes, I freaking sniffled, "I was so terrified and angry at what Towns had done to me and Booper, yes, I said that to him. I regret I said that."

I looked Towns straight in the eye and said, "Mr. Towns, I am sorry for saying that to you. It was mean-spirited, and I was wrong to say it."

Pelotzi did a double-take and grimaced. He wasn't expecting me to apologize. He recovered and said, "So, you admit that at the time, after you had stabbed him with a deadly weapon, you wanted my client to suffer?

"Yes, and I am very sorry," I said looking down at my folded hands. When I glanced up, I saw Lynne looked worried. I was, too, but the truth was the truth.

"Thank you. That will be all I have," he said and sat down.

Lynne quickly stood up. "Redirect, Your Honor?"

"Proceed."

Lynne said, "I'd like to ask you some sensitive questions to clarify the defense's outrageous claim you 'came onto' this man. Is that okay with you?

"Yes," I said, wondering what in the world she was going to

ask. She had to have a Plan B we hadn't prepared.

"First, do you have a boyfriend?"

"No, ma'am, I don't."

"Why not?"

"I just am not interested," I said truthfully. I saw where she was heading. I knew it was going to be embarrassing.

"I like playing sports—soccer and basketball. I spend my time going to school, practicing, playing, and studying. My Mom wants me to make good grades. I want to get a college scholarship to play soccer, but she wants me to be smart, too, so I can earn an academic scholarship if I need to. So, I don't have time for a boyfriend. I see the girls in my school who have boyfriends, and that's all they ever talk about or worry about. I think they're silly and wasting their lives."

Jeez, did I feel like a geek! Like I was some bookworm or stick-in-the-mud that none of the guys thought attractive. She didn't ask me if any of the guys had ever tried to be my boyfriend. Lots of them had, both at the Catholic school and now at Carver. Even some of the 9th grade guys who played on the same fields we did tried to hit on me, but I didn't find any of them interested in what I cared about. I didn't need a boyfriend just to have a boyfriend, but I would be happy to have one if the right one came along.

"Now, a very sensitive question. Have you ever been sexually active?"

"No, ma'am! Yuck!"

"One last question about this topic, and I'm sorry I need to ask it: When you were with the defendant in the truck, why did you appear to consider his comment about a 'roll in the hay'?"

"Ma'am, I was terrified for my life. He held his knife on me and kept pointing and waving it at me. He was drinking a lot—he finished one bottle right after he found Booper and me and threw it out of the truck. He started drinking the second one he ordered me to get out of the glove compartment. I was afraid he might pass out at the wheel and wreck the truck. I didn't know what he was capable of doing, and I just wanted to say alive."

"Thank you. I am sure that the jury now better understands what happened in the truck."

She switched gears to the fight at the farm. "The defense has claimed that at the farm you assaulted the defendant for no reason. Please review for the jury what actually happened between the time you reached the farm and the time you kicked the defendant."

"When we arrived, it was dark and scary. Sitting in the cab, he waved the knife at me and ordered me to stay in the truck until he could come around and open the door. He got out, walked around, and opened the door so I got out. He stood a few feet away, waved the knife on me for a moment, got a crazy look on his face, and began to come toward me. That's when I kicked him between the legs and ran into the barn."

"Okay. Now, what happened before you stabbed him?"

"I was hiding in the barn looking for a way to escape. But he had grabbed Booper out of the back of the truck and was threatening to kill him if I didn't come out. I couldn't let him harm Booper more than he already had. I would rather he try to hurt me—I knew I could at least try to defend myself. Booper was completely helpless. Booper was whining and groaning. I knew he was in awful pain, and I believed from the threats Towns had been making for months that he would kill Booper just because he could."

"Okay. Let's look again at Exhibit B, the screwdriver." She picked it up from the evidence table. She asked, "How long is this screwdriver?"

It was short and didn't look like a 'deadly weapon.' Geez, I wish in my heart it had been a lot longer!

I said, "At the time, it was dark in the barn, and I picked it up off the counter by the side barn door. I didn't know how long it was then. I have since learned that it is only two inches long."

Lynne walked over to the jury box and showed it to them for the second time. She had first held it up when she was questioning the police but had not walked it by the jury. She did not say anything; she just walked past each juror so all of them could see how small it was. Then, she returned it to the evidence table. She wanted them to see it was highly unlikely to be the 'deadly weapon' the defense attorney claimed.

"Thank you. Only one more question. How many minutes passed between the time you and your friends captured the defendant and the police and your parents arrived?"

"I honestly don't know. We stood around and talked about what to do. We were pretty freaked out. I did go over and make that remark. I had walked back to the group, and Rory had pulled out his cellphone and was literally dialing 9-1-1 when we heard the cars and the sirens on the road. They arrived within seconds after that."

"Thank you. That's all." She walked back to her chair, turned, and said, "The prosecution rests."

The judge excused me, and I walked back to my seat. I looked one last time directly at Towns and smiled slightly. I knew that frog was just about boiled, his skin all dark green and slimy, his legs ready for a dish of French-fried frogs' legs!

Lynne squeezed my hand and smiled at me when I sat down. Towns glared back at me with his hands clinched. He mouthed that he was going to get to me, one way or the other.

During the defense testimony, his attorney tried to play the victim card. Bull, we all have choices, even if we're in the throes of addiction like my Dad had been. There is a difference between being powerless over alcohol or drugs and not having a choice.

I learned from my Dad after he got into recovery in AA that the difference is a very fine and confusing line that wiggles back and forth based on your situation. Regardless, Dad said, by working the 12 Steps, he had to take responsibility for his actions—his choices and the harm they caused—when he was drunk.

That's exactly what Towns had always refused to do—take responsibility for the terrible things he did. He was filled with rage and hatred and blamed everyone else for his crummy life.

Towns' lawyer called only one witness, a psychiatrist who was supposed to be an expert in alcoholism and recovery from it. He testified that Towns suffered from a crippling emotional disorder caused by being abused as a child, from addiction to alcohol, and from severe emotional distress caused by his recent divorce and job loss.

On cross-examination, Lynne shot that down with only two questions:

"Doctor, in your opinion, does Mr. Towns know the difference between right and wrong? Is he sane in the legal and social sense?"

"Yes, he knows the difference, and he is legally sane."

"One more question, many people suffer from the same childhood traumas and adult difficulties that you say Mr. Towns suffers from, even far worse. Are you claiming that these conditions *caused* Mr. Towns to act as he did, that he did not have the power to choose his actions?"

"No, there is much research that shows childhood abuse contributes to many people abusing animals and other people when they become adults. But the research does not show, therefore I cannot testify, that Mr. Towns was *controlled* by his conditions and did not have the power to choose."

"Thank you, Doctor. That's all."

On his redirect, Pelotzi did get the 'shrink' to admit that Towns was one of the most extreme cases of alcoholism he had ever seen. Another, I hoped feeble, attempt to cast the smallest bit of reasonable doubt in one juror's mind.

That was it. Pelotzi did not call him to testify because he knew what a terrible witness he would make. Lynne would have had him cursing and screaming at her in minutes since he obviously was very angry at the world, especially smart, attractive women.

During their summations, both Lynne and Pelotzi gave it their best shot. Pelotzi harped on how I was a trespasser, a rebel, and a spoiled brat who took what she wanted. He stressed how I had been found guilty of trespass and theft, but 'somehow' neglected to mention the community service I was serving with dedication. The jerk! He focused on how I had attacked Towns when I came out of the barn and claimed the creep was unable to defend himself because he was protecting his rightful property. Jeez, if any of that were true, I'd be the frog and I'd be boiling alive any second!

Lynne went second, fortunately. She reminded the jury I was serving community service at the animal shelter and praised my dedication to the animals, my outstanding academic record, and my sports abilities.

She tore apart Towns' character and credibility, citing as much of his previous record as she was allowed to say. She emphasized his many probation violations and his additional jail time for those. I loved the one called "consorting with known felons"! That was the least of his violations, but it did have a certain ring that I thought hysterical. I'm lucky I didn't burst out laughing in court.

Then, Lynne compared his physical size, his strength, and his weapons to my smaller size, lesser strength, and punier weapons. I ground my teeth at that crap—the same crap that is used to prevent women from getting all kinds of jobs we can do as well as any man.

She flipped the law of self-defense against Towns, stating simply he should have just stopped me and called the police to handle the situation. Instead, he kidnapped me, threatened me, and drove me away with intent to harm me.

She focused on Towns' multiple threats against me and stressed my right to self-defense, his ill treatment of Booper on the road and at the farm, and his guilty plea and sentence for animal abuse.

She praised the guys' courage and got a chuckle from the jury when she repeated the line about how using their championship soccer skills was better than shooting him. She left no doubt in anyone's mind she wished Rory had shot him and prevented this entire farce of a trial.

She scored the winning goal at the end when she showed me she really "got it," how she understood what was right and good rather than just legal or convenient. "You, the members of the jury, have a unique opportunity today. You can show all the children in this room, and especially this brave girl, willing to sacrifice her own life for an abused dog, that you know that our laws are founded on a Higher Law. That law is not of man but derives from the heart of what it means to be human—the law of right over might, of true justice over an outdated rule, and yes, of love over not hate, but something far worse—apathy. Ms. Chapman did all she knew how to do to convince the adults to do something to stop this criminal's horrendous abuse. Her teachers ignored her— repeatedly. Her own mother grounded her for trying her best to do the right and moral thing."

I heard Mom gasp and begin to sob quietly behind me. I didn't know Lynne was going to say that. It was true, but it made my Mom look really bad when I knew she was just trying to protect me although she was pushed just about beyond her limits. She was exhausted, depressed, confused, resentful, and angry when she grounded me and I had lied to her far too many times. I deserved to be grounded, I knew, because I had been selfish and too wrapped up in my own misery. I peeked over my shoulder and felt shocked and happy because Kim was holding Mom's left hand and Dad had his arm around her shoulders.

Lynne concluded, "Ms. Chapman has admitted her responsibility, she is willingly serving the community, far more than the court has required, and she is learning valuable lessons in hard work, discipline, and compassion. She has dedicated her life to helping protect abused animals. She is NOT on trial here.

"That criminal, that depraved liar," she practically shouted as she whirled and pointed her finger at Towns, "IS on trial. And every law—moral, ethical and legal—convicts him of some of the most heinous crimes anyone can imagine. Kidnapping a young girl, terrorizing her with a long, sharp knife, threatening to kill her, assaulting her and severely injuring her. The list of his crimes against this girl and his own dog goes on and on. I respectfully ask that you look deeply into both your rational mind and your most sincere feelings to find this, this "man," she said, her word dripping with contempt, "guilty of all charges."

After Lynne's brilliant appeal to each juror's 'hot buttons,' the judge gave them her instructions about the law, what it meant, and how they should apply the evidence and the testimony to consider their verdict. Her instructions were slanted toward the prosecution because she said the jury could not consider a verdict of insanity or mental disease. The defense had not raised it as a defense.

She told them essentially that the "alcohol made me do it" defense was not established in law, but that they could consider the defendant's mental state as a contributing factor. Best of all, she told them they could consider his guilty plea to animal abuse charges. She then adjourned for the day and told the jury to come back in the morning to begin their deliberations. She reminded them not to discuss anything about the case with anyone and to avoid any news reports about the trial.

The next morning, I think the jury must have lingered over the free coffee and pastries in the jury room because they took all of three hours to come back with a verdict of guilty on all counts.

After the foreman read the verdict, Towns finally lost it. He had been an ugly frog sitting in the pot for days and he knew it. He could feel the temperature rising slowly and surely, but he couldn't find a way to jump up the slick sides of the hot pot. He jumped out of his seat, glared and pointed his scrawny forefinger at me, "Yew may think we're done, yer little bitch! But I got friends on the outside, friends a lot worse'n me! Yew better watch yer back 'cause we ain't done yet!"

Judge O'Shields angrily ordered the bailiffs to restrain him and get him out of the courtroom. He was handcuffed and dragged out screaming at me.

I felt mystified more than afraid of his outburst. I knew he hated me, but I was stunned that he was still so determined to hurt me.

After Towns' humiliating departure from the courtroom, the judge thanked the jurors for their service and dismissed them. She looked down at me and said, "You are quite a courageous young woman! And very sharp on the ball on the stand. Just be careful in the future about taking 'justice' into your own hands. That's our job, and I like my job at lot! Now, I 'order' you," she said with a smile, "to take excellent care of Booper, or you'll have to answer to me and my three King Charles spaniels." And she walked down the steps and left the room.

My Mom had been standing by the gate, waiting to lunge in.

She was terrified; she ran to me and grabbed me and held me tight. "Oh God, how are we going to protect ourselves from that lunatic?" she cried. "We'll have to move again and get away!"

Lynne reached over and patted Mom's arm. She reassured us a lot of criminals made those threats, but never followed through once they got to prison. They were too busy trying to stay alive, especially a loser like Towns with multiple convictions. "He's going to get a very long sentence, and he won't bother you," she said to calm my Mom.

I wasn't so sure. He had been obsessed with harming me since the first time he caught me in his yard. I think he's very dangerous, inside or outside jail.

Then, all the guys ran into the courtroom, rushed up to me, thumped me on the back, and babbled what an awesome team we made! Yes, we are an awesome team, and I will do my best to keep it that way.

Chapter 32
I Gain a Real Father

I thought the sentencing a couple of weeks later would be a simple matter of sticking it to Towns. But my Dad did something so amazing that I can still hardly believe it. I briefly testified about the trauma I have felt since I was kidnapped and threatened—headaches, nightmares, paranoia, and a few others I tossed in for good measure. Then, Judge O'Shields asked if anyone wanted to speak on Towns' behalf.

My Dad stood up and said, "Yes, I would like to speak." Mom and I were so shocked that we grabbed the railing, squeezed it tight, and almost jumped out of our chairs. But Kim just placed her hand on my Mom's arm, whispered, "Please listen. It's important for him to say this." We sat back down and stared at Kim; Kim just smiled at us and nodded toward my Dad as he walked toward the witness stand.

Dad took the stand and looked Towns in the eye. He said, "Your Honor, I am a recovering alcoholic. When I was drinking, I did many terrible things. But for the grace of my Higher Power, I could be sitting where Mr. Towns is sitting right now, or I could be dead from my disease. I lost my job, my wife divorced me—she was right to do so—and I almost lost the love of my amazing daughter." He smiled at us with what seemed like both regret and gratitude.

"Part of my job in recovery, what I have to do to stay sober, is to carry the message to other alcoholics and practice the principles of recovery every day. I am not speaking to excuse Mr. Towns' actions. I have taken responsibility for my actions and done my best to make amends to everyone I have harmed. I will continue to make amends to my former wife and my daughter for the rest of my life. I strongly believe Mr. Towns must do the same thing if he wants a chance at a better life, even in jail.

"I would like to make Mr. Towns an offer I hope he will accept. I am willing to visit him in prison once a week and attend AA meetings in prison with him. I will pray for him and for his recovery and be willing to help him if he wants. Thank you."

As Dad stepped down and walked by him, Towns snarled, "I don't need none of yer do-gooder crap. You can take your AA and shove it."

Dad stopped and looked at him, "I understand how you feel. I felt the same way for a long time, and I know the hell I created for myself. You have a right to choose your own heaven or your own hell. If you ever change your mind, my offer still stands."

He walked away and sat back down with us. Kim grinned and hugged him tightly. She murmured, "I am so proud of you!" Mom and I looked at him, speechless. I didn't know whether he had just made one of the most wonderful, most generous offers I had ever seen or one of the weirdest. I just felt so proud of him for standing up in public and having the courage to be willing to help a drunk and a criminal like Towns. I learned how much he had changed and how strong he had become. I finally had a real father.

Mom, on the other hand, didn't react so well. She leaned over to Dad and whispered, "How could you do such a thing? Offer to help the man who tried to kill your daughter? Are you out of your mind? Or are you just so 'high and mighty' now that you're 'Mr.

AA,' you think you're supposed to save the world. That man is evil and deserves every minute of punishment he gets."

Dad replied quietly, "I am sorry you feel that way. I haven't forgotten what he did. Part of me hates him for what he did to Harry, and I hope he gets a stiff sentence. But I can't stay sober if I hold onto my anger and resentment. I did what I had to do to be at peace with myself."

Mom snorted. She folded her arms in a huff and turned away from him. Well, so much for the progress I thought Dad and Mom had made since all of this happened. But Kim looked over at me and smiled with sad look. She whispered the words, "It's all right. I know how your Mom feels. It will be okay. It's going to take some time."

I sat back, torn between my strange pride in my Dad and a strong urge to protect my Mom. As Dad said, he had put her through so much trouble that I wondered if she would ever get over it. Dad had put so much effort into his recovery he really had shown us he was a different, much better person than he was before.

But Mom had suffered so much—living through years and years of worry and fear during his drinking days, losing our big house and Grandpa's farm, working so many hours at her lousy job, enduring our fall from prosperity to near-poverty, and of course, feeling terrified through the trouble all my mistakes had caused. She had a right to feel the way she did, too. Like Kim said, it was going to take time—and it has.

Towns was given an opportunity to speak for himself, but Pelotzi declined for him. "We will leave the sentence up to your Honor's well-known reputation for compassion for those so afflicted that they act in unfortunate ways."

After Dad's extraordinary statement, the sentencing was an

anti-climax. Judge O'Shields took no pity. She said Towns disgusted her for abusing Booper as badly as he had. She called him a coward for kidnapping me and threatening my life. She told him he was a menace to society who did not deserve any compassion from the court. When she said that, she stared directly at Pelotzi with a deep frown, like she was telling him, "Don't try that crap in my court!"

The judge gave Towns the maximum sentence for attempted murder and the other charges—25 years to life. He had plea-bargained the five more years for abusing Booper. Judge O'Shields made both sentences consecutive to his mandatory 5-year sentence for probation violation. That is, the minimum 30 years were added to the five years he was already serving. He will not have a chance for parole for at least 35 years, if he lives that long.

I dearly hope he doesn't. Does that sound insensitive of me? Do I lack compassion? Do I not believe in redemption? Don't judge my reaction until you have experienced the fear, terror, pain, and anguish I have. I have compassion for all the people and animals Towns will never hurt again and all those he will never have a chance to harm in the future.

If Towns somehow truly "sees the light" in prison, I'm sure my father will be more than happy to help him recover from his alcoholism. Maybe by then I'll be old enough and wise enough to consider forgiveness. Yet, I doubt he will change—I have looked into the man's eyes too many times and seen only rage and evil.

Most of all, I have to remember that he has threatened to take revenge on me, not once, but twice. He told me he has friends "on the outside" who are much worse than he. I hate that thought more than you can imagine. I often feel a twinge of fear anytime some adult I don't know gets close to me. I may have to keep looking over my shoulder and be hyperalert until I hear he is either dead or can't carry out his threat. What a creepy way to grow up!

Towns was led out—this time not even looking at me. That frightened me more than his threats! I wanted to wave at him and sing, "Sha na na, Sha na na, hey, hey, goodbye!" I restrained myself.

But at that moment, we celebrated a major victory, for sure! Mom, Dad and Kim cried for joy, relieved our nightmare had ended. They all hugged me tightly. Mom embarrassed me by stroking my hair and telling me how much she loved me and was so sorry she hadn't listened to me. I said, "Oh, Mom!" and pretended to wiggle away, but I really wanted her and Dad—and Kim—to hold me for a long, long time. It was going to take a while, maybe a long while, for me to feel truly safe again.

Lynne was thrilled with the outcome—she put Towns in jail practically forever, she beat Barry again, and she won a major media trial. She smiled widely at me, hugged me, and said, "You are one awesome young woman. I hope my little girls grow up just like you!

"Let me introduce you to my husband. He wanted to tell you something," a wicked grin on her face.

I turned and Barry Pelotzi stood there! I shook my head to see if I was in a bizarre new dimension. "Wha..??? You told me he holds a grudge against you for beating him!?"

Lynne laughed, "Oh, he does, but he leaves it here in the courtroom—if he knows what's good for him at home!"

Pelotzi—he was handsome!—took a few steps to be next to Lynne. He was about 6 inches taller than she, but they were an amazing couple. He stuck out his hand toward my Dad. They shook hands firmly. "Barry," I guess now, said, "Mr. Chapman, that was quite an offer you made. I have a lot of other clients who might respond a little better than Mr. Towns. It will take a miracle for him to want help."

Dad replied, "Well, miracles do come true—just look at what just happened here! I'll be happy to help anybody you want to send my way. Thank you for the chance to be of real service where it's needed most."

Barry then turned to me, "Well, Miss Chapman, you are one of the most formidable opponents I've faced in a long time. I thought I had you once or twice, but you—and my scheming wife!—beat me every time I tried to trap you. You are going to be something else when you grow up!

"Like Lynne told you before, we have a Labrador that we love like we love our daughters, and I'm sure you will love Booper in the same way. Good luck to you, and if you ever get in any trouble on the 'wrong' side of the law, give me call. It would be a hoot to defend you!"

All of us had a hearty laugh at that. Inside, I was laughing like "Huh, huh, huh" because I knew how close the trial had been. Towns could have gone free and kept Booper; I could have been the one going to jail for doing exactly what Barry had said I had done—and I felt no regrets. Through the grace of Whatever—and lawyers and judges who loved their dogs!—I was protected and my view of what was right prevailed. I knew then—and know far better now—that it doesn't always have to end up that way!

Chapter 33
Happy Days Are Here Again?

Do you think you have figured out what happened next? It looked like we were going to have a "fairy tale" ending where Towns rotted in jail and all of us lived happily ever after.

It started like that. Life has been great! I've been doing well in school again. My nightmares about Towns stopped as soon as he was shipped to prison hundreds of miles away. I've been working down my PBJ at the shelter faster than I thought I would. That didn't matter much as I was going to keep working at the shelter anyway. I love the dogs and cats, and so many of them need all the love and care they could get.

Best of all, the day after the trial, Lynne had a quiet word with Marion Kerry and "somehow," we went to the top of the list and yes! Booper came home with me! Kerry wasn't at all happy and made my work even more demanding, sometimes disgusting, like cleaning out the huge trash containers in the back parking lot when it was below zero.

That didn't bother me at all. At last and for real and forever, the incredible dog I had always wanted and would never let go! But Booper is *not* my property. He is a beloved member of our family—and lots of others in our neighborhood, too!

Booper is safe, healthy and happy. Booper healed to become a gorgeous creature, deep black with a German shepherd's curved tail. He's big—more than two feet tall from his paws to his back—and weighs about 100 pounds of muscle. The vet said he is probably mixed Labrador and German shepherd—the perfect combination for a gentle warrior.

He normally is the sweetest dog. He just wants to run everywhere and chase me and the guys with a big smile on his face, his thick tail wagging, and his pink lips drooling dog sweat. He loves to be hugged and cuddle up with me on my bed and with Mom and me on our couch.

Mom had been a tough nut to crack at first, but it was love at first sight as soon as she saw Booper after I brought him home, cleaned him up, and brushed him until his black coat shone like obsidian.

But Mom will never admit it! She still pretends to grouse when Booper gets up on the couch while we watch TV and eat popcorn. After she tells him to get down, he slinks down to the floor as he looks at her with his "pitiful" face. In a few minutes, he sort of slowly oozes back onto the other end of the couch.

I don't know how a 100-pound dog oozes, but he moves back onto the couch like a thick snake. Mom usually gives up after she tells him twice. Once he's back on the other end of the couch, he scrunches and oozes over me and uses his massive head to shove me to one side so he ends up between Mom and me. Mom's hand usually ends up on his head, rubbing it and scratching him behind the ears. Sometimes, a few pieces of popcorn seem to fall right out of Mom's hand and into Booper's mouth. I think it's hilarious!

He's not a softie, however. My "gentle warrior" is fiercely protective of Mom and me. You do NOT want to appear to threaten either one of us or my friends! We never had him neutered. He remains "all man" and he is quite proud of it. We do have to keep him away from the female dogs in the neighborhood! The world does not need more unwanted dogs that will be abandoned, dumped in our shelter, or killed!

During the last few weeks of winter before spring soccer practice began, Booper and I spent most afternoons running the ball fields at school, playing pick-up games with the guys and whoever else showed up from the neighborhood.

By the way, we had a winning basketball season, but the distractions of the trials, the guys' PBJs, our extra chores, the media craziness, and everything else took a toll on the team so we didn't win the championship—this year! Just wait 'til next year!

Playing around on the soccer field, Booper is always on my pickup team—of course! He is getting darn good at hitting the ball back to me with his head and "playing defense" by running around and through the other team, barking at them!

With spring soccer practice about to start on March 1, the guys talked a lot about our prospects. It looked good. All the Redhawks are coming back, so we have a great chance to beat the Wasps again for the spring league championship.

We're growing much closer as a team, too. Since the guys rescued me at the farm, I've begun to talk with them—well, the girls most of the time—about everything. Rory and the PBJs keep teasing us and giving us a hard time. But we girls give the guys as good as we get—all in fun.

The boys just don't get how to talk to us or be honest with us quite yet. They are all good hearted and obviously courageous. Yes, I'll admit they've become as close to me as brothers, and I know how much trouble many of the girls have with their brothers!

Chapter 34
Torrents and Portents

Freezing rain and biting winds swept the field like demons chasing errant souls on the first day of March as soccer practice began. As I ran onto the field—first as usual, I stopped and stared up at the dark gray clouds racing across the sky and got a chill that made me tremble. It wasn't the weather, I'd been playing for weeks with Booper in weather like this.

No, this chill felt personal. I fervently hoped the shiver down my spine was just the cold rain dripping down my shirt and not a terrible omen. I had an awful thought, "Was Towns already conspiring from prison to send someone to hurt Booper and me?"

I really doubted it, Lynne had told us he had more problems to worry about. But the tiny fear niggled deep in my brain and sometimes popped out on days like today.

One thing I had learned from our victory over Towns; the universal law would continue to be the ultimate truth: Be careful what you wish for! You might just get it and a whole lot more than you ever expected! Some would be great, some would be terrible.

The Redhawks' test with Towns certainly had proven that actions based on good intentions always have unintended consequences! All of us suffered in some way to bring about the best consequence possible.

I had gotten exactly what I had wanted—my incredible Booper. I also got a lot more and better than I ever expected—my teammates who love each other like brothers and sisters. We had paid a very high price to not only get what we have, but we have to care for each other every day to keep it. All of us knew in our hearts that was true. That's why what we have today is so precious.

By the end of winter, we were ready to move on and look back at the Towns' debacle with "fond memories." We wanted to brag about how we banded together to capture a truly terrible criminal. Something to tell over and over again to the sixth graders and pump up our reputations as the coolest kids at Carver! The elementary school nearby asked us to visit and talk to their classes! What a great way to teach them the values of teamwork and friendship as well as an excellent way to be able to skip class for a morning!

I wasn't thinking about all of our fun as I stood in the rain and gloom. I looked up at the sky. For an eerie moment, I thought I clearly saw a face exactly like Towns, with a monstrous grin on his face, his sallow chin, his sunken cheeks, and his evil eyes staring down at me. I quivered like a slender reed in the harsh wind that pierced through my sweats. I shook myself and tried to laugh it off, "Man, my imagination has run away with my good sense."

I looked again and Towns was gone. I thought, "There, see scaredy cat! Nothing but clouds."

As I watched, the clouds slowly twisted and turned into a new shape. It looked vaguely like an ugly spirit with a vulture-like head and beady eyes that had a ravenous look. I had had nightmares about something like this, but it had always been a distant presence that was hiding from me and I never saw clearly. It swirled and twirled and seemed about to become clear enough to recognize.

Then, the wind changed direction abruptly, and the shape changed into an opaque, round shape that sort of looked like a human head. Before I could recognize who it looked like, a strong gust of wind blew it into wisps, and the trails of the shape melted into the cloud bank.

"Wow," I thought, "very creepy! Must be all the stress, darkness, and cold weather." I hate the S-A-D days of winter when there is so little sun and so much darkness. As I was creeping myself out, Rory and the guys ran onto the field past me, yelling something inane and insulting as usual. Coach Bill, who never called off a practice unless the snow was a foot deep—and we couldn't clean the field off ourselves!—blew his whistle and I ran to join *our* championship team.

This menacing day, though, would give way to flowers blooming soon, days growing longer, the sun getting warmer, life getting better. I just wanted to bask with Booper in the promises of spring come true and swat the Wasps again with my team!

A lovely dream to cheer me up on a miserable day! A bright dream of sparkling days of love and laughter to come! Remember: I always have been a dreamer.

But the future doesn't have to care about my dreams. It doesn't have to make my dreams come true or my happy, peaceful life with Booper last forever. The future always brings new tragedies and new opportunities to triumph. Sometimes—well, maybe all the time—I never know which is which! How much can I shape the future, or will the future do more to shape me?

I don't know, but I suspect I will find out—both a tantalizing and terrible thought. However, for this freezing, soaking wet, miserable moment, life is about as good as it gets and I'm going to run with it toward the goal! Ole´!

The End of the Beginning

COMING SOON!
The Next Adventure
Booper and Harry -
Book 2

Evil Wears Comfortable Shoes

Can Booper, Harry and the Redhawks End A Reign of Terror
Against Innocent Creatures Before The Evil Overwhelms Them?

Turn the page to join Booper and Harry's
next rousing adventure!

…Making my most cherished wish to have Booper come true cost me a very high price I don't wish on anyone: painful physical wounds, severe anxiety over the trials, vicious personal attacks by the news 'vultures' and social media monsters, and severe guilt I felt because of the enormous fear, stress, and worry I had dumped in my Mom's lap.

Has that steep price been worth all of the results—I call them blessings—I've received? Yes—period. No doubts, no regrets.

How could I possibly complain? Despite the "collateral damage," I had found, defended and given a safe home to the incredible creature I wanted more than anything else—ever: my wonderful dog Booper to love and care for.

Booper has been all that and so much more—a gentle, yet fierce protector of my family; a happy, hyper mascot for the Redhawks; a welcome solace for my mom as she slowly recovers from her many traumas; and my constant companion and comforter.

In a cool way, my love for Booper is only a small part of the wonderful results of all our trying consequences. My Mom and I are closer to each other than we've ever been. I've stopped lying to her—well, most of the time. She trusts me now and treats me more like a mature young woman rather than a hormonally crazed tween.

Mom and Dad are on friendly speaking terms, something I never thought I'd see! They fought through a nasty divorce four years ago just before my Grandpa died because my Dad hit bottom as an awful alcoholic after he had just about destroyed himself and us. But he's been in Alcoholics Anonymous since then and works hard on his recovery "one day at a time." Last fall, just before all the "poop hit the fan," he married a great fellow AA member, Kim, who helped save Dad's life when he was in rehab.

I was back at the top of my game at George Washington Carver Middle School—making A's as I could have been doing all along—and on the soccer field and basketball court. Last and certainly not least, the Redhawks and I had truly become a family in the best sense of that word. We are the best of friends and teammates. We continue to love each other—even if the guys will never admit it—and we always have each other's back. "One for all and all for one" doesn't even begin to describe what we've been through and what we mean to each other. We make The Three Musketeers look disloyal and selfish!

That's how good I thought my life was on that bright, clear Saturday morning in late March. For the first time in six months, I felt truly happy as I practically skipped across town toward the shelter. I left Booper at home because he had spent more than three months in the shelter after I saved him and while we waited for my and Towns' trials to end. Booper hated the place, I couldn't even drag him in the door. Just try to pull 100 pounds of all-muscle dog that doesn't want to budge! I tried and I can't do it. I thought his long time cooped up in a cage was why he hated it, but I was so wrong…

I planned to spend eight enjoyable hours taking care of the animals and especially "gussying up"—that's Southern slang from my Grandpa for grooming—the dogs and cats for their new owners. Saturday was our big adoption day. I loved to see the puppies and kittens go to new homes when the families obviously wanted them and had the means to love them and give them happy lives. The kids were always starry-eyed and fell in love every time they got to cuddle their new dog or cat for the first time. That alone made all the filthy chores I had to do worthwhile!

Right on time at 8 a.m., I bopped in the front door to say hello to Marion Kerry, the shelter director.

She had never been nice to me since I started at the shelter last October. The first time I met her, I felt something was very strange. Something about her voice made the hairs on my neck stand on end. I blamed my reaction on being so nervous about my first real job—my PBJ service—and the stress that had given me nightmares since my ordeal with Towns. I should have listened to my inner voice. It was screaming at me, and I dismissed it as a silly fear. The signs were always there, and I missed them.

She had strongly objected to keeping Booper there so he could heal and we could complete my and Towns' trials. Lynne and a judge had to intervene to save Booper. Kerry definitely didn't want me to work off my PBJ service there, but the juvie judge didn't give her a choice.

Instead, she had done her best to drive me away; she always gave me all the worst jobs, but that was fine with me. After what I'd been through, her scowls and rudeness and the dirtiest jobs were no big deal—or so I believed foolishly.

After all, I was happy because I got to spend lots of time with Booper—and sneak him treats—as he healed from his terrible injuries and was protected by the court. And I was helping to keep dozens of abandoned and abused animals alive and well. I was sure I could endure Kerry's quirks for their sake.

But after only a few weeks at the shelter, I began to suspect Kerry hated the animals. She only seemed to get any pleasure from her work when she was putting an animal to sleep. She never gave any of the puppies or kittens cute names to make them more adorable and more adoptable. She never called any animal by a pet name. No "sweet Fido." No "cutesy Kitty." Only "it" and "that animal."

With 20-20 hindsight—you know where that begins, right?—I believe even now that I could have helped prevent the worst, but even more obvious conflicts I missed were yet to come.

Whenever Kerry decided to descend from her "throne," a large chair in her office, and deigned to grace us, her "humble subjects" in the cage room, the animals went crazy. The dogs howled and thrashed in their cages. The cats screeched and hissed. The cats, even the kittens, puffed their bodies as large as they could so they would look more fierce. They arched their backs and bared their teeth and spit at us through the wires. They often tried to attack us, too, throwing their bodies against the sides of their cages.

The snakes slithered into their dens inside their hollow plastic logs and hid. If she came close, they hissed and struck out from their logs, their fangs bared and venom flying at us. The occasional monkey we took in squealed and chattered and raced to the very top corner of its cage and pushed its body against the side as far away from us as it could. If we came near, it would literally crap onto its platform and throw the feces at us.

And the poor terrified guinea pigs and hamsters suffered worst of all from her presence. They ran on their wheels like maniacs as they had no shelter to hide in. I'd even watched in shock as a few died of what I have realized must have been panic attacks. Their fear made their little hearts pump so fast that they burst. Ghastly!

How did I miss all those terrifying signs of evil? The animals told me repeatedly, loudly, fiercely that Marion was evil. I must have been so preoccupied with saving Booper and staving off my own troubles that I had never thought my first reaction was the truth. I thought foolishly that she knew she was unfit for the job and hated it, so she chose to act like the "Cruella Deville" of the shelter.

Undoubtedly the worst for me was the cruel way Kerry forced me to help her put animals, especially dogs, to sleep. If I didn't, she would have thrown me out and I'd had to leave Booper there while I took on another PBJ service. I feared for his life so I chose to participate. It felt indescribably atrocious.

Either the poor creatures were very ill or very crazy, or worse, the shelter had become overcrowded and we could not find another shelter to take the oldest dogs and cats. The oldest or sickest were always put to sleep first because they were so hard to get adopted.

Every time was hideous. I felt so sad while I held a poor animal as Marion, with a slight twitch of a smile, injected it with the deadly awful "blue shot" of an overdose of narcotics. I grieved every one of them and I grew to hate Kerry more and more. But through my sorrow, I made a deep commitment that one day, I would either lead or set up a rescue league or lifetime shelter that would never put an animal to sleep.

The "blue shot" was supposed to be a "humane" way to die— the animals just did go to sleep and pass away peacefully. But it was an incredibly lame excuse for depriving a living creature— with feelings as deep as our own, I believe—of a long life being loved by someone who really cared for him. As I said, Life is *NOT* fair.

I learned that again—when would I ever learn once and for all?—as soon I walked through the shelter door on that beautiful March day. I didn't understand then that blue skies and crisp cool days do not mean happy days. Remember: The September 11, 2001 attacks that killed 3,000 people in New York, Pennsylvania, and Washington, DC, happened on a perfectly blue, cloudless, late summer day.

As I stepped in the door, Kerry looked up from some papers on the front counter, saw it was me, squinted her eyes, and said sarcastically, "Well, my hero, are your 15 minutes of fame over?"

"Ma'am?" I asked, puzzled.

"Is the trial over and everything done? Have the news stories about how brave and wonderful you are stopped? Have you finished your celebration dances for getting your way? You've got the dog and life is all peaches and cream, I assume?" she practically snarled.

Crap, I thought, she's really annoyed. Now what!?

"Yes, ma'am," I said as politely as I could. "The trial is over. Towns is headed to jail upstate. Things at home are getting back to normal one day at a time. We're doing well. Thank you for asking."

I should have stopped talking then, but me and my big mouth. "I certainly didn't seek out or enjoy my '15 minutes.' I could have done without them," I sort of snapped back.

"Right! I bet," Kerry said with a sneer in her voice. "All that attention, all that publicity, being praised to high heavens as the leader of a courageous band of tweenie titans! The Redhawk Rangers ride to the rescue! Didn't you enjoy it just a little bit, deep down in your heart of hearts?" she probed.

I stuck my foot in it. "Well, I am glad Towns was punished for what he did to Booper and me. I'm glad the shelter received a lot of favorable publicity, and I believe we received more donations than usual. I'm happy to be here, helping the animals as much as I can. All of that is a lot more important than anything I may or may not have felt."

"I 'appreciate' your help in improving the shelter's finances. I couldn't have done it without you. You are very 'humble' for such a remarkable girl," she scoffed, not meaning a word of it.

She peered at me over her *pince nez* glasses, her dark blue eyes blazing bright with something I had never seen before. Had I seen anger? Yes. Annoyance? Yes. But rage? Jealousy? Hatred? Worse?

As I stood there transfixed, her face seemed to take on a hungry, greedy look I had only seen once in my life. I was at the zoo when I was 10 years old with my Mom. We had come upon a zookeeper about to feed three endangered Indian white rumped vultures perched on a platform about 10 feet above the floor. She threw the tiny carcass of a dead fawn, probably killed on a nearby highway, into their cage. The scavengers stared at that carcass with their shining black eyes focused hungrily on their meal. Kerry was looking at me with exactly the same shiny, hungry eyes, intent on pouncing on her prey. Except she was much worse; her piercing dark blue eyes seemed to have no living feeling in them at all— just darkness.

From my sudden, intense fear, a new name insanely sprang into my mind as a cold bead of sweat rolled down my spine like an ice cube—Marion the Carrion! That's her! A vile, voracious creature!

At the zoo, I recalled with terror, the trio of vultures calmly plopped from their perch onto the carcass and began to pluck its eyes out. They gobbled the "softest, tastiest appetizers" first and then ripped out the guts for the main feast. I felt stunned and fascinated by how fast they were devouring that poor fawn. My Mom had to drag me away from the wretched scene.

That event had stuck in my mind as a symbol for how callous and cruel greedy, heartless people can be. At that moment in the shelter, I realized the Carrion was one of them. Maybe one of the worst of them. I knew I could be in grave danger if I didn't finesse this dicey situation. I recoiled from the Carrion, taking a step away from her, hoping against all hope that somehow, some way I could escape the fawn's fate. "Oh my God, what does she plan to do to me"? I cringed at the thought.

I almost turned and fled from the shelter to call for help, but the Carrion saw my fear and instantly, her scowl and her tight lips changed to a warm smile, and her dark blue eyes lightened and seemed as innocent as an angel's.

"Well," she said pleasantly, "I am so happy you are free to help even more now. How many hours of community service do you have left?"

"What in the world had just happened?" I thought frantically, keeping a straight face with great effort and resisting a huge desire to start shaking. I gripped my fingers into the palms of my hands until they hurt like the devil.

"From a rapacious vulture to the face of an angel in seconds? What is she?" my mind shrieked!

Somehow, I replied respectfully with a steady voice, "Oh, please don't worry about that. I have a lot of hours left. Even after my community service is completed, I'd still love to keep helping the shelter. I love taking care of the animals, especially the dogs."

My wiser inner self screamed at me, "Fool! Idiot! What did you just do?" I had just told her I was her slave for at least 8 hours a week for the rest of eternity!

However, another terrible yet wonderful idea flashed through my mind. At least I could help and protect as many animals as I could; if it took an eternity to discover and stop the evil the Carrion was doing, I would do it. I would spend more time at the shelter and keep a very close eye on the animals and how the Carrion treated them. I would gather evidence and find a way to trap her and crush her horrendous schemes—whatever they were. After all, I told myself boldly, I had outfoxed Towns and beaten him. I could do the same to the Carrion. Super Girl flies to the rescue again!...*Or so I thought!*

About the Author

Robert L. Perry is the author of the compelling young adult series, *The Booper and Harry Mysteries.* His mission? To encourage 'tweens and teens to learn how to triumph over the difficult challenges they face in an increasingly troubled world. His vivid stories portray the ordeals Harry, a troubled teenage tomboy, and Booper, her beloved rescue dog, must overcome to protect her family, her friends, her school, and her hometown. This mighty duo must rely on their own daring and the courage of the Redhawks, her diverse, dogged soccer team, to prevail over every adversity.

Before turning to fiction to fulfill his new mission, Robert published 23 non-fiction works, many of them for young people. These non-fiction works focused on addiction prevention, computing, career choices, and entrepreneurship. He also taught professional writing at a major university and served as the chief speechwriter for the director of a federal agency.

When he's not working with Booper and Harry to create their next adventure, Robert loves to swing dance and embark on his own adventures. His love for adventure has taken him to 32 countries on six continents, including Antarctica! Only Australia left to visit! He climbed Mt. Kilimanjaro for one of his "zero" birthday landmarks! He loves to hike and explore as Mother Nature always feeds his boundless curiosity. "She" has given him amazing experiences on the Galapagos Islands, African safaris, the Amazon River, Machu Picchu, Vietnam, Indonesia, Cambodia, Ireland and many more. Closer to home, he loves to hike mountains, the nearby Shenandoahs, Blue Ridges, and Great Smokies and especially, the Rockies.

He lives in Northern Virginia and hangs out with a group of crazy and loving friends whose lives are constant reminders that personal greatness results when you learn to turn tragedy into triumph!

To join Booper, Harry and the Redhawks in their adventures, go to www.booperandharry.com, on Twitter at @AndBooper, and on Instagram at https://www.instagram.com/booperandharry/